Double Take

Books by Melody Carlson

WORDS FROM THE ROCK SERIES

True

Life

Always

Just Another Girl

Anything but Normal

Never Been Kissed

Double Take

A Novel

DISCARD

Melody Carlson

Revell

a division of Baker Publishing Group
Grand Rapids, Michigan

© 2011 by Melody Carlson

Published by Revell
a division of Baker Publishing Group
P.O. Box 6287, Grand Rapids, MI 49516-6287
www.revellbooks.com

Printed in the United States of America

Library of Congress Cataloging-in-Publication Data
Carlson, Melody.
    Double take : a novel / Melody Carlson.
        p.   cm.
    Summary: Two look-a-like, discontented seventeen-year-olds—one a sophis-
ticated city girl and the other an Amish farm girl—decide to trade lives for a
week.
    ISBN 978-0-8007-1964-7 (pbk.)
    [1. Mistaken identity—Fiction. 2. Amish—Fiction. 3. Wealth—Fiction.
4. Self-realization—Fiction. 5. Spiritual life—Fiction. 6. New York (N.Y.)—
Fiction.] I. Title.
PZ7.C216637Do 2011
[Fic]—dc22   2010053530

11   12   13   14   15   16   17   7   6   5   4   3

1

"Why does everything have to be so complicated?" Madison shook her Blackberry at her mom as she entered the Manhattan penthouse. "I'm sick of it! Sick of the stress—sick of everyone pushing and pulling on me. I can't take it anymore!"

"Calm down." Her mom set what looked like a new Falchi handbag on the side table. Tossing her cashmere cloak onto a chair, she strolled into the living room and gracefully settled herself on the sofa with a calculated smile. "Tell me what's going on, dear, and I'll see if I can fix it."

"You cannot fix it." Madison folded her arms across her front. "You are part of it."

"Oh, Madison, are you still complaining about spring break? Do you know how many girls would love to be in your shoes?" Her mom's brows arched as she nodded to Madison's feet. "By the way, aren't those my Manolos?"

"You can have them." Madison kicked off the wedge sandals and flopped down on the ottoman with a loud groan. "I would rather go shoeless than be controlled by you or anyone else. I'm serious, Mom. I'm sick of it. Sick of everyone telling me where to go and what to do, and how they're planning my future for me."

Her mom's smile was fading fast. "Don't be such a drama queen. Honestly, I never heard anyone complain as much as you do . . . over nothing."

"Nothing?" Madison stood up. "You and Grandma keep pressuring me to give up spring break to go to Tuscany with you—so I can hang with a bunch of old people." She rolled her eyes. "And Vivian insists I *must* go to Palm Beach with her and her family. Plus I've got Garret pushing me just to stay home and do some *things* in the city." She held up her Blackberry. "Now Dad calls up and tells me he's decided that it's time for a father-daughter bonding vacation, which is really a thinly disguised excuse for visiting Harvard—"

"What?" Her mom leaned forward. "Are you serious?"

Madison nodded. "He wants me to come to Boston to stay with him. He said we can spend some time on campus and meet his—"

"Harvard?" Her mom grabbed her handbag and jerked out her phone. "Your father knows good and well that you are going to Yale, Madison, and if he thinks he can waltz in and—"

"Please, don't call him, Mom." Madison paced back and forth, sorry she'd even brought this up. "That will just make everything worse."

"Your father cannot start dragging Harvard into the college conversation. Not at this stage of the game. We've already been all over this, and he knows—"

"See!" Madison stopped pacing and held her hands up. "*This* is what I'm talking about. Everyone is treating me like I'm five years old, or like they think I'm their puppet!"

"Oh, Madison!" Her mom looked seriously irritated now. "Just grow up."

So much for the "I can fix it" spiel.

"I wish everyone would just leave me alone." Madison hurried to her room, and just as her mom began speaking into the phone, she slammed the door behind her. Immature, yes, but if everyone was going to treat her like a child, she might as well act like one.

She went into her bathroom, closing and locking the door, trying to get as far away from her mother as possible. For a long moment, she stood in front of the mirror over the sink, just staring blankly. On the outside, she looked like the typical spoiled little rich girl. Impeccably dressed, long and sleek blonde hair with roots that looked natural, clear skin, blue eyes, good teeth—her mother was right, lots of girls would like to be Madison. Just not Madison! Sometimes it felt like she'd been born into the wrong family . . . or the wrong century.

As if to remind her that this was the twenty-first century, her Blackberry rang again. As badly as she wanted to flush the stupid phone down the toilet, she saw that it was her best friend. Weren't BFFs supposed to be understanding? Madison could use a little understanding right now.

"Hey, Viv," she said in a forced cheerful tone.

"Why didn't you call me back?" Vivian demanded. "My parents are already on their way to the airport. Are you coming with us or not?"

"I can't, Vivian."

"*Can't?*" Vivian's voice grew shrill. "Don't you mean *won't?*"

Madison attempted to explain all the pressure on her just now, including her dad's Harvard plan, but Vivian cut her off. "That means I'll be stuck down there all by myself, Madison. Do you know how boring that's going to be?"

"Oh, I'm sure you'll find someone to entertain you." Madison wasn't surprised that, as usual, her friend was primarily thinking of herself. It was like Vivian hadn't even heard her. One more reason Madison was relieved to pass on Florida. "Anyway, have fun down there, Viv. If I change my mind, I'll call you, okay?"

"Yeah, right!" Vivian hung up.

"Great." Madison flopped on her bed and tried to figure out just when life had gotten so complicated. Wasn't being seventeen supposed to be fun and carefree? And spring break—wasn't that supposed to be, like . . . a break?

Madison could hear her mom's voice now—loud and angry. She was obviously talking to Madison's dad (aka Mom's ex) on the phone, and she was obviously enraged over this Harvard development. Madison wrapped a down pillow over her ears, attempting to block out the sound. It took her straight back to childhood, to times when Mom and Dad could fight like this for hours. Why had she even mentioned Dad and Harvard to Mom? No good would come out of it for anyone.

A part of Madison was tempted to do what she used to do—just give in to keep the peace. Except that giving in was probably what had gotten her to this feeling of frustration in the first place. No, she decided, no one was going to stick up for Madison except Madison. The sooner they all figured that out, the better it would be.

The truth was she didn't want to go to any of the Ivy League schools. Not Yale *or* Harvard. If Madison could have it her way, which was highly unlikely, she would rather go to college in Colorado or Oregon or somewhere equally remote—someplace different from here. A school that valued things like individuality and creativity and respecting nature and living green—and not the green of the almighty dollar either. Not that anyone was listening to her . . . or cared. All this stress over spring break seemed like the tip of the iceberg to her. Like a bad omen—as if the pressures in her life would only get worse if she didn't resist.

"Madison?" It was Mom, and she was trying to make her voice sound sweet and kind—enticing. It was a familiar tone.

"What?" Madison called back in an irate voice.

"I need to speak to you, dear. May I come in?"

"I don't care." Madison knew it was useless to say no.

Her mom came in and sat down in the lounge chair by the window. Crossing her legs, she leaned back and smiled. "I tried to talk some sense into your father, although I'm not sure it's possible. That man can be such a mule."

Despite feeling slightly relieved that Mom was dealing with Dad, Madison was tempted to tell her to butt out and that she'd deal with it herself. Even if it made no sense, a part of Madison wanted to argue with her mom, to declare that maybe she *did* want to spend the week with her dad and maybe she *did* want to go to Harvard. Not that that was true, but what if it was?

She knew that was nuts. Plus she didn't have the energy to go there right now. She was so tired of conflict.

Her mom cleared her throat. "Now, I need to know what you've decided to do for spring break."

Madison groaned. She considered the family vacation homes. Maybe if they weren't already rented out, she could sneak off to one of them.

"You know Grandmother Marabella isn't getting any younger," Mom continued. "She would very much like you

9

to join us in Tuscany." She smiled in a catty way. "I know she wants to show you off, darling."

Madison sat up. "What if I don't want to be shown off?"

Her mom waved her hand. "Madison, what is going on with you? I thought you'd outgrown teenage angst by now. Is it PMS?"

Madison let out an exasperated sigh.

"It's just that you seem so touchy lately," her mom continued. "You're taking everything so personally—"

"Personally?" Madison frowned. "It's *my* life. Isn't it supposed to be personal? Maybe the idea of Grandma Marabella parading me around in front of her old friends feels a little personal to me."

"Why not just humor her, darling? You know you're her favorite, and you know she'll probably leave much of her fortune to you. Why not cater to her whims for once?"

For once? Madison stood up and began pacing again. How many times had Madison given in to various members of her family? Try *always*. How many times had she heard her mom say this—like she thought money was the answer to every single question?

"What if I don't want to cater to anyone's whims, Mom? What if I don't even want Grandma Marabella's fortune? What if I want a different kind of life altogether?"

Her mom laughed. "A *different* kind of life? You mean a life without money? Seriously, Madison, what kind of life would that be?"

"It would be a life of my own."

Her mom stood, looking directly at Madison. "You want a life separate from your family? A life with no trust fund, no inheritance, no credit cards, allowance, college tuition, or expense accounts? Do you really think you could make it on your own, Madison?"

Madison shrugged.

"What I *need* to know"—her mom's voice was getting that sharp edge again—"is whether or not you'll be going with us to Italy. Yes or no?"

"No." Madison braced herself for the fit that would follow.

Her mom took in a deep breath, holding it for a few seconds. "Fine." She narrowed her eyes. "But just so you know, if you stay home, your father will be calling. He will expect you to come up to Boston."

"I'll deal with it." Madison turned away.

"Have it your way." Her mom's voice was icy. "I will inform your grandmother of your decision." This was followed by the clicking of high heels across the hardwood floor and the solid closing of her bedroom door—a sound of finality.

Madison questioned herself—what if she'd made a mistake? Should she run out and tell her mother she was sorry and that she was willing to go to Tuscany after all? Besides, if staying home meant dealing with Dad and Garret—plus she knew Vivian wouldn't let her off the hook—what was the point?

Madison knew that Dad wouldn't give up on Harvard easily. She could hear it in his voice this morning. Garret would continue to pressure her to forgive him for yesterday and to go to his parents' vacant beach house. Viv would probably call every hour and text every few minutes in an attempt to entice, guilt, or coerce Madison into flying down to join her. Eventually one of them (Dad, Garret, or Viv) would wear Madison down, and she would cave. Right now, caving was what her mother expected too. Mom was probably just waiting for Madison to slink out and sheepishly backtrack, recant . . . apologize.

"Not this time," Madison whispered as she went over to the window. Looking out, she longed for some form of escape, some place to get away to. Despite the weatherman's promise of spring in the air, Central Park looked gray, gloomy, and cold in the morning light. Even so, Madison thought she'd rather be stuck in New York than placating her mother and grandmother over in Tuscany. Except that New York had its own set of challenges—namely, Dad, Garret, and Vivian's pestering calls. Madison sat down on the window seat and wondered what to do. Stay . . . go . . . run away?

She heard a *tap-tap-tap* on her door. Nadya. Their live-in housekeeper had been with them only a week and was still trying to figure things out, but at least she didn't come blasting in without knocking the way Maria used to.

"Come in, Nadya," Madison called pleasantly.

Nadya timidly stepped into the room, looking down at the floor in an apologetic way. "Excuse, please. Your mother . . . she ask me to help you pack, Miss Van Buren."

Madison blinked. "Pack?"

"For Italia."

Madison rolled her eyes. "I am not going to Italy, Nadya. My mother was mistaken. Sorry."

Nadya tipped her head to one side. "Oh?"

Madison forced a smile. "My mother and grandmother are going to Italy. I am staying home."

Nadya's expression was a mixture of confusion and disappointment. Madison suspected that the housekeeper had been looking forward to some peace and quiet and having the penthouse to herself. Perhaps Nadya had already invited

12

friends or family to join her. Madison had heard stories about housekeepers doing all kinds of things while home owners were absent.

Just then Madison's phone rang again, and with downcast eyes Nadya made a fast exit. This time it was Garret. She'd been avoiding his calls and ignoring his texts for almost twenty-four hours now. She suspected he'd be knocking on the door before long if she kept up the freeze-out.

"What is it, Garret?" Her voice was flat.

"Are you still mad at me?" he asked in a hurt tone.

"Maybe."

"Come on, Maddie, let's move on, okay?"

She didn't respond.

"Did you decide yet what you're doing for spring break?"

"Maybe . . . maybe not. What's it to you?"

"Come on, Madison," he pleaded. "I told you I was sorry."

"Sorry that you were flirting with Constance Westfall? Or sorry you got caught?"

"I told you—she was the one flirting with me. I already explained the whole thing. Why won't you believe me? You know I love you."

"I *saw* the photo, Garret." The image of her so-called boyfriend and that loser girl in what looked like a completely mutual embrace flashed through her mind again. Why was she even speaking to him? "A picture's worth a thousand words, and it will take more than that to erase it from my brain."

"Which brings me to another subject. Madison, why are your friends suddenly spying on me?"

She laughed, but not with real humor. "Spying? Vivian happened to be minding her own business going to journalism when she ran into you two. I'm just thankful she had the sensibility to snap a shot." Okay, the truth was Madison had been hurt and shocked when Vivian sent the photo to her Blackberry. But if she hadn't seen it for herself, Madison probably wouldn't have believed it.

"I told you that Constance kind of trapped me yesterday—everyone knows she's been after me since eighth grade. Seriously, the only reason she came to our school was to get her hooks back into me."

"And I thought our school had higher standards than to admit someone like her."

"Her aunt's on the board. Anyway, Madison, you know my heart belongs to you. If you let me, I'll prove it to you this week."

Madison closed her eyes and shook her head. She didn't need to be having this conversation right now. More pressure.

"So, did you decide to stick around then? I've already ordered a bunch of food and stuff to be sent to Nantucket and—"

"Sorry, Garret." Madison made up her mind. "I won't be around during spring break."

"You're going to Tuscany after all?"

"I'm not really sure."

"Well, you're not going to Palm Beach, right? You said you'd rather—"

"No, I'm not sure where I'll be, I just don't think I'll be around here either." She hung up, turned off her phone, and tossed it in her bag.

She was getting out of here. She had no idea where she was going, but she knew she had to get away—and fast. Her guess was that Garret, who lived only a couple blocks away, might be here any minute. And if he looked at her with those chocolate-brown eyes and started sweet-talking, running his fingers down her arm, she would begin to melt and lose her resolve. She had to make her getaway.

Tempted to escape without saying a word to her mom, Madison knew that would simply lead to more trouble—possibly the cancellation of the vacation in Italy, which would be blamed on Madison for the entire spring break.

She knocked on her mom's door, planning her strategy as she waited for her to answer.

"Have you come to your senses?" Her mom sounded hopeful as she opened the door.

Madison let out a sigh. "I really don't want to go to Tuscany, Mom. I feel bad about it, but you told me it was *my* decision, right? I hope Grandmother will get over it in time. I just can't deal with all the pressure. Can you understand that?"

Her mom frowned. "Are you feeling okay?"

"I just need some downtime." Now this was the honest-to-goodness truth. "I don't want to go to Italy and I don't want to go to Palm Beach and I don't want to go to Boston. I feel stressed and I need a break. Okay?" Madison felt on the brink of tears.

Mom put her hand on her shoulder. "Okay. I'm not thrilled with your choice, Madison. But I understand. Nadya will be here, and you can always call your dad if you need something. Or if you change your mind, just call me and I'll arrange for your ticket."

Madison hugged her mom. "Thanks for understanding."

Mom looked at Madison's bag. "Are you going out?"

"I just need some fresh air to clear my head." She smiled. "Tell Grandma I'm really, really sorry. You guys have a great trip!"

"Our flight leaves around two." Mom looked at her Chanel watch. "I still have a million things to do."

"Have fun, Mom!" Madison turned away, hurried out of the penthouse and into the elevator, and counted the seconds as it went down. The sooner she got away, the better she would feel.

Relieved not to have collided with Garret in the lobby, she went directly to the under-park and waited impatiently for the garage guy to bring her car out. The Mini Cooper had been a present for her sixteenth birthday. Naturally, everyone questioned her choice—she wondered how many other teens had to fight their parents to get a less expensive car—but she liked that it was green. Of course, it had taken her another six months just to get her license, but that was behind her now. Although her driving skills weren't stellar, and despite the fact that her mother thought she was crazy to keep a car in Manhattan, Madison liked the feeling of being behind the wheel—in control.

Of course, that control was questionable as she pulled out onto the busy avenue where taxis were blaring horns and traffic was moving at a snail's pace. Still, she knew it would've been worse on a weekday during the business commute. Driving in the city required two basic things—patience and courage.

As she turned onto a less busy street, she had no idea where she was going or when she would come back, but to start with, she would go with the flow of the traffic. After that she intended to just drive and drive—like she was running for her life. Maybe somewhere out there, on the open road, she would find what she was looking for. Perhaps she would even find herself.

2

Anna Fisher was bored. But she knew better than to say that out loud—especially when everyone was busy with farming and fixing and all the additional chores that came with springtime. Anna knew from experience that her mother's response would be simply to heap more work on her. Not as punishment, mind you, but as discipline—or so Mamm would say. Despite being seventeen, Anna still had trouble distinguishing between punishment and discipline. In fact, it seemed the older she got, the more confused she grew about much of the Ordnung.

As a child she hadn't questioned the community rules, but now she was unsure. To make it even more confusing, as a teenager she wasn't even subject to the rules. According to the bishop, Anna needed to discover for herself whether or not she wanted to be part of this community. If so, she needed to be baptized. In the meantime, no one seemed to really care what she was doing. Call it *rumspringa* or just plain indifference, but Anna felt caught in the middle, and there was much she did not understand. Yet she kept most questions to herself.

Now as Anna hung the morning wash, she felt unusually

restless, and as she looked down the road toward the Glick farm, she felt exceedingly sad. Anna's heart ached whenever she thought about Jacob Glick. The two of them had been best friends since childhood. As they entered adolescence, Jacob had become the love of Anna's life, and everyone in the community seemed certain the two would marry.

But Jacob had always questioned everything, and not just silently. He sometimes argued with the deacon about doctrine and faith and the ever-changing rules of the Ordnung. Then last fall his attitude and actions were described as rebellious. Jacob had been nearly eighteen when his parents decided to take action. Although their community's form of *rumspringa* didn't usually include exiling a teen, when Jacob explicitly informed the bishop that he never intended to be baptized, Jacob had been allowed to leave. He'd seemed glad to go, but Anna felt it was unwise.

"We let Jacob leave so he can return," his father had announced at a December meeting. "As you know, the apple will fall but not roll far from the tree."

Anna wasn't so sure about that. For all she knew, Jacob might never roll back to the tree. That felt wrong—and it made her begin to secretly question things even more. One of the things Anna had always loved about Jacob was his questioning mind. He was always thinking deep thoughts, searching for answers. Like she'd read in a book recently, Jacob thought "outside of the box." And now he was living outside of the box.

"I want to experience New York City," he had told her last summer on one of the evenings when they'd sneaked out to meet by the irrigation pond. "I want to see the Statue of Liberty and the Empire State Building. I want to walk through the Guggenheim Museum and Madame Tussauds."

"How do you know about all these places?" she asked.

"My great-grandfather's photo album," he confessed. "He wasn't born Amish. He was born in New York and then he went to war—World War II. I think it was hard on him. He became antiwar—I'm sure that's why he came here to live."

"I did not know that."

"It's an old story. My family doesn't speak of it. But someday I will visit New York City. I know it deep inside of me."

As much as Anna enjoyed listening to Jacob, his dreams had sounded impossible to her. Yet it was possible he was living them out right now. She hoped he was all right, safe from danger and not starving . . . but perhaps just hungry enough to roll back to the tree. Every night before going to bed, Anna said a secret prayer for Jacob, praying he would return to his senses, return to the community—and return to her.

In the same way Anna longed to see Jacob again, she longed for something different in her own life too. She couldn't put her finger on it exactly, but deep inside of her she desired something exciting or unusual or interesting to happen. Although she knew that was unlikely, since every day seemed to be almost the same as the one before. She knew she was supposed to practice contentment and give thanks for the goodness in her life—she was supposed to appreciate what God had given her. Sometimes she did, but not today. Perhaps it was spring in the air, or perhaps it was missing Jacob, but Anna was not simply bored and restless, she was discontented.

Anna knew this was a time in her life to practice some independence—this era was called *rumspringa*, and all teens were allowed to experience some safe exploration of life within the confines of the community. But that was as far as Anna planned to take it. She had no desire to be exiled out into the English world. She had heard horror stories about other teens, and the mere idea of being cast out like that was unsettling. To be out in that great big world all alone, fending for oneself, exposed to God only knew what . . . no thank you. Anna was not that bored. Better to be content with the morning sun on her back and the smell of the ripe earth, knowing today was pie-making day.

As Anna pegged the last towel on the line, she wished she hadn't finished her novel last night. She had read too fast. She should have been able to make it last at least one more day, perhaps even two. Now she wouldn't get another new book for almost a week. Why hadn't she considered that instead of selfishly devouring the words as fast as her eyes could move?

This "guilty pleasure" (a phrase she'd learned from last night's book) was something Anna and Mamm had shared for more than a year now. While the practice of reading novels was frowned upon by the deacon in their settlement, it was not against the rules, thankfully. However, her father did not approve.

"Why do you let your daughter read English trash?" her father had asked her mother the first time he'd caught Anna with one of the bright-colored paperbacks.

"It is not trash," her mother had patiently responded. "Grace Riehl recommended this book to me. Her Leah has already read it. Grace says it improves her reading skills." The Riehl family was respected in the community, so her father would not fault them. Still, Anna knew he was not convinced.

"Is it a true book?" he had demanded as he waved the book in the air.

"It is a *story*," Mamm had quietly explained.

"So it is not true." Her father's dark beard jutted out even farther, a sign that his stubbornness was kicking in.

"It is a story," her mother said again. "A story about life."

"But not real, not true," he insisted.

Her mother simply shrugged, returning to her darning.

For the sake of reading these books, Anna decided to step forward. "Jesus Christ told stories," she offered. "Jesus told stories to teach principles. Is that not right, Daed? Is that not real?"

His blue eyes grew troubled. "*Ja, ja.* What are you saying?"

"Were Jesus's stories true?" Anna persisted. "Were his stories real?"

Her father simply nodded. He reluctantly handed the paperback back to Anna and returned to fixing a harness. Fortunately, that had been the end of that discussion. Just the same, Anna had sewn herself a plain brown removable book cover that she claimed was to protect the books from wear and tear, but was in actuality her way of protecting her father's eyes from the book covers.

A few women in the community shared books, but the best resource for "Christian fiction" was found in the general store in the nearby town. Mrs. McCluster kept quite a large rack of these books right next to the kitchen utensils section. To Anna's delight, new books seemed to arrive with the same regularity as the fresh eggs and produce that Anna's family delivered to the store. Thanks to money earned from Anna's sewing plus the reselling of her gently used books, she always made sure she had the funds to purchase a new book or two whenever she got the chance to go to town. Unfortunately, her next trip wouldn't be until late next week.

"Anna!" Mamm called from the back porch, waving a white dish towel to get her attention. "Come—come fast!"

Using one hand to hold the empty wicker basket, Anna used the other to hold up the full skirt of her dress so she could run full speed. Her mother did not usually call with such urgency—not unless something was wrong.

As Anna sprinted across the dew-dampened grass, she wondered if her mother's anxiety was the result of the jangling of the telephone Anna had heard while hanging the wash. Their telephone, like that of their neighbors, was kept in the barn. There were many reasons for this inconvenient location, but primarily, Anna suspected, it was to discourage its casual use. Everyone knew the telephone existed primarily for business, and occasionally for emergencies.

"What is it?" Anna breathlessly asked her mother as she set the basket down on the boot bench.

"My sister Rachel is in a bad way."

"What happened?"

Mamm patted her tummy. "Aunt Rachel is with baby—she must not work so much."

"Oh dear." Anna tried to recall how many children Aunt Rachel had. Was she expecting her fifth or sixth?

"You know how Rachel is regarded in her community."

Anna nodded. She had seen it herself the last time she went to help Aunt Rachel. For some unknown reason—whether love or desperation—Aunt Rachel had chosen to marry into a different community. One where the Ordnung was Old Order and much more conservative. Unfortunately, Aunt Rachel did not always agree with the Old Order. As a result, she had been warned by the bishop, and although she hadn't been shunned back then, Anna didn't know how she stood in her community now. Many women in her settlement had distanced themselves from Aunt Rachel, almost as if she'd been shunned. But she did not seem to mind, except when she needed help. The last time Aunt Rachel had been in need—a couple of years ago—Anna had been called upon. It had not been an easy time then, and it might be worse now.

"You must go help Aunt Rachel, Anna."

Anna wanted to protest. She wanted to argue and say it was unfair and ask why someone else couldn't go help her aunt. But she knew it was worse than pointless. Perhaps Anna had brought this on herself. Was this God's answer to her boredom?

"Run and gather your things," Mamm urged. "Hasten! Daed is gettin' the wagon ready. Matthew will drive you to town, but you must be quick. Daed and Matthew must to finish planting the west field."

With a heavy heart, Anna hurried up to her room. Why this? Why now? Anything would be better than getting stuck at Aunt Rachel's. The last time Anna had visited, she had begun to suspect another reason Aunt Rachel's neighbors avoided her—her uncontrollable children. Who could stand to be around such wild things? The twins, Ezra and Noah, had been four or five and full of mischief. Two-year-old Jeremiah had been unstoppable and into everything. Even baby Elizabeth had been colicky, crying day and night. And her solemn uncle Daniel, unless he came in to eat, which he did silently and sullenly, had spent all his time in the barn. Anna had been so relieved to leave that place.

As she stuffed her clothes and nightgown into the duffel sack that her mother had placed in her room, Anna was tempted to tuck a couple of previously read paperbacks inside as well. Except that she suspected they'd be confiscated if discovered by her uncle. Anna felt certain that English novels were verboten in Aunt Rachel's rigid community, and not wanting to forfeit what she could possibly sell later, she reluctantly left the precious books in the drawer. Hopefully Aunt Rachel's baby would come soon. Last time Anna had been stuck there for two whole weeks, and it had seemed like two years. But she was older now. Perhaps she could endure more.

"I'm ready," she told her mother as she came down the stairs.

"I wish I could go," nine-year-old Katie said as she expertly slipped a round pie crust into the pan.

"I wish you could go too." Anna kissed her sister's rosy cheek. "Someday."

"Here is food." Mamm shoved a brown paper bag into her arms. "You must to wait in town until Uncle Daniel can fetch you. He cannot leave the farm until the work is done. Not until late midday."

Anna suppressed the urge to show her delight at this news. A whole day in town—all by herself! Well, that might almost be worth the sacrifice she was making for Aunt Rachel. Perhaps she'd risk buying a new book. She might even have it read before Uncle Daniel picked her up.

"How long will I stay with Aunt Rachel?" she asked as she and her mother went outside. "When is her baby coming?"

Her mother frowned. "Rachel says late April."

Anna blinked. That was a month away—and last time Rachel's baby had come late.

"I did not promise you for all that time, Anna."

Anna wanted to ask how she'd been promised at all—without agreeing to it herself—but she knew that was futile. It was not as if she had any say in these things. When someone needed you, you went. If a neighbor's barn burned, you helped build another. If a friend needed food, you shared from your table. That was how it was in the community—helping others. And if the others were your own family, even more so. But so many weeks with Aunt Rachel's irrepressible children? Anna blinked back tears.

"You will miss us." Mamm hugged her. "We will miss you too, dear daughter. But God will be your strength. When you return, you will be stronger. God will make you a strong woman, ready for marriage and children of your own."

Anna just nodded, swallowing against the hard lump that was growing in the back of her throat. It was bad enough being sent to Aunt Rachel, but her mother's talk of Anna becoming ready for marriage and children—combined with knowing that her parents had recently been favoring Aaron Zook for her match—well, it was all too frightening!

3

By nine thirty Madison was driving west on the highway. At first she questioned herself—why west? Then she realized it was the only direction where no one was pulling on her. Dad was north in Boston, Mom would be flying east by this afternoon, and Vivian was heading south. West spelled freedom. It seemed the natural choice for escaping everyone.

With the city traffic behind her and the highway lanes decreasing, she began to notice the countryside changing. Replacing the cityscape, urban sprawl, and industrial wastelands, housing developments, rolling hills, and small communities began to appear. She sighed to contrast this peacefully pastoral setting to her normal world of city traffic, blaring horns, and flashing neon signs. She knew by the barns and silos that she was in the agricultural section of Pennsylvania now, but it was like a totally different world. It hardly seemed possible that these seemingly endless lush green fields and cows were only a hundred or so miles from Manhattan. When she spotted a horse-drawn carriage on a side road, she realized she was in Amish country.

The only reason she recognized Amish country was because her dad had brought her out this way when she was about nine. On his way to visit a client with a large equestrian business, Dad had stopped in a charming little town for ice cream cones. Upon seeing the horses and buggies and oddly dressed people, Madison actually believed they'd stepped into a time machine and had been transported back to the 1800s. But Dad popped her bubble by explaining about the Amish people, and how they lived a simple life without modern "conveniences," including cars or electricity or cell phones or Nintendo.

After recovering from the disappointment that it was still the new millennium, Madison had been so captivated by this peculiar culture that she couldn't help but stare. Of course, that made her dad uncomfortable as he paid for their ice cream. When he said it was time to go, she was reluctant, but Dad promised to take her to another place, "even better than this," he assured her. Of course, it turned out to be one of those fake frontier towns where the people were wearing costumes and simply pretending to be early settlers. Madison had wanted the real thing.

So here she was again—in a similar sort of place anyway. She wished she could find that same town. Or at least stumble onto one that was like it.

Finally hunger and the need for coffee got the best of her, and she stopped in a small town that, while quaint, wasn't quite like the one she remembered. Although she was pleased to see a horse-drawn buggy parked on a side street.

Madison entered what appeared to be the only coffee shop in town and looked around to see fairly ordinary people sipping their mochas and lattes. Deciding to use the restroom before ordering, she took her time. Out of habit, she touched up her lip gloss but was interrupted by someone knocking on the ladies' room door. Madison tossed her lip gloss into her Kate Spade bag, then quickly exited and plowed straight into the woman who was standing outside. The impact caused Madison's still-open purse to slide off her arm. Tumbling down, it emptied its contents all over the black-and-white tiled floor, which now resembled a pawed-through sale counter at Macy's.

"Excuse me!" The startled woman knelt down, helping Madison to gather her Blackberry, Chanel sunglasses, wallet, and various beauty products. "I am so sorry."

"It was my fault," Madison admitted as they both stood. That was when Madison noticed the long cotton dress, black stockings, and homely black shoes.

"No, no. I stand too close to the door." The woman handed Madison the tooled silver bracelet that Grandma Marabella had gotten in Taos and smiled. "Very pretty."

"Thanks." Madison studied the young woman more carefully as she dumped the last items back into her purse, then securely closed it. She didn't seem as old as Madison had first assumed. Perhaps she was even the same age as Madison. But something about this young woman—something beyond her plain lavender dress, crisp white bonnet, and bright smile—made Madison stare, almost as if she were nine years old again.

"You are all right?" the girl asked with concern.

"Yes." Madison smiled. "I'm fine."

"Excuse me." With her head down, the girl hurried into the restroom, and the lock on the door clicked.

Madison just stood there, staring at the closed door and wondering, what was it about that girl? What was it that captured Madison so? Was it that she dressed differently?

Spoke differently? The innocent simplicity of her plain clothes and her sweet expression? Or was it something about the blonde hair and blue eyes? Sure, the girl was pretty, but that was no reason for Madison to obsess like a stalker. Really, she should go.

Yet despite feeling silly and conspicuous and slightly nutty, Madison couldn't help but just stand there, waiting for the girl to emerge from the bathroom.

"I'm sorry," Madison said as the girl came back out. The girl seemed caught off guard. She obviously didn't expect to see Madison lurking here, waiting for her. Why should she? This was just too weird.

"Is something wrong?" With a concerned expression, the girl glanced around the tiled floor again. "Did you lose something else?"

"No. It's just that . . . " Madison stared intently at the girl, slowly figuring out what was so compelling. "I couldn't help but notice *something*."

The girl's brow creased. "Notice something?"

Madison felt more than a little ridiculous, not to mention way out of her comfort zone, but it was like she couldn't stop herself. Besides, this was a day for doing strange things—like hiding out from her boyfriend and running away from home.

"Maybe I'm imagining it . . . " Madison paused. "But do you think we look alike?"

The girl's hand flew to her mouth, and she sounded like she was suppressing laughter.

"I'm sorry," Madison said again. "You probably think I'm crazy."

The girl shook her head, but her big blue eyes twinkled. "No. Not crazy. But maybe you need spectacles."

Madison smiled. "Really? You don't think we look alike?"

The young woman opened the bathroom door again. She gently tugged Madison in with her and they stood in front of the mirror above the sink. "See. You are very, very pretty. And I . . . I am plain."

Madison blinked to see them standing side by side. Unless she was losing it, which was entirely possible, there seemed to be a most definite resemblance. She was surprised this girl couldn't see it for herself. Madison reached for a couple of paper towels, using one to wipe off her lip gloss and dampening the other to remove the rest of her makeup. All the while the other girl watched with wide-eyed amusement.

Finally, with her face devoid of makeup and slightly blotchy from rubbing, Madison pointed to the mirror. "Can you see it now?"

The girl blinked, then leaned forward, looking first at her own reflection then over to Madison. She turned and looked directly at Madison and nodded soberly. "Yes. You could be my sister."

Madison laughed nervously.

"Like twins," the girl said.

"See," Madison proclaimed. "That's what I was talking about."

The girl continued to stare. "It is . . . what is that word? Freaky."

Madison laughed, then stuck out her hand. "I'm Madison Van Buren. What's your name?"

"I am Anna Fisher."

"You're Amish?"

"*Ah*-mish," Anna said.

"Right. *Ah*-mish." Madison said it correctly this time. "I

came here to get some coffee," she told Anna as they emerged from the restroom. "Can I get you a cup too?"

Anna looked a bit uncomfortable.

"Maybe you don't drink coffee," Madison said quickly. "Juice or soda perhaps?" Mostly Madison wanted an excuse to keep Anna here, to have a conversation with her.

"No, no, I drink coffee."

"Oh, good." Madison nudged Anna over to the counter now, waving at the board on the wall. "Pick out whatever you like."

"Coffee with milk," Anna told her.

"Okay." Madison ordered two lattes. Hoping she might entice this intriguing girl to sit a bit longer, she ordered a cranberry scone and chocolate muffin as well. She carried the tray over to a corner table, and suddenly Madison found herself sitting across from a person from a completely different world. As they sipped their coffees—which Anna said was very good—and ate the pastries, Anna explained that she'd been dropped off in town by her father and was waiting for her uncle to pick her up sometime before sunset.

"What will you do here all day?" Madison asked.

Anna shrugged. "I will look around. Perhaps I'll read my new book." She gave a mischievous smile. "I love to read English novels."

"English novels?" Madison liked some British authors too. "You mean like Jane Austen or the Brontë sisters?"

Anna shook her head, then reached into her bag to remove a flashy-looking chick lit book. "I mean like this."

Madison laughed. "I've read that one. It's pretty good." They started talking about books, and it turned out they'd read several of the same titles. "I guess we aren't as different as I'd imagined," Madison said.

"But we live in different worlds." Anna set down her coffee cup with a wistful look. "Where do you live, Madison?"

"New York."

Anna blinked. "New York City?"

Madison nodded. "Manhattan."

Anna's big blue eyes got a bit sad.

"Is something wrong?" Madison asked.

"I think my . . . my, uh, my boyfriend is in New York City."

"Really? Is he Amish too?"

Anna looked unsure. "Yes. I mean no. I mean he may be living a different lifestyle now. I'm not sure."

"He hasn't kept in touch?"

Anna shook her head.

Madison didn't know what to say, so she changed the subject. "Why are you going to visit your aunt and uncle?"

Anna explained that her aunt was about to have a baby and needed help with her other children. "I am not looking forward to it."

Madison sighed. "I know what you mean."

Anna seemed confused. "How is that possible?"

"I'm not looking forward to going home."

"Why not?" Anna blinked. "You must have a very exciting life."

"Oh yes, it's exciting enough. Sometimes it's too exciting. The reason I drove off this morning was to get away from all that excitement." Madison forced a laugh. "As I drove past all those sweet little farming communities, I felt envious."

"Envious?" Anna looked skeptical. "Of farms?"

"Of that whole lifestyle. I've always wished I could go back in time. The idea of a simple life . . . well, it's very appealing. All that peace and quiet, the slow pace."

Anna's expression grew thoughtful. "Yes, it is all that. Just this morning I told myself to enjoy the sun on my back as I pegged clothes to the line. I wanted to go to the pond and pick some daffodils, and today is pie-making day and—"

"See!" Madison exclaimed. "I think that sounds perfectly lovely. Hanging out the laundry to dry in the sun, picking daffodils, making pies."

Anna laughed. "Here I am thinking I would like your exciting and colorful life. I imagine it's like the books I love to read. So many are in New York City—all the talk of pretty clothes, going to the theater . . . *shoes!*"

Madison smiled as she stuck out a Louboutin short boot. "Yes, we Manhattan girls do enjoy our shoes."

"Jacob used to talk about New York. It made me want to see it too. I think that is why I love to read those books."

"You should come visit New York," Madison suggested.

Anna looked as if Madison had just suggested she should fly to the moon and sample the green cheese there.

"I know," Madison declared. "You could come home with me."

"No, " Anna said slowly. "Not possible. My aunt needs me."

"Oh, right." Suddenly Madison started to giggle. She couldn't believe what she was considering. Really, it was insane.

"What is it?" Anna asked. "What is funny?"

"It's just that—" She burst into laughter. "I just got this crazy idea, Anna."

"What sort of idea?" Anna leaned forward.

"We could switch lives."

Anna's pale brows shot up. *"What?"*

"Like that old children's story—*The Country Mouse and the City Mouse*. Did you ever hear it when you were little?"

Anna shook her head, so Madison began to explain the concept of trading lives. She even told Anna about some of the reality TV shows that did this very thing, although that just seemed to muddy the waters.

"I would become you," Madison said slowly, "and you would become me. We already look alike—maybe it's fate."

"It is not possible." Anna sighed wistfully. "But I wish it could be."

"It can be," Madison insisted. She told Anna about how she would mostly be home alone in the comfortable Manhattan penthouse. "Nadya, our housekeeper, is so new, she probably wouldn't even figure out that you're not me. You could wear my clothes and do whatever you liked—see the sights, go to the theater, just have a good time."

Anna's eyes grew big. "Oh no, I could not do that."

"You might find Jacob." Madison grinned. "You can use our phones and computers and whatever to look for him."

Anna's blue eyes looked almost hopeful now.

"What if you found him, Anna?"

Anna took in a quick breath and seemed close to tears.

"And while you're in New York being me," Madison continued, "I would be helping your aunt with her children."

Suddenly she imagined herself living the simple life—taking some cherub-faced children to pick daffodils, hanging the laundry in the sun, or making a big cherry pie. It was like a scene from *Little House on the Prairie*—the kind of "comfort TV" that she often watched in secret to avoid being teased by her friends. But if this trading places plan worked, she could be living the simple life for real!

"Oh, please, Anna, just think about it. What if we did it—just for one week?"

"But how?" Anna looked down at herself. "How can I be like you? You are sophisticated, a city girl . . . and I am simple, a farm girl."

Madison pulled out her Blackberry. "We'll exchange all the information we can today. We have several hours to do it. Then we'll stay in touch by phone."

Anna held up her hands. "I have no phone. Our community is not as liberal as some. Our bishop says no good will come of all these phones."

"Well, you'll have plenty of phones to use in New York, Anna." Madison winked. "I mean *Madison*."

Anna started to giggle. "Do you think we can do this?"

"Absolutely." Madison stood. "Back to the restroom, where our work will begin."

As Anna followed her back to the ladies' room, the wheels in Madison's head began to spin. She felt certain their clothes would fit since they seemed to be almost exactly the same height and weight. The shoes could be a problem, but Madison figured there could be a way around that too. After all, there were a few shops in this town.

This whole thing felt like playing a fun new game, and somehow she just knew they could pull it off. If all went well, she might even write about this experience for her sociology term paper. Not only could it be the perfect escape from her life, it might help her grade-point average.

With the restroom door locked, and with their backs turned to each other because Anna insisted, they stripped down to their underwear. Anna drew the line there, and Madison was actually relieved—it was weird enough trading clothes, but underwear . . . well, that was downright creepy. Then, with backs still turned, they exchanged their clothes and proceeded to dress.

Madison wasn't sure how she felt about the heavy black stockings, but the shoes fit. Although they were uglier than sin, at least they were comfortable. So was Anna's cotton dress. The pale purple fabric felt cool against her skin. It was probably softened from washing and wearing, and it was cut so loose that it almost felt like a nightgown. The smell was odd, kind of a mixture of body odor and sunshine. Not terrible. Just different. But Madison was having difficulty fastening the funny little wrap that went on top. Finally she looped it over her shoulder, but it still hung loosely around her middle. She asked Anna if she was ready.

"I guess so." Anna sounded dubious.

"Turn around then."

They both turned around and immediately started to giggle. "I never wore boys' trousers before," Anna said. "It is very strange."

"Those jeans look better on you than me," Madison told her.

Anna stepped up to adjust the apron around Madison. "The apron is attached with straight pins."

"Straight pins?" Madison frowned. "How is that possible?"

"I will show you."

Madison watched as Anna fastened several pins.

"You need help with your cape too."

"Cape?"

Anna pointed to the black piece of fabric draped over Madison's shoulders. "This is your cape, and it goes like this." She wrapped and crossed the straps around Madison's front, then pulled them behind her. "You use these straight pins to fasten them in back."

"More straight pins?" Madison tried to look over her shoulder to see. "That's all that holds it on?"

"Yes. You must do it right."

Next Madison assisted Anna with the wide Gucci belt and other accessories, except for her earrings, which she simply dropped into her purse. She looked at Anna and laughed, pointing to Anna's head. "What about your bonnet?"

Anna touched her white bonnet. "My *kapp*?"

"Is that what you call it—a cap?"

Anna nodded. "I am supposed to wear it always when outside of the home."

Madison frowned. "But you can't wear it and pass for me in Manhattan."

Anna looked stumped.

"And I can't be you without it either," Madison told her. "If we're really trading lives—even just for this week—don't we have to do this the right way? I can't pretend to be you without your bonnet—I mean your cap."

"But there is so much more. How will you talk like me?" Anna asked. "My community is a conservative one, and we speak mostly English." Anna looked worried as she adjusted the bracelet on her wrist. "But Aunt Rachel and Uncle Daniel's settlement is even more conservative. They do not use much English inside the home. Mostly they speak Pennsylvania Dutch."

"Pennsylvania Dutch?" Madison frowned. "Is that some kind of Dutch?"

"It is a German dialect."

"Great." Madison nodded. "I'm third-year German."

"Third-year German?" Anna looked confused.

"I studied German for three years in school. I spent six weeks of last summer over in Germany too. And I even know a smattering of Dutch." Madison spoke some German, and Anna actually understood some of it. "And your speech isn't that different from mine," Madison said to bolster Anna's confidence.

"Thank you. It is from reading English novels. I practice speaking it inside my head sometimes."

"We can do this, Anna," Madison urged her. "And if we do it right, you might not just have a fun break, but you might find your boyfriend." Okay, Madison knew that was ridiculous, but Anna didn't have to know that.

Anna reached up to her white cap, slowly removed it, and handed it to Madison. "I am you . . . you are me."

As Madison stood in front of the mirror, allowing Anna to comb and flatten her long hair—which was almost exactly the same length as Anna's—part it in the middle, and tightly pin it up, she wondered what on earth she was doing. Anna showed her how to wear the cap, positioning it just so on the crown of her head, pinning it securely, and letting the strings hang loose on the sides.

Madison leaned forward and stared at her image. She was someone else. While that was oddly appealing, she still felt uneasy. What if this was a mistake?

4

Anna could not believe she had agreed to this strange idea. In fact, as Madison did something with her hair, making it look fluffy like an Englisher girl, Anna reassured herself that this was only a game. A way to pass the time. They would play this odd game for a few hours, then exchange clothes again and go their separate ways.

"Madison," she said as Madison was showing her how to put on makeup, "what if I decide I cannot do this?"

Madison shrugged. "Hey, I can't force you to do it if you don't want to."

"So, if I cannot do this, you will understand?"

"Sure." Madison stepped back to study Anna's face. "Perfect." She smiled. "I'll understand. Really, I mostly offered this for your sake. I thought you'd appreciate the chance to visit New York and maybe find your boyfriend." She put the makeup back into the orange purse, snapped it closed, and handed it to Anna. "Because I could visit a farm if I wanted to. It sounds like your life is a lot more limited."

Anna nodded. That was true enough. Still, she was unsure.

"Now let's practice walking around town like this," Madison suggested. "We'll just see how it feels."

"And we'll see if I can keep from falling over in these high heels." Anna giggled as she looked down at the brown suede boots. She felt like the characters in some of her books. She often thought like them, but after just this short time spent with Madison, she felt she was starting to talk like them too.

"I have an idea," Madison said. "To make this realistic, we'll go different directions. You walk around town like you're me, and I'll walk around like I'm you. Then we'll meet back."

Anna felt nervous. Was she foolish to agree to this? What if Madison was tricking her? What if someone from her community came to town and saw her?

"Don't worry." Madison pointed to the purse hooked over Anna's arm. "You've got my money and credit cards and car keys and phone and everything. So you know I can't ditch you here or anything like that."

Anna picked up the duffel bag with her clothes and things and handed it to Madison. "Now you have my things, not that they will get you anywhere."

"So you want to try this?" Madison asked.

Anna giggled. "I think so."

"Let's meet at the café down the street for lunch, okay? At one."

"One o'clock." Anna turned to go.

"Hey, can I have a few dollars first?" Madison held out her hand. "In case I need a soda or something."

Anna handed the purse back to her. Madison opened a wallet and extracted a twenty-dollar bill, slipped it into the pocket of Anna's white apron, and grinned. "Have fun, *Madison*!"

"You too, *Anna*." Anna laughed nervously as they exited the bathroom and the coffee shop, turning to go in opposite directions. As Anna walked through town, she kept expecting people to stare at her as if they knew she was an imposter. But other than a few smiles and hellos, no one seemed to notice.

The more Anna walked, the more she started to relax. Even the shoes started to feel somewhat normal. Maybe she could do this. But was it wrong?

Of course it was. She was no fool. She knew it was wrong. But wasn't it also wrong for Jacob's parents to send him away as they had? And wasn't it wrong for Anna's parents to send her to Aunt Rachel's to work like a slave—for more than a month? What if she returned to discover they were intent on matching her with Aaron Zook? Didn't Anna deserve a short break? What would it really hurt? Plus Madison seemed so eager to sample "the simple life." Why not allow her this?

Anna paused in front of a small clothing shop called Lulu's. She had glanced in the windows before, often wishing she could sneak in unobserved and just look around the colorful racks of clothes. Today she could. So she did.

"Can I help you?" a woman with orange hair asked cheerfully.

"Oh, no." Anna glanced over her shoulder. "I want to only look."

The woman nodded. "Sure, just let me know if you'd like to try anything."

Anna wondered what that meant—to try anything—but hoping to play the convincing role of a normal Englisher girl, she slowly strolled around the racks and shelves and simply looked at all the different kinds of garments. So many colors and textures . . . so many choices. How did the English make all those decisions?

As she fingered the softest fabric she had ever felt, the

orange-haired woman returned with a wide smile. "You have good taste."

"Oh?" Anna nodded as if she agreed.

"One hundred percent silk," the woman assured her. "From France."

"Very pretty." Anna held up one with tiny pink rosebuds and green leaves and vines printed on a sky-blue background.

"Let's try it on you." The woman took the soft fabric and draped it around Anna's neck, then directed Anna toward a mirror on the wall. "It's lovely with your coloring."

Anna nodded again, just staring at the strange girl in the mirror. Really, that was not Anna. That was Madison Van Buren, the sophisticated New Yorker.

"Would you like it?" the woman asked.

"Yes." Anna nodded firmly. "I would."

The woman led Anna to the counter, and with trembling hands, Anna took Madison's wallet out and opened it.

"That will be ninety-seven dollars."

Anna blinked in surprise as the woman wrote something down on a receipt pad.

"Will that be cash or credit?" The woman looked up at Anna.

Anna stared down at the interior of the wallet, where a neat row of plastic cards glistened. She felt sure they were credit cards; she'd read about people using them to make purchases. Even so, she knew she couldn't use one. She didn't even know how that was done.

She looked to where she'd seen Madison remove that twenty-dollar bill. There were more bills there, but surely not nearly a hundred dollars. Even if there was, how could Anna possibly spend that much money on a flimsy piece of fabric, no matter how pretty it was? This was crazy. It wasn't even her money. What was she doing?

Then, as if she were a marionette with someone else pulling her strings, she extracted a crisp stack of bills to discover they were all twenty-dollar bills, and there were at least ten of them.

Steadying herself, she decided this would be the test. If Madison truly wanted to trade lives—just for one week—how would she react to Anna spending money like this? If Madison threw a fit, Anna would demand that they switch back their clothes and part ways. Really, wouldn't it be a relief?

She counted out the bills and laid them on the counter as the woman chattered away, wrapping the fabric in tissue paper and slipping it into a shiny pink bag. She gave Anna the change and thanked her. "Enjoy your scarf," she called as a dazed Anna exited the shop.

The bag felt as light as Anna's head as she walked down the sidewalk. Soon she began to feel a sense of excitement, a sense of adventure, and a sense of confidence—she could do this!

At one o'clock, Anna entered the café to see that Madison was already there. Still wearing Anna's best lavender dress, she was sitting in a booth and bent over as she wrote something in a notebook. "Hey," Anna called out, imitating how she imagined a character in one of her books might sound. "What's up?"

Madison looked up and chuckled. "Hell-o, Anna," she said in a slow, slightly stilted way. Was that how Anna sounded to her? "*Wie geht's?*"

"What are you doing?"

Madison nodded to the other side of the booth. "*Sitzen sie.*"

Anna smiled as she sat. "Pretty good, but not quite the same."

"That's why I have these." Madison held up a little paperback called *A Guide to Amish* as well as one that looked like a Pennsylvania Dutch booklet. "I've been doing my homework." She pointed to the notebook.

Anna leaned across the table to see what Madison was writing.

"I'm trying to write down everything I think you'll need to know in New York. Names, addresses, phone numbers, things like the security code to the penthouse, the doorman's name . . . I think it's all here." She flipped the page to a boxy-looking drawing. "This is the floor plan to the penthouse. See, you come in this door, and my room—your room—is the second door to the left, just past the powder room."

"What *is* a powder room?" Anna had read this in books but never quite figured it out. Was it a place where women powdered their noses? That was talked about sometimes too, but it never quite made sense.

"It's a small bathroom with just a toilet and sink."

Anna nodded.

"Hey, what did you get?" Madison pointed to the pink bag.

Anna suddenly felt uneasy. "A scarf."

"Let's see."

Anna pulled it out and handed it to Madison, who looked it over carefully. "Wow, it's Hermes. You have good taste, Anna."

"It was very costly."

Madison studied the little price tag still on it. "For Hermes? That's actually a good buy. It must be last year's design." She held it up. "Still, it's pretty."

"You do not mind how much it cost?"

Madison laughed. "I do need to show you how the credit cards work before you run out of cash."

While they ate lunch, they both took notes. Working fast and furiously, as if in class, they wrote down names and facts and anything they thought the other one might need during her week. Anna told Madison the most commonly used slang words, ones that might not be in the book. She spelled them out and helped Madison pronounce them correctly. She also drew a house plan, as best she could recall, of Aunt Rachel's two-story house. "I'm not sure if the boys are all in the same bedroom."

"How many boys?"

Anna held up her hand to count on her fingers. "Noah and Ezra are twins—they're probably around seven years old now. Jeremiah must be four. Elizabeth is two."

"Four kids?" Madison blinked.

"Do you want to change your mind?"

"No, I like kids."

Anna chuckled and wondered just how much she should tell Madison. But the further along she got with this game, the more she wanted it to continue. Maybe it was selfish or stupid, but more than ever Anna wanted to go to New York.

Madison slid a piece of printed paper across the table. "This is your bus ticket into New York. It leaves at 5:10. After you get into the city, you'll take a taxi home. I've written it all out for you."

They continued filling pages of paper as they exchanged more information. Every few minutes, they gave each other what Madison called pop quizzes, until it was half past four and Anna was feeling really nervous. If she wanted to change her mind, the time was getting short. Her uncle might be here in just an hour or so. But as the minutes ticked by, Anna felt more and more certain she was going to do this.

Madison was talking quickly now, as if she too was getting concerned about the time left. "Now even though I told Garret that I didn't plan to be around, there's still a chance he'll try to call me both on my cell and at home. I'll field the calls on my Blackberry, but you might have to deal with him in Manhattan, and I'll warn you he is a persistent guy."

Anna nodded. She knew Garret Stuart was the boyfriend who'd been caught with another girl named Constance Westfall, and that Madison's BFF had caught them in a photo together and that Madison was fed up.

"If he does call, feel free to dump him."

"Dump him?" Anna frowned.

"Yes. Tell him you don't want to see him. It's fine. I'll deal with him later."

"Right." Anna made note of the term *dump him*.

"Naturally, you'll be dependent on taxis to get around town since you don't drive, but that's what I usually do in the city anyway." Madison explained how she'd paid to park her car in a lot in town for the week. "They looked at me a little funny." She chuckled. "I guess they don't get many Amish girls driving cars in these parts. Anyway, I'll just pick it up when we switch our lives back a week from today."

"That's right." Anna felt slightly panicked when she realized they would have to meet and go through this whole exchange again. "How are we going to do—" Her words were stopped by the sound of a man's voice calling out her name.

"Anna Fisher?"

"Oh, oh." Madison's eyes grew wide. "Don't look now, but

a man in a straw hat and a brownish-gray beard just walked into the café. He's looking directly at me."

"Tall, thin man?" Anna whispered. "Narrow face?"

"Uncle Daniel," Madison exclaimed with a wave. *"Wie geht's?"*

Anna's heart pounded against her chest as she sat frozen in the booth. Her back was to her uncle, and although he couldn't see her, she felt certain he would figure this out. Then she would be in serious trouble.

Her uncle sounded impatient as he informed her that it was time to go, and everything in Anna said to stand up and go with him now, to stop this nonsense before it was too late. But she felt as if her blue jeans—rather, Madison's blue jeans—had been stitched to the padded bench seat. She could not move. Even if she did move, what would he say to see her dressed like this? No, it was too late.

Madison stood, and speaking in her odd-sounding German, she assured Anna's uncle she was coming. Nodding to Anna with a look of confidence, Madison picked up the notebook pages and stuffed them into the duffel bag. "Nice to meet you, Miss Madison." She hooked the cloth straps of the bag over her arm and hurried off.

Anna held her breath as she listened to the jingling of the bell on the door, followed by the solid sound of the door closing. Anna knew they were on their way, that it was too late to stop this craziness. With a pounding heart, she slowly stood, watching Uncle Daniel as he strode over to his black buggy parked by the general supply store. And Madison—Anna—was right on his heels.

A fresh ripple of fear rushed through Anna. This was wrong and reckless and completely irrational. Even though she would be severely reprimanded, she should run out there, confess her bad judgment, and put an end to it. No good would come of this switch.

Feeling panicked, she hurried out the door and rushed out into the street. But it was too late. The buggy was already a block away and moving quickly.

She watched as it grew smaller and smaller, then stared down at the wrinkled slip of paper still in her hand. Her bus ticket to New York. She pushed up her sleeve and looked at Madison's pretty silver watch to see it was already close to five o'clock. It seemed her only option was to go to the bus station and proceed with Madison's crazy plan. What choice did she have? And what did she have to lose anyway? What if she was able to find Jacob in New York City? Wouldn't that make all of this worthwhile?

As Anna sat on the bus station bench, studying Madison's notes and trying not to feel too guilty, she remembered something her father sometimes said when something strange occurred on the farm or in the community. *God works in mysterious ways.*

Was it possible that God could do something with this mysterious mess that she and Madison had created? Anna bowed her head and attempted to pray. Suddenly she became aware that her head was uncovered—not only that, but she was wearing boys' trousers! How would it be possible for God to listen to her prayers now? Oh, what had she done?

5

Madison leaned back in the seat of the buggy and sighed. So far so good. Anna's uncle hadn't even given her a second glance. As she looked out the window, watching the houses along the street slowly pass by, she felt transported to another time. The rhythmic rumble of the wheels rolling down the uneven street, the gentle swaying of the carriage, the afternoon shadows of trees and sunlight—all made Madison very sleepy. She briefly considered a nap, but unsure of the length of the buggy ride, she decided it made more sense to study her notes.

She reached for the duffel bag and suddenly remembered something. She had forgotten to get her Blackberry from Anna! That was going to be her lifeline. She had meant to hide it somewhere, just in case. She'd meant to pocket a Visa card too. But in those last minutes in the café, as they tried to exchange information, it happened so fast—the uncle arrived early, and now she was cut off. She smoothed the front of her apron and took in a deep breath, slowly letting it out. Wasn't this exactly what she'd wanted—to disconnect from all the pushing and pulling in her life? Well, here she was.

She pulled out her notes and booklets and spread them out on the worn leather seat. She decided to practice a phrase that she planned to use to explain her loose grasp of Pennsylvania Dutch language—her everything excuse. *I fell and hurt my head . . . I cannot remember some things.* Hopefully it would work.

Madison's childhood friend Lucinda Tompkins had suffered a head injury while skiing, and it had changed her personality as well as her language skills. If Madison could just convince Anna's relatives that this had happened to her, perhaps they would overlook some things.

But the more she thought about this whole mad scheme, the crazier it all seemed. Had she lost her mind? She wondered what Anna would do when the week was up and it was time to change places again. How would Anna explain her sudden ability to communicate clearly again? Would she have to pretend she'd fallen and hit her head again and returned to her senses? Really, this whole thing was nuts. Yet it was fun too. Madison decided she would coach Anna when they met in town—create a reentry plan.

Of course, this brought up a whole new set of challenges. How would Madison schedule this exchange meeting without the convenience of her cell phone? And without revealing her true identity, which would get Anna into trouble, how would Madison convince Uncle Daniel, who seemed a bit on the grumpy side, to bring her back to town next Saturday?

Madison shook her head and turned her attention back to her pages of notes. She would have to think about her exit strategy later. Right now she needed to do all she could to pull this off successfully. Fortunately, she'd taken a couple years of drama and loved participating in productions. For this performance, she should win a Tony! She tugged up one of the black stockings and went over her notes.

After about an hour, the charm of riding in the buggy had worn off. They were well into the countryside now, and the road was bumpier than ever. Madison's backside was starting to ache, and she desperately needed to use a restroom. She pulled out the house plan that Anna had sketched and searched for the location of the bathroom. Hopefully there would be one on the first floor and near the front door because she needed to go—bad. But she couldn't find a bathroom on either the first or second story. Anna seemed to have forgotten to include this.

Madison was tempted to call out to Uncle Daniel, asking him how far it was to the house, or if he might care to make a rest stop, but he was just turning down what appeared to be a long driveway. She peered out the window to spot a red barn and a tall white farmhouse at the end. In the dusky light, with the periwinkle sky and the golden light in the windows, this charming, quintessential scene could've been on a calendar or postcard.

As the buggy drew closer, she spotted a small structure between the house and barn, a shedlike building that looked very much like an outhouse. Not that she'd ever actually seen a real outhouse in person, but she'd seen them on shows like *Little House on the Prairie*. Was it possible that this outhouse was the family's bathroom? If so, why hadn't Anna mentioned this? Madison shuddered. Why hadn't she considered this possibility?

The buggy finally pulled to a stop near the house, and Madison fumbled with the door, rushing to get out. Uncle Daniel was saying something to her, but she just waved her hand at him. "Toilet!" she exclaimed as she hurried toward the small structure, which did indeed appear to be an outhouse.

Opening the wooden door, she held her breath and felt thankful that she wasn't wearing her normal clothes, because she discovered that when you're in a hurry, a simple dress with a full skirt could be thrown over your shoulders, which made using the toilet much faster and easier. The small space was definitely rustic and the smell was disgusting, but all in all it was better than having an accident. How embarrassing would that be?

However, as she finished up, fumbling in the dusky light to find a roll of sandpaper-grade toilet paper, she wasn't too sure she'd care to make a trip out here in the middle of the night. Seriously, what had she gotten herself into? And how long would it take to get out of it? She pulled down her dress, straightened her apron, and quickly emerged from the smelly outhouse, gasping for fresh air as the door slammed closed behind her.

Uncle Daniel was waiting nearby, peering curiously at her. He said something she thought was an inquiry as to what she'd been doing, which seemed rather obvious.

She pointed to the outhouse. "Toilet."

She blinked as he questioned her judgment in his odd-sounding German. Then he told her rather explicitly that there was a toilet *in the house*. Well, go figure.

He pointed to the outhouse now. "That is for *Yuchend*."

She couldn't help but laugh. He was informing her that the outhouse was for the boys. She held up her hands and gave him a helpless look, again speaking in German, saying, "I don't know." It was a phrase she would probably use often this week. If she made it for a full week.

With her bag in one hand, Daniel waved toward the house, telling her to come to dinner.

She rubbed her stomach for dramatic effect, telling him in German that she was very hungry.

He frowned curiously at her as he held the back door open. She suspected her German was not working for him. Or else he was questioning her identity, but she hoped not. Certainly she hadn't blown it already.

She followed him into an old-fashioned kitchen that was lit by several kerosene lanterns. There he greeted a very round woman with tired eyes, obviously Aunt Rachel, then he went out of the kitchen, saying something about putting Anna's bag in a room. He seemed eager to get away.

"Anna! Anna!" The plain-looking woman put a lid on a black pot, then rushed over and wrapped her arms around Madison and pulled her close.

"Aunt Rachel." Madison returned the hug. Her nose was being assaulted by so many different aromas now. Food cooking, perspiration, mustiness—not terrible smells, but they would take some getting used to.

Rachel held Madison at arm's length, staring into her eyes, and in that same odd German she said that Anna was different. Madison nodded nervously. How could it be that Rachel was already suspicious? Anna said it had been two years since she'd seen her aunt. Wasn't it possible that Anna had changed somewhat since then? As a distraction device, Madison pointed to Rachel's bulging midsection, inquiring to her well-being.

Rachel shook her head, telling her she wasn't feeling too good.

Madison made a sympathetic face, then hearing the voices

of children in the other room, she nodded her head toward the doorway, asking about the children. *"Un die Kinner?"*

Rachel let out a sigh, pushing a loose strand of mousy brown hair behind her ear, saying that as usual the children were loud and busy. As if on cue, the young voices in the other room grew shriller, and Madison was unsure of what to do. She wanted to look around, study the old-fashioned kitchen, figure things out. But that might draw Rachel's attention. What would Anna say or do now?

Before she could think of anything, Rachel took Madison's face in both her hands and examined her closely. Her words said that Anna looked older, but Rachel had a question in her gray eyes, as if something was not quite right.

"Ja, ja," Madison said in a dismissive way. Was the jig up—had Rachel already figured it out? Before Rachel could press deeper, Madison offered to go check on the children. Thankfully, this seemed to please Rachel.

Madison hurried from the kitchen into the next room, which was boxy and plain. Although the wide plank floors were attractive and a big rock fireplace dominated one wall, the general impression was sparse. There were a few pieces of rustic-looking wooden furniture lining one wall. There were no paintings, and other than several strategically placed kerosene lanterns, there were no decorative touches of any kind. On a worn rag rug in the center of the floor, three boys dressed in old-fashioned trousers with suspenders were arguing loudly, it seemed, over a wooden board game.

"Hello," Madison said cautiously.

One of the older boys jumped to his feet. "Nicht Anna!" She recognized the word for *cousin* and paused for a moment, trying to recall the twins' names. She took a wild guess as to which one this was. "Ezra?"

"*Ja!*" He laughed as she ruffled his blond curls.

"And Noah." She pointed to the identical boy. That was easy. She'd gotten lucky with the twins, but it wasn't likely to happen again. She pointed to the younger boy. "And Jeremiah."

He smiled shyly, then, while his brothers were distracted, he grabbed up some pieces from the board game and took off running. The two older boys yelled something unintelligible and chased after him. Jeremiah ran into a little dark-haired girl who had just toddled around the corner, knocking her onto her bottom on the hard floor. She burst into loud sobs. Just like that, chaos erupted, with the older boys yelling at Jeremiah and the toddler wailing. Madison wanted to cover her ears.

Instead she went over and picked up the crying girl, attempting to soothe her, but little Elizabeth's wailing grew more intense, probably from being held by a stranger. Then the volume of the boys' voices increased. Ezra shouted instructions at Madison, telling her to put down Elizabeth, who was now kicking her feet. Meanwhile Noah was demanding that Jeremiah return the game pieces.

As Madison set the struggling toddler back on the floor, she knew she was in over her head. This was too hard. She would not last one full day in this house. What on earth had she been thinking?

But there was no time to think. Rachel was calling them to dinner now. "*Schnell!*"

Like magic, all the children, including the sobbing toddler, raced to the kitchen and scrambled into their wooden chairs.

Rachel helped Elizabeth into her high chair, but the child was still fussing, and the boys continued to bicker over the board game. When their father entered the room, the decibel level went down considerably. Other than a few more whimpers from Elizabeth, the table grew amazingly quiet as Daniel bowed his head as if to pray. Everyone followed his example, including Madison. No words came from his mouth, although he appeared to be praying silently. Still, she was astonished at how long he kept his head bowed, and she was certain the food would be cold by the time he finished. But most astonishing was how his previously uncontrollable children waited patiently, especially when she was feeling fidgety.

When he finally lifted his head, the meal proceeded in a quiet and controlled fashion. It seemed obvious that these children respected, perhaps even feared, their father. Conversation was minimal, and the main focus was on the food and eating. It seemed that a special meal of baked ham, scalloped potatoes, and green beans had been prepared in honor of Nicht Anna's visit. The food, while plain and simple, was fairly palatable, or else Madison was just hungry.

When dinner was over, it seemed clear that the expectation was that Nicht Anna would wash the dishes while Aunt Rachel went to put her feet up.

The family had barely left the room when Madison knew this was going to be hopeless. Not only was there no dishwasher, which she barely knew how to operate anyway, but after running the tap water into the big stone sink, she realized there was no hot water either. How could there be with no electricity? She studied the sink area, trying to think how to best tackle something like this. A large enamel pan already had some gray soapy water in it, but it was cold and disgusting. She dumped it down the sink, then went over to where a big black wood-burning stove dominated the back wall of the kitchen. On it was a large cast-iron kettle. When she lifted it, she discovered it was extremely heavy—but it was also full of hot water.

Feeling like a clueless alien, Madison slowly put together a plan for washing the dishes. She would fill the enamel pan with this hot water, add soap—or what she hoped was soap—then wash the dishes in the hot soapy water and stack them in the sink. After that she would pour more water over them, and hopefully that would rinse off the soap. It seemed feasible. But as she attempted to carry out this plan, everything took exceedingly long. By the time she finally started to dry the dishes—which, thanks to the stubborn soap, had to be rinsed several times and eventually in cold water since she'd used all the hot—her arms were exhausted.

"Oh, Anna, Anna." Rachel frowned as she came into the kitchen.

Madison held out her now soggy apron, staring hopelessly at the dishes spread around the counters of the still messy kitchen. She was so frustrated she felt close to tears. And her hands looked like prunes.

Rachel looked truly disappointed as she asked Madison what was wrong.

Madison attempted to answer, explaining in a mix of broken German and English what she was doing, or attempting to do. But knew she sounded like an imbecile. Rachel shook her head and rambled on about how Anna was doing it all wrong—*all wrong*.

Madison held up her hands hopelessly, admitting that she knew it was wrong but couldn't help it.

Rachel studied Madison with a creased brow, then asked in German, "What happened to Anna? Did she get taken away, replaced with another girl?"

At least that's what Madison thought she said, but she wasn't sure because this dialect was so different from what she'd learned in school and what she'd spoken in Germany last summer. Anyway, it seemed obvious that Rachel had figured her out. She appeared to know that Madison was an imposter. What now?

Madison just shrugged, ready to quit this crazy game. She felt slightly sick to her stomach, not to mention tired.

Rachel put a hand on Madison's forehead as if to see if she had a fever. That's when Madison remembered her "get out of jail free" line. Perhaps it was worth a try. She would do her best for Anna's sake. Using her best German mixed with English, and showing a sad expression, Madison told Rachel a whopper, saying she'd suffered a concussion that had damaged her memory and language skills. Not unlike a device employed in a poorly written soap opera. Would Rachel buy this story, or would she see right through her and throw her from her house?

Rachel looked concerned, asking when this fall had happened.

Madison thought fast and then continued her pathetic little story in broken German and English, saying how she'd slipped on the ice last winter, falling and hitting her head on a rock and lying there unconscious for some time. Rachel nodded as if she understood how this might happen. Madison pointed to her mouth, saying her words got jumbled at times, and it was very odd, but she now understood English better than German.

Again Rachel nodded. Finally Madison pointed to her head, saying her thoughts were jumbled too and that she forgot many ordinary household things like how to wash dishes. Rachel put an arm around Madison's shoulders and squeezed her. "Poor Anna. I know something is *unnerschittlich*—I mean you are *different*."

Madison begged Rachel not to tell her mother about this. "Mamm will worry," she said, going on to say how her mother had been anxious about letting Anna come to help, but that she'd assured her mother she would be all right. Most of all, Madison wanted to ensure that Rachel didn't report this tangled tale back to Anna's mother.

"*Ja*. I know what we will do." Rachel gave her a firm nod. "I will help you. And you will help me. Together we will work this out."

"Together?" Madison asked hopefully.

"*Ja, ja*." Rachel pressed a forefinger to her lips. "It is our secret."

Rachel helped Madison to finish up the kitchen work in the proper way. She showed her "simple" tasks like how to store perishable foods in the icebox. She reminded her of the right way to dry the dishes and where the dishes went. How to save the food scraps into the right containers—blue bucket was for compost, black bucket was for pigs and chickens. Rachel was basically treating Madison as if she were learning impaired. Maybe she was.

After that they worked together to put the boys to bed, all the while Rachel instructing Anna step-by-step how to do this and that, which pegs to hang which clothes, where to place the dirty clothes, where the boys were to set their boots, how to help Jeremiah wash his face with a rough cloth, how to listen to their prayers, and to be sure not to leave the kerosene lantern behind since Jeremiah nearly set the curtains on fire recently. Finally they stood in the hallway next to the door to the bedroom that Madison was to share with Elizabeth.

"*Denki*, Anna." Rachel clasped her hand. "Good *Nacht*."

Madison told Rachel good night and thanked her too. With a kerosene lantern in hand, she tiptoed into the room where Elizabeth was already tucked into her small wooden bed. Madison paused to listen to the even breathing of the baby, and not for the first time, she felt guilty for being an imposter in this family. She shuddered to think of how these people might react, especially the sullen father, if they discovered she was not Anna but an interloper from the outside. It was frightening.

But Madison was so exhausted, she didn't have the energy to consider these things too seriously. By the time she searched through Anna's duffel bag—not bothering to hang anything on the pegs by the window, just digging until she found what she assumed was a nightgown since it was plain white cotton—all she wanted to do was sleep. The narrow bed creaked as she climbed into it, and despite the grainy feel of the rough sheets, the hardness of the mattress, the musty smell, and the strangeness of everything, Madison was thankful for this bed. Every bone in her body felt tired. As she was drifting off to sleep, she knew she would not be able to continue her charade. It was impossible.

In the morning she would come clean about everything. She would confess the truth to Rachel, beg to be taken to a phone since there was none in the house, and call Anna and tell her to come back here. Really, it was ridiculous to think she could pull this off. As for taking a break from her real life . . . well, she'd been wrong, wrong, wrong. For starters, this was no break. Even if her real life had some forms of stress, compared to living the Amish life, it was easy-breezy. It seemed her illusions about the simple life were just that—illusions!

6

Anna's heart pounded as she stepped onto the big silver bus. She'd never been on a bus before, had no idea what to expect. She hurried to find a seat, setting Madison's purse in her lap and waiting to see what happened next. The bus started to move, slowly at first and then faster. Suddenly she was clutching the seat, fearful that this big bus might go so fast it would fly right off the road.

To distract herself, she looked out the window, watching the countryside whizzing past. Fields, barns, horses, cows . . . What if a loose cow wandered in front of the bus? Surely there would be a horrible wreck. What then?

A young woman dressed in gray pants and a red jacket sat across the aisle from Anna. She opened a black leather satchel—or perhaps it was a briefcase—and slid out a smooth black object, opening it up like a book, only sideways. Anna peered at it curiously. Was it a computer? She knew what computers were—sort of—and she knew that Mr. Riehl supposedly had one (strictly for business use and something he never spoke of). She'd read of them in books, but she'd never actually used one herself.

Anna tried not to stare as the woman peered intently at

a blue screen, pausing now and then to do something with the buttons. Anna wished she was brave enough to ask the woman what she was doing. It was taking all her confidence and self-control simply to sit there—to not stand up and scream, "Stop this bus and let me off!"

Anna looked ahead of her to see an elderly man reading a newspaper. On the other side, a woman about her mother's age was reading a hardback book. Anna wished she'd had the foresight to have purchased a book before boarding this bus. That would have helped to pass the time. She couldn't imagine how long it would take to reach New York. Wasn't it an awful long ways away? Perhaps she wouldn't even be there until morning. Yet if that was so, where would she sleep? Right here on the seat? Why hadn't she thought to ask? Madison had written it all down—perhaps that was the "book" Anna needed to read right now.

As she dug for her notes, Anna wondered how Madison was doing with Uncle Daniel. Had she tried to engage the silent man in conversation? It would be futile. Anyway, they should be nearly home by now. What would Madison think of Aunt Rachel? Would she be disappointed?

Now, it wasn't that Anna didn't like her aunt. She did, but she just didn't understand her. Anna had grown up hearing whispered things about Aunt Rachel—words like too lazy, too fat, too old, too clumsy . . . she'd never find a husband. As a result, Anna had probably lost some respect for her aunt. Then being in Aunt Rachel's home and seeing that her housekeeping skills were sloppy at best, her cooking just so-so, her children ill-behaved . . . well, Anna had come to her own conclusions. Still, she had wondered why Aunt Rachel hadn't tried harder to make friends within her community.

Or perhaps she had tried. Perhaps the other women simply didn't like her. But this wasn't Anna's problem today. Right now she needed to get ready for her own challenges. She opened up the notes and started to read.

Soon after, Anna heard a jangling sound. It seemed to be coming from Madison's purse. She opened it to see the little purse phone all lit up. She picked it up and stared, trying to figure out what to do. Hadn't Madison meant to take it with her?

One of the little squares said talk, so Anna pushed it and said, "Hello?" Perhaps it was Madison, calling to tell her that she'd changed her mind.

"Madison?" a male voice said.

Anna bit her lip. "Yes?"

"Are you okay?"

"Yes." Anna glanced around to see if anyone was looking at her. She felt so strange talking into this tiny purse phone, not even knowing who she was speaking to.

"You don't sound okay. Are you still mad at me?"

"No," Anna said slowly.

"I told you I'm sorry, Maddie. Really sorry. Can't you find it in your heart to forgive me?"

She didn't know what to say. She'd been taught from an early age to forgive everyone, but she suspected this was Madison's boyfriend, Garret.

"Can't you give me one more chance?"

"I don't know . . ."

"Where are you anyway?"

"On a bus." She looked out the window where the countryside seemed to be changing or getting tighter, because the houses were closer and the fields were smaller—or was it simply because the bus was going so fast?

"A bus? Where are you going?"

"New York."

"Where are you right now?"

She told him the name of the town they'd just passed through, and when he asked why she was there, she got nervous and confessed she'd been in Allentown, but that only increased his curiosity. What had Madison said she should do about Garret? That she should dump him out? That didn't sound quite right, but her notes were folded up and zipped in a pocket of her purse right now. "I am very busy, Garret," she said crisply.

"So you won't forgive me?"

Anna frowned. Really, what could it hurt to forgive someone? "Yes," she said slowly, "I do forgive you. Now I must go."

"You sound kinda weird, Maddie. Are you really okay?"

"Yes. I said I am fine. Now I need to say goodbye." She pulled the phone away from her ear, wondering how to turn this thing off.

"Wait—wait!" She could hear his voice still calling to her.

She put the phone back to her ear. "What do you want now?"

"I want to make it up to you, Maddie. What can I do?"

Anna remembered now that Madison had said Garret was persistent. "Promise to never do that again."

"Sure, of course I won't. But I need to do something else."

"You need to say goodbye," she told him. She pulled the phone away and looked closely at the buttons. Although she could still hear his voice, she pushed the one that said END. That seemed a good choice. End the conversation and end the relationship with the cheating boyfriend—end of story.

Thinking about boyfriends sent her mind straight to Jacob.

She looked at the purse phone still in her hand and wondered if this might somehow help her to find him. Was it possible that he had a phone too? If so, how did one go about finding the right number? How did one go about locating someone in a big city like New York?

She looked out the window and was surprised to see that she was no longer in the country at all. Now there were buildings of different shapes and sizes clustered together with barely any room between them. She saw roads filled with cars, red taillights strung together in a long line. The bus must be coming into the city.

She pulled out her notes, trying to organize them so she could study them, perhaps even memorize some things. Why hadn't she done this already? She hadn't realized the bus would be so fast. She looked at Madison's watch to see that it hadn't even been two hours, yet she had a feeling she would soon be there. To come so far this quickly made her feel dizzy.

She stared at Madison's handwriting, memorizing the numbers of the building where Madison lived, the name of the housekeeper, phone numbers. She wanted to plant them like seeds in her head. She would need them.

But as she looked out at the buildings, which seemed to be growing taller, she knew it was impossible. She would be lost in this huge maze of cement and bricks. How did Madison do this day in and day out?

Anna closed her eyes. It was something she'd taught herself to do as a child whenever she felt overwhelmed. Not that it happened too often, but if a school test was too difficult, or if a sewing project seemed impossible, she would simply close her eyes and imagine clear blue sky and fluffy white clouds, and she would breathe deeply. That would calm her.

With eyes closed, that is what she envisioned now—blue sky, fluffy white clouds rolling gently, a summer breeze, the sound of birds.

She was startled back to reality when she realized the bus had stopped moving. The woman across from her was already gone. Others were gathering things, making their way off the bus. She knew she needed to do the same, and she should have felt glad to escape this big, fast, moving bus, but that meant she'd have to do something else completely foreign to her, something equally frightening—she would have to ride in a car. Worse yet, a taxi car driven by a complete stranger! Oh, why had she agreed to this?

The driver was standing now, looking at her. "Isn't this your stop?"

"Yes." She stood, clinging to the strap of Madison's purse. "I will get off here." With trembling knees, she made her way to the door and down the steps to where lots of people were walking around. So many people . . . It reminded her of the time she'd poked a stick into an anthill and all the little creatures had gone in all directions, some even climbing up the stick, which she'd thrown. At the time she'd wondered if they'd all find their way back home, but now she knew ants never got lost. Still, she wondered how all these people would find their way in such a big, busy city.

As she walked through the bus terminal, she noticed a mom with a baby in a pack and a toddler in a stroller. The young woman didn't seem worried about all these people, so Anna decided perhaps she should relax a bit too. She began to watch other people—people of all ages, sizes, and colors—and all of them seemed unconcerned about getting lost. In fact, many of them seemed quite happy to be here.

Then she noticed a man sitting on a bench who seemed to be staring right at her. He had grimy clothes and a dirty face, and when he smiled at her, she saw that his teeth looked dark and rotten. He reached out his dirty hand toward her, and she jumped back in fear, turning to walk in the other direction. What did that man want from her? Was he a beggar? She'd never seen a real beggar.

"Madison!"

Anna paused. Had the beggar man called out that name? If so, why would he know her—or Madison—or whoever? She looked over her shoulder as she continued to walk the other way.

"Madison!" the voice called again.

This time she looked to see a young man waving at her. Smiling brightly, he hurried toward her—and her heart leaped to see those big brown eyes. *Jacob!* Waving eagerly, she rushed toward him and then realized he had called her Madison—not Anna. She stopped suddenly. This was *not* Jacob.

"Madison!" He threw his arms around her. "Why didn't you answer your phone?"

"I, uh, I didn't hear it."

"I decided to surprise you," he said as she tugged away from him. "I looked up the arrival time on your bus and figured out that you'd—" He stopped speaking, peering curiously at her now. "I still don't get why you're riding on a bus. And why you were out by Allentown."

"It's a long story," she said, remembering how she'd read that line in a book once.

He put his arm around her shoulders. "Well, you can tell me at dinner. I made reservations at Palo's."

Suddenly Garret—at least, she assumed it was him—was

leading her onto a very busy street with vehicles everywhere and lots of honking and people and noise. He waved to a shiny black car, which somehow managed to squeeze past the other cars, pulling right in front of them. Garret helped her into the back of the car. It was roomy, similar to a wagon, only much nicer, and the seat was very comfortable—softer than a bed. The next thing she knew, she was actually riding in an automobile. Thanks to all the other cars clogging the street, they weren't going very fast.

"I assume you'll want to change." Garret leaned back and smiled at her.

"Change." She nodded as she tried to absorb his meaning. She had already changed from Anna to Madison. But she suspected he meant her clothing, that she would want to exchange it for other clothes, something suitable for dinner. How strange this all was. "Yes. I want to change."

"Don't worry, there's plenty of time. I know how you don't like to be rushed."

She looked at Madison's watch and nodded. She needed to get into this role better. Having him pop up like that had caught her off guard.

"So you didn't go to Tuscany." He sounded pleased about this. "You didn't go to Palm Beach or Boston either, so . . . what does that mean?"

Anna had no idea what that meant. She just shrugged and opened her purse as if something in there was highly interesting. She wanted to pull out her folded notes and study them closely, but she knew that would only make him curious. Thus far, she felt he was so pleased about being forgiven that he was slightly blinded—or maybe he wasn't a very observant fellow. If so, that was good.

He leaned over, gently placing his hand on the side of her face. "Did I tell you how beautiful you look?"

She felt her cheeks grow warm as she pulled away. Somehow she had to slow this down with him. "Just because I forgave you does not mean I—"

"I'm so glad you did forgive me, Maddie. Do you know how hard this has been on me? You know how much I love you."

She snapped her purse closed and looked evenly at him. "We have gone through a rough patch," she told him, again using words she'd read in a book. "For that reason I want to take things slow now. If that's not accept—"

"That's fine, Maddie." He threw back his head and laughed. "Why are you talking weird like that? You sound so different."

"Maybe I am different." She stared directly at him now, almost as if to challenge him to question her real identity, but he looked baffled.

"Okay, I get you." He frowned slightly. "You're acting all prim and proper just to keep me at arm's length. You probably expect me to prove myself to you. Right?" He looked at her with those big brown eyes so much like Jacob's—puppy dog eyes.

She nodded. "Right."

"That's what I plan to do." He folded his arms across his chest and leaned back. "You'll see."

Anna turned to look out the window. She had really meant to observe everything as she rode through the city. Perhaps she'd even imagined she would spot Jacob walking by, that she would tell the driver to stop, and she would jump out and call his name and they would embrace and all would be well. But as she watched people and cars and buildings moving

70

past her, she began to question the likelihood of a scene like that actually unfolding.

"Here we are," Garret said as he reached across her to open the door. "Want me to walk you up?"

She considered this. It might simplify things to have his help finding her way through the building. But what if she forgot the doorman's name or needed to pull out her notes to help with the security code in the penthouse? "No thank you," she said.

"The reservation is for nine," he told her.

She turned away to hide her shock. Dinner at nine o'clock? Her family would be asleep in bed by then.

"Can you be back down here by, say, 8:45?"

"Yes." She forced a smile as she got out of the car. "8:45." She hurried up to the building, under the awning that was just as Madison had described. She smiled at the doorman. "Hello, Henry."

"Good evening and welcome home, Miss Van Buren." He smiled back at her as he opened the door.

Beyond the glass doors, she stepped into a space as big as Daed's barn, but instead of dirt, there was a shiny floor made of some kind of stone and an enormous, elegant carpet, plus several chairs and a huge hanging lamp overhead that would easily fill Anna's entire house. Anna tried not to look too stunned or overly impressed at what Madison had explained was a lobby—a place to wait or just pass through—as she went over to what she assumed were the elevators.

"After the lobby, you go to the narrow part of the building," Madison had told her when Anna had questioned how she would possibly recognize an elevator—unless it was a grain elevator, which was not the situation. "There you'll see three sets of brass doors and buttons that are lit up. You use the elevator that's on a wall by itself, then you push up for up and down for down."

At the time, Anna had giggled, thinking that it all sounded rather obvious and easy. Now she was glad Madison had been so specific. Push up for up, she told herself as she pressed the button next to the single set of doors.

"When you're inside, the doors will close—"

"By themselves?" Anna had asked.

Madison laughed. "Yes. They open and close by themselves. When you're inside, you slide this card"—she showed her a silvery card—"into the slot until you see a green light, and then you push the button with the number 26 on it."

Now that Anna was inside, she looked around for a place to slide the card. After some time she found it, and after two tries she saw a green light. Then she pushed the number 26 button and waited, wondering why everything was so complicated here.

Suddenly it felt as if she were shooting straight up into the air. She reached for a rail on the wall, clinging to it as her head grew lighter. Did anyone ever faint in an elevator? There was a whooshing sound, and after a few seconds the doors opened, again by themselves. As she got out, she felt a strange popping inside her ears. This was all very odd, and she was thankful she'd asked Garret to wait downstairs. He would have thought she was crazy if he'd witnessed her just now.

As Madison had explained, Anna emerged into a foyer, which was another place to wait. This space had no windows, but it had a black leather couch and a black-and-white chair as well as a big, strange painting on the wall. There was a pair of big red doors off to the side. "Punch the code numbers into the keypad by the red doors," Madison had instructed.

Anna had tried to memorize the code numbers, but so much had happened that she didn't trust her memory right now. She pulled the pages out of her purse and looked for the numbers, then carefully pressed them in. She heard a clicking noise, then she tried the door, and—just like that—it opened. She had made it—all the way to New York City, to Manhattan, and into Madison's penthouse!

"Ah." She closed the door, leaned against it, and sighed joyfully. "Home sweet home."

"Miss Madison?"

Anna stood up straight as if at attention.

"You are all right?" A short, stout, dark-haired woman in a neat gray dress looked curiously at her.

"Yes." Anna nodded, trying to get her bearings. This must be the housekeeper. What was her name?

The woman came closer now, peering curiously with dark brows furrowed. "You are *all right*?" she repeated, a bit more firmly this time.

"Yes." Anna forced a smile. "I am fine."

The woman still looked troubled. Or maybe she was suspicious.

"I need to get ready for my date," Anna said in what she hoped sounded like Madison. She headed toward the left hallway. She knew Madison's bedroom was down that hallway and her mother's room was down the opposite hallway. But there were two doors in the left hallway. Anna glanced over her shoulder to see the housekeeper still watching her. Wanting to escape those dark, prying eyes, Anna nervously opened the first door but was dismayed to discover it was not a bedroom. It was a small bathroom—the powder room. Even so, she went inside, closing the door behind her. As ridiculous as it seemed, she thought perhaps she could pretend that was where she'd meant to go.

Anna's heart pounded as she turned on the shiny silver water faucet, allowing the water to go to waste down the sink, which looked like a giant glass bowl. This was her sad effort to appear to be using this pretty powder room. She had a feeling the housekeeper—what was her name?—was out there waiting for Anna to emerge for further questioning. After all her hard work, Anna could not believe she was about to be found out by the housekeeper. Perhaps she was on the phone right now, calling Madison's mother and alerting her to the intruder trying to pass herself off as Madison Van Buren. Worse yet, perhaps she was calling the police!

7

To Anna's relief, the housekeeper, Nadya (whose name she discovered by searching her notes), was nowhere to be seen when Anna finally exited the powder room. This time Anna went straight for the other door, but as soon as she went in, she thought she'd made another mistake. Because this room, on first impression, didn't look like a bedroom. At least not like any bedroom Anna had ever seen. Then she noticed there was indeed a bed—a big, beautiful bed with soft blue and gold bedding that looked fit for a queen. Not that Anna had ever met a queen, but she'd read about one once. This room seemed prepared for royalty. Was it possible that Madison was actually a princess?

Anna walked slowly across the large room, going directly to the big window. With wide eyes, she looked out to see a scene that resembled the night sky—only it was brighter and flashing and a bit frightening. She gasped to see all the lights and colors and shapes. She finally reached for the thick soft curtains, pulled them shut, and stepped back to catch her breath. It was just too much!

Turning away, she continued to take in the room, studying the details of luxurious furnishings, beautiful lamps, big mirrors, thick rugs. Everything was so fancy, she couldn't imagine how anyone actually lived here. She was afraid to touch anything. When she finally put her hand on the silky bedding, she jumped at three quick knocks on the bedroom door.

"Miss Madison?" called the housekeeper's voice from the hallway.

"Yes?"

"You need my help?"

Anna glanced around, wondering what she could possibly need help with when everything in this room looked perfectly immaculate. Unless the housekeeper could give her some fashion advice, which seemed unlikely.

"No thank you, Nadya," Anna called out. "I am fine." *Quit sounding so "prim and proper," as Garret put it*, she warned herself as she removed the short boots that were starting to hurt her feet. *Talk like Madison. Otherwise everyone is going to be suspicious.*

Anna noticed what she assumed was a television. Oh, she'd seen a television before, in a store, but it had been small and boxy whereas this one was large and flat. She knew from reading books that televisions were operated with things you could pick up and hold in your hand—things that were called *remotes*—but she had never seen one. She went over to the big black screen and studied it closely. If she could only figure how to turn this thing on, it might be helpful. She could listen to the way the English spoke and see how they acted and do a better job imitating.

Next to the television, she spied a black object that resembled Madison's phone. Was that the remote? She read the tiny words by the buttons. Although they made little sense, she tried pressing them: INFO, TOOLS, RETURN, MENU . . . nothing. Then she pressed POWER, and suddenly the black screen came to life. She jumped back as she heard a woman talking. Anna studied her curiously. She was telling about how she lost weight using something called Metaboglycemic and how "for only $19.95, you can too." Anna stared at two images of the woman—or so the television was telling her—one before, one after.

Anna blinked and stepped away. The English used pills to lose weight? Perhaps she should tell Aunt Rachel about this. But right now she needed to change her clothes.

Where did Madison keep her clothes? Certainly not hanging on pegs like at Anna's house. She opened a door and was surprised to see that it was another bathroom. She remembered the floor plan Madison had drawn. All the bedrooms had their own bathrooms, and this one was much bigger than the powder room. Everything in it was white and sky-blue and beautiful. The bathtub was huge and shiny, and there was a giant glass box that Anna supposed was a shower. She'd heard of such luxuries before, but besides the spray hose in their bathtub, her house did not have one. Unless she counted her father's cleaning station out by the barn, where he and her brothers sometimes hosed off the mud before coming into the house.

She opened some of the drawers to see all kinds of curious things, and she opened some cupboard doors to reveal stacks of beautiful linens, but she saw no clothes in here. Then she remembered another door in the big bedroom—perhaps it was a cupboard with clothes. When she opened it, she thought it was yet another room, except that it was filled with shoes and purses and clothes that were hung up with wooden hangers, like the store where she'd purchased the scarf.

With her mouth open, Anna just stood and stared. This room was obviously Madison's clothing closet, but it looked bigger than the bedroom Anna shared with her little sister Katie. All this for clothes? Anna just shook her head in wonder.

Now she needed to pick out something to wear. But where to begin? Anna started by removing her clothes, and it felt good to get out of those blue jeans. Oh, she knew from reading English novels that they weren't really boys' pants, but they weren't all that comfortable either. She missed her loose cotton dresses. As she recalled from books, girls often wore dresses on dates.

She went to the section of the closet that had dresses—at least she thought they were dresses. They were all quite short. She studied the dresses of every color and every fabric imaginable. Or even unimaginable. She blinked at a red one that glittered like jewels, then put it back where she'd gotten it. Next she pulled out a black one that glistened with hundreds of tiny glass beads. How long it must have taken to sew all those beads on. It was pretty, but how could she wear a dress that was so short? She held one up that seemed longer, but still it would be well above her knee. What would Mamm and Daed say? Well, she couldn't think about that now.

Anna heard something like bells chiming in the bedroom. Madison's phone! She ran to the purse and dug for the phone. "Hello?" she breathlessly answered.

"I know, I know," said an unfamiliar female voice. "I wasn't going to call you—and really you don't deserve to be called—but it's been almost twelve hours and I am totally desperate. Madison, you have got to come down here. I mean it. Seriously, I cannot do this without you. You must come immediately!"

"I . . . I can't." Anna took in a breath. This had to be Vivian, the best friend who wanted Madison to come stay with her.

"You mean you *won't*," Vivian snapped. "You're supposed to be my best friend and that's the best you can do? You are useless."

"I am sorry." Anna didn't know what else to say.

"Please come." Her voice softened. "I'm begging you."

"I'm sorry. I cannot come. It's impossible."

"I am dying here, Madison. You have to come!"

"Dying?" Anna felt alarmed.

"It is so freaking boring! I want to drown myself in the pool right now. Please come, Madison. It'll be fun. I promise."

"I can't." Anna was standing in the doorway to the closet. She needed to get off the phone and find something to wear. "I have a date with Garret and—"

"Are you insane? Why are you going out with that lowlife? You said you were going to take a long break from him. It's been like one day. What is wrong with you?"

"I don't know."

"Why do you sound so weird? Seriously, Madison, you do not sound like yourself. Are you sick or something?"

"I . . . I'm well. I just need to get dressed." Anna was tempted to ask Vivian for some fashion advice but suspected that would be a mistake.

"Fine! Be that way. Next time you want me to do something for you, you can just forget it. I am so over you, Madison!"

"I am sorry," Anna said again.

"If you're sorry, why don't you—"

That was it. No other words came out, just silence. Anna looked at the phone to see that the little screen was dark. She shook it and looked again. Still dark. Was it broken? Or had she done something wrong?

She shrugged and set it down, then turned toward the television, where several women were all talking at once in agitated voices. The women looked little older than Anna, but in the next picture, they were all smiling and they all wore dresses similar to those in Madison's closet. Anna watched as words came across the screen—*The Real Housewives of New York City*. She moved closer to the television, studying how these real housewives looked. Certainly nothing like the wives in Anna's community. But then she knew that everything was different here. This was how people in New York dressed.

She returned to the closet, finally picking out a sleeveless dark blue dress in a shiny fabric. This would be an acceptable color in her community. Almost all shades of blue, many shades of purple, and some subdued red tones, as well as pastels (on younger women) were common. Dark blue was quite respectable for most any age and any occasion. Of course, that was nearly all that would be respectable about this garment.

Anna looked through some of the drawers to find very interesting sorts of undergarments, hosiery, and other things. She picked a pair of black stockings, hoping that would help make up for the length of the dress, then she found a pair of black shoes. After a few minutes, she managed to dress herself, but when she looked at her reflection in the mirror, she couldn't help but laugh. She did not look right. Her white cotton undergarments peeked out from beneath the dress, and the black stockings and shoes . . . well, she was no expert, but she knew they were all wrong too.

Still wearing this outfit, she studied the television, hoping to get some fashion direction, but now there was a woman dancing around in undergarments—very skimpy undergarments that were red as blood. Anna blinked then stared. She was shocked that someone would want to be on television dressed like that—for all the world to see. But now she realized that if she was going to dress like a modern Englisher girl, she would need to wear Madison's undergarments as well.

Starting over, she returned to the closet and peeled off the clothes, this time putting on some of Madison's skimpy undergarments. It felt strange, and she could not imagine ever letting anyone—certainly not the whole television world—see her in these things. Then she put the blue dress back on.

Now that looked better. Except for her bare legs, which, unlike the TV women's, were pale. She picked up the black hose again, deciding she didn't care if she was less fashionable than Madison. If she felt more covered in these stockings, that was her choice. Instead of the high-heeled shoes, she picked out a pair of brown suede boots that were actually quite comfortable. Then she found a little purple sweater that she put on over the dress.

She looked at her image in the mirror again and frowned. She looked nothing like the housewives of New York City. Knowing it was probably hopeless, she decided she didn't care. Perhaps she would pretend that Madison had experienced some kind of life-changing revelation, that she had decided to toss fashion to the wind.

Because she was missing her *kapp*, Anna looked through a collection of hats, finally selecting a bright pink one. Before she put in on, she braided her hair in two pigtails just like her mother used to do when she was a little girl.

She laughed to see her reflection now. She would probably

scare Garret off with this strange getup. Perhaps that would be a good thing. Just for fun, she put a shiny red belt around her waist, then looked through Madison's jewelry collection. Finding a big brooch filled with lots of colorful jewels, she pinned it to the sweater and nodded with satisfaction. She looked a bit like a rainbow, or perhaps like one of the more colorful quilts that she sometimes helped to put together with the other women in her community.

To this colorful collection of garments, she added the orange purse that she'd been carrying all day. When she emerged from the bedroom, Nadya, who was standing nearby pretending to dust, stared at her with a shocked expression. As if she couldn't believe what she was seeing.

"How do I look?" Anna asked, suppressing the urge to giggle.

Nadya nodded with a bewildered expression. "You, uh, you look good, Miss Madison."

"Thank you!" Feeling Nadya's eyes still on her, Anna opened the front door. "See you later," she called, hoping she sounded more like Madison than she looked.

Anna pushed the only button by the elevator and waited for the doors to open and close. Nothing happened. She looked at all the buttons with all the numbers and wondered what to do. Put in the card and push 26 again? She was about to dig out the notes, but suddenly the elevator started to go down all by itself. She felt a bit nervous but thought maybe the elevator knew what it was doing. It stopped and the doors opened. Thinking it must be the lobby, Anna started to get out.

"Cool your jets." A short, dark-haired girl gently pushed Anna back into the elevator. "This isn't the lobby, silly."

"Oh?" Anna blinked at her. She had very short hair, big

dark eyes, and was wearing a black dress topped by a bright jacket of yellow and red.

"Didn't you push it?" The girl reached over to the row of lit-up number buttons, pushing the one with an L on it, and just like that, the elevator began going down again.

Push the L button, Anna told herself, *to go down. L must be for lobby.*

"What *are* you wearing?" The girl stared at Anna curiously.

Anna shrugged. "This and that."

The girl laughed. "It looks like a Madison Van Buren original."

Anna tried not to look shocked. Obviously, this girl knew Madison. But who was she?

The girl looked more closely at her. "Seriously, Madison, it's not a bad look. Kudos to you for trying something new."

"Thank you." Anna nodded, wondering what kudos were.

"Too bad you're not interested in helping with Fashion Fling this year."

Anna frowned. What was a fashion fling? Throwing clothes, perhaps?

"But then I guess you don't care about starving Haitian orphans or—"

"I do care," Anna insisted. Just then the elevator stopped and the doors opened, and there standing in the lobby was Garret. At first he smiled, but then as if seeing her better, he looked somewhat confused.

"Hey, Madison," he said as he stepped toward the elevator.

"You're not still with that loser, are you?" The strange girl said this quietly, then shook her head as if disappointed.

"Hello, Lucinda." Garret spoke in a flat-sounding voice, as if merely being polite but not caring much for this girl.

Lucinda just rolled her dark eyes at him and continued walking, her red high heels clicking on the stone floor ahead of them. Once outside, she was joined by several other young people who must have been waiting for her.

"Too bad you had to run into *Ms. Tompkins*," Garret said with mock sympathy. "Hopefully she didn't spoil your appetite."

Anna gave him a smirky smile. Now she knew the girl's name was Lucinda Tompkins, and that Garret and Lucinda were not friends. "No, I still have an appetite," she assured him as they went outside.

"Interesting ensemble you're wearing tonight." He glanced curiously at her.

"Thank you very much." She faked a smile. "I felt like doing something different."

He nodded. "You can say that again."

"Haven't you heard? Change is good." She waited as he opened the door to the black car. She remembered reading that line in a book, always wishing she could use it.

He gave her a sideways glance. "Seriously, Madison, did you just say change is good?"

She nodded as she slid across the smooth seat, pushing the hem of her skirt closer to her knees and trying not to cringe at the shortness.

He laughed as he sat down next to her. "That does not sound like my Maddie."

She shrugged. "Maybe it's because I'm changing."

"I'll say."

"Lucinda asked me about Fashion Fling," Anna began carefully. Mostly she wanted to change the subject, but she was also curious about that girl.

"Don't tell me you're thinking about modeling for her ridiculous fund-raiser?"

"What's wrong with raising money for Haitian orphans?" She imitated Lucinda in her challenge to him.

"Just make a donation like you did last year."

She folded her arms across her front and leaned back.

He turned to study her. "Okay, Maddie, I have to know. What is going on with you?" He plucked at one of her braids, then shook his head. "I mean first you run off to—what, Amish land? Then you're riding around on a bus? What's up with that?"

"It's a long story," she told him again. As the words came out of her mouth, she knew exactly what kind of a story it was going to be. Part true, part imagination . . . and hopefully helpful to her mission. Because that, she had decided, was what this week was going to be. A mission to find Jacob.

"I'd like to hear it," Garret said.

She repeated the tale Madison had told her, saying how she was fed up with everything, how there was too much stress, and how she'd driven west and gone looking for the simple life. Because it was true—for Madison anyway—it sounded believable.

He laughed. "Seriously? You did that?"

She nodded.

He still looked skeptical. "Where's your car then?"

Anna took in a slow breath, wondering how to answer this one. "Well . . . it broke down."

"Broke down?"

Fortunately, the driver had pulled over, and it was time for them to get out and go into the restaurant, which allowed her more time to stitch the story together in her head. It was similar to quilt making, fitting in different shapes and sizes, sewing them neatly together to make one whole quilt. She would attempt to make one whole story.

After a bit, they were seated at a table in the crowded and noisy restaurant. Although she'd read about people ordering food in books, she had no idea how to go about it. Despite being in English, or partly, the menu seemed like a different language. The only restaurant she had eaten in, and only a couple of times, served simple foods like steak and potatoes or macaroni and cheese. Nothing like this. To her relief, Garret offered to order for both of them.

"Unless you've changed about liking that too," he said cautiously.

"No, no," she said quickly. "Not yet anyway."

"Right." He spoke directly to the waiter, ordering strange-sounding things she'd never heard of before. She just hoped she could eat them without looking too ridiculous—or getting sick.

The waiter left, and Garret turned back to her. "So your car . . . where is it?"

"I had to leave it in Friedrich," she told him. "Until it's fixed."

He looked dubious. "Don't tell me you're trusting some small-town mechanic with your beloved Cooper?"

She thought for a moment. Perhaps Cooper was another word for car. "A very fine mechanic," she said. "But I thought you wanted to hear my story, Garret. Or do you prefer to talk about Cooper?"

He nodded. "Yes, please, continue your story. It's like something from *The Twilight Zone*."

She wasn't sure how to respond to that either, so she simply continued. "While in Allentown I met a girl who was Amish, and we spent quite a bit of time together. You see, I was waiting for the bus to come." She paused to take a sip of some of the strange fizzy water that he'd ordered for her.

He still looked puzzled, but thankfully, he kept his mouth shut.

"The girl's name was Anna, and she told me about her boyfriend who is living in New York City."

Garret's perplexed expression seemed to be bordering on boredom now.

She needed to hurry her story. "I told this Anna that I would try to find her boyfriend for—"

"Hey, is he one of those guys like on that MTV show with the weird name? You know, where Amish force their teens to go out and live on their own, and these guys do all kinds of wild and crazy—"

"No. Not that kind of *rumspringa*," she said quickly.

"Yeah, that's what it's called. *Rumspringa*."

"It is not like that," she told him. She considered how much to say without revealing her true identity. "Anna told me that Jacob didn't agree with his family on some things. He had a grandfather who'd come from New York. So Anna felt sure that Jacob would be here."

"Did Anna have an address or phone number?"

Anna frowned. "No. Just his name."

Garret gave her a hopeless look. "Finding an Amish guy with just a name? Let me guess, his last name is Smith. That should make it really easy."

"No. His last name is Glick. Jacob Edgar Glick."

"Even so . . ." He shook his head. "You'll never find him."

"How can you be so sure?"

Garret went on and on in a rather arrogant way, talking about how many people lived in the New York City metro area, how there were so many boroughs, so many places for people to hide who didn't want to be found. "And with no phone . . ." He held up his hands. "Impossible."

"For someone who sounds so smart, like he's such an expert, you certainly give up easily."

"I'm an expert?" He frowned.

"You talk as if you know so much about it, Garret. As if you are so much smarter than I am. Doesn't that sound like an expert?"

He shrugged. "Not really."

"Just not smart enough to actually find someone though." She was hoping to challenge him. It was a tactic that often worked with her brothers—to act as if something was too hard for them—and then they would attempt it.

"I don't know." With a thoughtful expression, he broke a piece of bread in two. "I *might* be able to find him."

"Really?" She tried not to look too hopeful.

"Why is it so important to you anyway, Madison? Since when did you start to care about poor little Amish girls?"

"They're people too, aren't they?"

His eyes narrowed slightly, almost as if he suspected he wasn't really speaking to Madison.

"Remember what I said, that change is good." She smiled. "I thought you liked that."

To her relief, he smiled back. "I do like it. I'm just trying to get used to it."

Their food was served, and as she imitated how he ate and tried to pretend she was enjoying some strange-tasting foods, she also worked to keep him distracted. She hoped she was getting him involved by plying him with questions about how one would hunt down a missing person in New York. By the time they were served dessert, some kind of a chocolate cake that was actually quite tasty, Garret almost seemed to be growing interested in helping her. Unfortunately, he seemed equally interested in getting her to come to a vacation house with him—one that was owned by his family and was vacant for the entire week.

"I can't think of going anywhere or doing anything," she told him when they were back at Madison's building, "until I do everything possible to find Jacob Glick. I promised Anna."

"So you're saying that if we locate this Glick dude, you'll come to Nantucket with me?"

"I thought you said it would be impossible to find him," she said in a teasing tone.

"Well, maybe I want to prove myself wrong."

She gave him her biggest smile. "If you do that, Garret, you will be my own personal hero."

His eyes lit up. "Really?"

She nodded.

"Can I come up with you?" he asked as he helped her out of the car.

"No." She shook her head. "All I want to do is go to bed right now."

He made a face like a small boy might do. "It's not even late."

"I am very tired."

"Okay. I'll call you in the morning."

"Oh yes." She remembered something. "My phone is broken."

"Broken?" He looked dubious.

"Yes. I was talking to Vivian and it quit working."

"It was charged?"

She frowned. "Charged?"

His brow creased like he questioned her sensibility or, worse, her identity.

"Thank you for dinner," she said quickly. "I need to go to bed so I can get up early tomorrow. I will start looking for Jacob Glick."

He gave her a mystified look, but it seemed tinged with something else too. Perhaps admiration. "You know, Madison, I'm liking this change in you. I don't think I've ever seen you so concerned about someone else. It's kind of attractive." He leaned toward her, but before he could kiss her (she felt certain that was about to happen), she slipped away, shooting him a big grin as she waved and dashed toward the doorman.

"See you, Garret."

"I'll call you in the morning," he yelled after her.

"Thank you!"

Anna knew she was being false. She knew it was wrong to trick Garret into helping her like this, playing as if she would reward him somehow if he found Jacob. But it seemed her only chance. It seemed a safe risk. As badly as she wanted it, what were the chances Garret would actually find Jacob? If he didn't, she would owe him nothing.

On the other hand, if he did find Jacob . . . well, wouldn't that just change everything? Naturally, her real identity would be revealed then. How could she keep it a secret with Jacob in the picture? And if he was in the picture, it would no longer matter what she'd promised to Garret. All that would matter would be starting a new life with Jacob.

At least that's what she told herself as she fell into a bed so soft she imagined it was a cloud, like a heavenly bed she might sleep in someday. That is, if she ever straightened out her life enough to have a chance to be received in heaven. That seemed highly unlikely now.

8

Something had disturbed Madison's sleep. Not that she'd been sleeping very soundly since this mattress must've been stuffed with potatoes, or maybe rocks. She had been having an interesting dream that she wanted to finish—traveling in a foreign country, she'd been speaking and thinking in fluent German.

"Mamm! Mamm! Mamm!"

Madison sat up and rubbed her eyes. What was that? Blinking to see a dull gray light peeking beneath the bottom of the white linen curtain on the window, she realized it was predawn. Had she ever been up this early before? Maybe at summer camp. She heard a rooster crow, followed by the sound of a child crying. Then she remembered where she was—realizing this wasn't just a dream.

"Mamm! Mamm!"

"Shush, shush," Madison told Elizabeth. She spoke in perfect German—just like in her dream. Although telling this fussing child to go back to sleep was probably like telling the sun not to come up.

With great reluctance, Madison got out of bed. Shivering, she crept across the drafty pine floor to peer into the wooden crib. Elizabeth looked at her with a curious expression, watery eyes, and a drippy nose.

"*Guder Mariye*," Madison said in a gentle voice. "What do you want?"

Elizabeth held her hands out to be picked up.

"You want Nicht Anna to hold you?"

Elizabeth nodded as if she understood English. Maybe she did. Madison reached down and picked the child up, holding her close and attempting to soothe her with a mix of English and German. To her relief, Elizabeth seemed comfortable with her this morning. She even smiled, patting Madison's cheek with a chubby little hand. That's when Madison realized that her nightgown was growing damp.

"Oh!" Madison held Elizabeth back to see that both of their nightgowns were soggy and smelling of urine. She wrinkled her nose. "You are wet."

"*Wie geht's*, Anna?" Rachel yawned as she came into the room. "*Wie geht's*, Elizabeth?"

"She is wet," Madison said.

Rachel laughed, saying something in German slang to Elizabeth as she gingerly removed her from Madison's arms. Setting the little girl on the floor, Rachel peeled off the soggy nightgown and tossed it toward the crib. She pointed to the pegs by Elizabeth's bed. "You can dress her."

Madison nodded. Rachel padded out of the bedroom, leaving Madison to figure out how to do this. Shouldn't the child have a bath? Would that involve heating water? Elizabeth was shivering, so Madison decided just to get some clothes on her before she developed pneumonia. After a brief struggle, Madison managed to get the child into fresh undergarments and a dress, but no shoes, before Elizabeth dashed from the room.

"Good riddance." Madison shut the door and looked down at her own dampened nightgown, wondering how she would get herself clean without the comfort of warm water. Seriously, how did people live like this? And why?

She gathered up Anna's dress, the same one she'd worn yesterday, and went down the hall to the sparse bathroom. Using a rough rag, cold water, and some soap that smelled like old tennis shoes, she attempted to clean herself and dress. She had to get out of this place—the sooner the better. If only she'd remembered to keep her phone.

As she went back to her room, tossing the soiled nightgown next to the child's on the floor, Madison remembered something.

"Uncle Daniel has a phone in the barn," Anna had told her yesterday. Was it only yesterday they'd sat in the café together?

When Madison had asked why anyone would keep a phone in a barn, Anna had explained that it was only for farm business and emergencies.

"Well, this is an emergency," Madison said as she slipped her feet into Anna's shoes. "Anna better answer the phone!"

Madison tiptoed down the stairs, but the wooden treads creaked here and there. She hoped the sounds of the boys' voices would camouflage her noise. It sounded like Rachel was getting them up, telling them to get dressed and get to their chores. Madison crept through the living room and peeked into the kitchen to make sure Daniel wasn't lurking in there, but other than a big pot boiling on the cast-iron stove, the kitchen was still. She quietly opened the back door and surveyed the farm, which seemed stark and harsh in the light of day, much less romanticized than it had appeared last night in the purple dusky light. Some chickens squawked and a cow mooed, but no one seemed to be in sight.

She looked every which way, then sprinted across the hard-packed soil to the barn. Once she was inside, hiding in the shadow between the door and a wooden wall, she could hear someone doing something up above her. The sound of footsteps and scratching sounds and loud thumps told her Daniel was probably working up there. Hopefully he'd be occupied for a while.

She noticed an old-fashioned black phone, the kind with a curly cord, hanging on a post by a door. Did she dare do this? How could she not?

Holding her breath, she waited, listening to the noises overhead, and finally decided that if she spoke quietly, Daniel might not even hear her. She reached for the phone, quickly dialed the numbers of her cell, and heard the rings and the sound of her own voice saying, "Hey, it's me, you know what to do."

Irritated that Anna wasn't answering, she quickly launched into a desperate message. "It's me," she said softly. "I've decided we need to switch back, Anna. Immediately. I can't do this. I want out. I don't want to get you in trouble, but we have to undo this. I'll call you in about an hour if I can. You better answer then."

As she hung up, she realized the noises above her had stopped. Worried that Daniel had overheard her conversation, she waited, but now she heard what sounded like someone working outside. She slipped out the side door, then peeked around the corner to see not middle-aged Daniel but a much younger man doing something with hay bales on the backside of the barn.

The shirtless man hoisted one hay bale on top of another as if it were an oversized building block. Madison gaped at his perfect abs and ripped muscles as he shoved the bale into place. His torso was tan and glistening in the sun, and with his shaggy blond hair, chiseled profile, perfect nose, full lips . . . seriously, this guy could model for the front of a romance novel.

As if he could feel her eyes, he turned and stared back. Madison's hand flew to her mouth and she considered running, but instead she started to giggle.

As he reached for a light blue shirt that was lying on a nearby hay bale, he asked in German who she was.

She paused to gather her thoughts. The sincerity in his eyes almost enticed her to say her real name, but then she remembered the switch. "Nicht Anna," she said as she cautiously moved closer. Curious if he was as attractive up close as from a distance, she explained how her mother and Rachel were sisters. In response, he told her that Daniel was his uncle, his mother's brother.

For a long moment, they just stood looking at each other, transfixed. Then his slow smile revealed straight white teeth and his blue eyes sparkled in a way that told her he found her attractive too. She took in a quick breath. This guy was so good-looking! He smiled as he said something else to her, but it was like her inner translator had checked out and the words went right over her head.

She held up her hand to stop him, brokenly explaining that English was more understandable.

"You speak English?" he asked.

"Yes." She pushed a strand of hair from her face, wishing she'd taken the time to comb and pin her hair. She realized she'd forgotten her cap too, but hoped that wasn't offensive.

His eyes lit up. "I speak English . . . fluently."

"Oh, good." She tried not to jump up and down for joy. He was fluent in English! But instead of launching into her normal speech pattern, she controlled herself. She needed to keep her character believable. "That is good. We can speak English together."

He nodded as he adjusted his suspenders over his shirt.

"What is your name?" she asked.

"Malachi Stoltzfus." He stuck out his hand. "And you are Anna—Anna what?"

She thought for a moment, trying to recall. "Anna Fisher," she declared. It was weird, but as she said this, she actually wanted it to be true. Right now she wished she really was Anna Fisher.

"Malachi!" Daniel hurried around from the other side of the barn with a severe expression, as if he were extremely displeased about something. Perhaps Madison shouldn't have been talking to Malachi like this. She remembered Anna said the rules in this community were quite strict.

"*Wie geht's*, Uncle Daniel?" she said nervously.

"Uncle Daniel." Malachi's smile faded when he saw his uncle's grim expression. Daniel launched into what sounded like a severe scolding, pointing at the bales of hay and shaking his head. Was he complaining because Malachi wasn't working hard enough? Was it some unpardonable sin to take a break? What was wrong with these people anyway?

Madison didn't know what to do. Maybe this was her fault.

Daniel stopped chastising Malachi and turned his attention to Madison. He pointed at her and growled something unintelligible. Then, shaking his head like she was hopeless or some kind of degenerate, he muttered something under his breath and stormed away.

"What did he say?" she asked Malachi. "Did I get you in trouble?"

Malachi chuckled. "No. I make my own trouble."

"Why?"

"It is Sabbath," he explained. "No work is allowed. Only daily chores."

"Oh." She nodded.

"I was meant to move this hay yesterday." He nodded to the bales. "I forgot. So I came over this morning and then I forgot it is Sabbath." He shrugged. "It seems I am nothing but trouble."

Madison was still trying to process what Daniel had said to her and why he was so angry. It couldn't be that she was working on the Sabbath. Then she remembered how he'd pointed to her head. She reached up and remembered her cap was missing. "My cap," she said quickly, trying to do this right, like Anna would do. "I must go to house."

"I will see you again?" Malachi smiled.

She smiled back. "I hope so."

As if embarrassed, she turned and hurried back to the house, feeling light-headed. Malachi was an unexpected surprise. Equally surprising, he seemed to like her as much as she liked him. Perhaps she'd been too hasty in wanting to get away from this place.

"Hello?" Rachel's brows arched with curiosity as Madison came into the house.

"I was outside," Madison explained. "Fresh air."

Rachel nodded, then turned to stir a pot of what looked like oatmeal. "It is almost done. You can set the table now."

Madison tried to get the dishes and silverware in the right places, but even this task required coaching from Rachel. Meanwhile, Elizabeth was pulling pots and pans out of a cabinet. It seemed Madison's best contribution was to keep Elizabeth out of trouble so that Rachel could finish cooking.

"I met Malachi," Madison told Rachel as she balanced Elizabeth on one hip so they could both watch Rachel cracking brown eggs into a white ceramic bowl.

Rachel smiled and nodded. "Malachi is a good boy. Hard worker."

Madison decided not to mention the working on Sunday bit. "Malachi is Uncle Daniel's nephew?"

"*Ja*. He is Daniel's sister's boy." Rachel poured the eggs into a cast-iron pan, stepped back as they sizzled in the grease, then quickly stirred them with a wooden spoon until they started to get fluffy.

Madison was about to ask how old Malachi was and where he lived, when Daniel and the boys spilled into the kitchen. Before long, all were seated at the table, where Daniel again bowed his head and prayed silently for a long time, and then everyone concentrated on eating oatmeal, muffins, scrambled eggs, and ham.

After breakfast, as they were cleaning up in the kitchen, Rachel told Madison it would be time to get ready for meeting soon.

"What kind of meeting?" Madison asked.

Rachel gave her a funny look, then chuckled. "*Ja, ja*, I remember now." She lowered her voice. "Meeting is a long sittin' for young'uns."

Madison nodded as if she understood, but she still wondered what the meeting was about. As she helped the boys to get cleaned up, and as she combed and pinned up her own hair and fastened her white cap into place, she began to suspect that meeting was church. She had been to church only a few times in her life, and that had always been with Grandmother Van Buren, and only on Easter or Christmas when they'd been visiting her in Boston.

She hadn't disliked the religious experience. In fact, as a child, she'd been somewhat enchanted by the old stone church and the beautiful stained-glass windows. She remembered sitting there and feeling very small as she looked up at the high cathedral ceilings, and she had wondered about God . . . wished she could know more about him . . . perhaps even pray to him. But then her parents divorced, Grandmother Van Buren passed on, and Madison had not been inside a church since.

As it turned out, she didn't end up in a church today either. Meeting, as they called it, was held in a neighboring farmhouse. About two hundred people (men, women, and children) sat shoulder to shoulder on wooden benches in a large living room and sang hymns in an old-fashioned German dialect, some of which she understood. Then a couple of men took turns speaking, praying, and reading from the Bible. Everything was done exceedingly slow.

Madison had been surprised that Rachel hadn't come with them. She and Elizabeth stayed home, and Daniel never even batted an eyelash. Now that she was here, Madison suspected that Rachel didn't like this torture by boredom any more than Madison did. She totally did not get how the boys were able to sit there so quietly, although Jeremiah eventually succumbed to the monotony and warmth of the room by falling asleep on his father's lap.

The only thing that kept Madison from standing up and screaming to be let out of here was the fact that she and Malachi, on opposite sides of the room since males and females were separated, were able to gaze fondly at each other. She spent most of the meeting locking eyes with him and wondering what kind of a kisser he might be. Thankful that no one could read her mind (her fantasies were probably verboten), Madison wondered how much she'd be willing to sacrifice if love actually tapped her on the shoulder in a place like this.

Not that she thought she was seriously falling in love with this stunning creature, but it was interesting to consider, and they would certainly have beautiful children. Still, since there was little else to think on, she wondered, would she surrender a luxurious lifestyle, college, career, freedom . . . for true love?

9

Except for the time when she'd had chicken pox, Anna couldn't remember ever sleeping in this late. According to the silver clock by the bed, it was 8:17. Anna was wide awake and ready to start her day. As she started to remake the wonderful bed—of such proportions she could hardly believe—she paused and decided to try something first. Still wearing Madison's silky pink pajamas, or what she assumed were pajamas since she'd worn only cotton nightgowns before, Anna stood on the unmade bed and began to bounce up and down.

Anna giggled. It was just as she imagined it would be, almost as springy as the trampoline the Riehls used to have in their barn. Anna didn't recall how they had acquired such a treasure, but it wasn't long before their barn became the favorite gathering place of young people. But one day the deacon questioned the idea of adolescent boys and girls jumping up and down like that together. After that the trampoline disappeared.

Just as Anna was going up, she noticed the bedroom door opening, and Nadya entered the room with a silver tray in her hands. Anna ended her jump by landing on her backside, but she tried to act normal as she slid off the bed and smiled. "Good morning, Nadya."

Nadya's brow furrowed as she set the tray on the dresser. "Your breakfast," she said stiffly.

"Thank you." Anna tried to sound natural, as if someone brought her breakfast like this every morning, but she was stunned. Maybe Madison really was a princess.

"I forgot it's not school day." Nadya looked slightly apologetic now. "I hope is all right I bring this."

Anna nodded enthusiastically. "I'm hungry."

Nadya backed away now, almost as if she were afraid of Anna, or perhaps she was questioning Anna's true identity. Madison probably didn't jump on beds.

"Thank you," Anna said again.

"You are welcome." Nadya hurried out the door.

Anna looked at the breakfast tray, and although it was nice being served like this—the little flower in a crystal vase was a nice touch—it sure didn't seem to be much of a breakfast. A small pot of coffee, grapefruit juice, and dry-looking toast. No butter? Who ate like that? Especially at the start of the day, when your body needed fuel to do chores. Although Madison probably didn't have many chores. Still, to eat like this? It was odd.

Perhaps not everything about Madison's life was so luxurious after all. Just the same, Anna ate every bite. Then she went back to remaking the bed, still marveling at the height of the mattress—it was equal to four or five mattresses in Anna's house. What would her mother think?

After finishing the bed, which did not look like it had before she slept in it, Anna went to the closet to get dressed. Another dilemma. What to wear? Why did it have to be so complicated?

Finally, she decided on an outfit similar in its colorful combination to what she'd worn last night. She wasn't sure what Madison would think if she could see it, but thankfully, she could not. Anna was determined not to be concerned by things like clothes today. Today was about finding Jacob. If only she knew where to begin.

Before she left the bedroom, Anna carefully put away the clothes she'd worn yesterday and made sure everything was in its proper place. She checked Madison's floor plan drawing, and when she felt sure of where the kitchen was, she carried the breakfast tray there. For a moment she just stood in the doorway, staring in wonder at the beautiful kitchen. The dark wood cupboards looked like fine furniture, and everything was shiny and new looking.

Nadya came in through a back door. Anna knew from the floor plan drawing that Nadya's room was back there behind a laundry area. Anna smiled as she set the tray on the counter by the sink.

"What are you doing in here?" Nadya demanded.

Anna wasn't sure what to say, so she simply thanked Nadya for breakfast again. Unfortunately, this only seemed to further aggravate the housekeeper, but instead of saying so, she turned away and began scrubbing the already clean countertop. Anna suspected Nadya did not like sharing her kitchen, so she left.

Anna took her time in the living room. First she looked at all the elegant furnishings. So many things—layers and layers of things. Upholstered couches and chairs with pretty pillows and blankets. Tables with lamps and vases of flowers and all sorts of things to stare at. She went over to feel the luxurious curtains that hung alongside the incredibly huge windows. There were layers of different fabrics and trims. So much sewing for something as simple as curtains.

She looked out the window but was shocked to see how high up the penthouse was from the ground. The cars and people and trees, all far down below her, looked small and unreal. The scene made her dizzy, and she grabbed the edge of a table to steady herself. Anna had never been up this high, and for a moment she imagined that the whole tall building was swaying. What if it fell? She slowly backed away from the window, stood in the center of the room, and just tried to calm down.

Worried that Nadya might come out and discover her acting like a country bumpkin, Anna hurried back to the bedroom. Just as she closed the door, she heard a ringing sound. Not like Madison's purse phone, but more like the telephone in her father's barn. Before she could figure out its source, the ringing stopped. Anna sat down on a chair and wondered what to do next. Should she go down to the streets of New York City and begin looking for Jacob? Or, as Garret had suggested, was that totally ridiculous?

Three little knocks on the door told her it was Nadya again. "Come in," Anna called as she stood.

"Telephone for Miss Madison," Nadya announced as she handed her what seemed a larger version of Madison's purse phone. Nadya frowned at the bed, causing Anna to worry that she'd done a less than satisfactory job. As Nadya left the room, she murmured something in a different language.

Anna said hello into the phone.

"Madison?"

"Yes." She knew it was Garret.

He chuckled. "You still sound different."

She tried to think of a response but couldn't.

"Do you still want to proceed with your manhunt?"

Manhunt? Oh, he meant Jacob. "I do," she said eagerly.

"Okay then. I'm in."

Anna was about to ask him what he was in, but he continued.

"I tried your cell phone, but it went to voice mail. Is it really broken?"

"I, uh, I don't know." So much she did not know.

"It won't charge?"

Anna pressed her lips together as she tried to understand what he meant.

"Why don't you just use the other one? I mean you'll need it if we're going to start calling around, right?"

Anna wasn't sure what he meant. Wasn't she using the other one now? Again she felt in over her head. This game seemed to get harder and harder. "Yes," she told him. "I will do that."

"Want to meet at Viva?"

Viva—that word rang a bell. She felt sure it was in her notes. "Yes," she told him. "I will meet you at Viva." Who, what, where was Viva?

"In, say, twenty minutes?" he asked.

"Yes," she said again. "That sounds good."

She had no idea what Viva was, but Garret must have assumed she could get there. As soon as she hung up, she dug out her notes, scanning the pages until she saw that Viva was a coffee shop located right across the street. Well, that was handy.

Now about this phone business. He had mentioned another phone—was it the phone that Nadya had just given her?

Twice Garret had said something about a charge in regard to the purse phone, but what did that mean? Was it possible that something as small as a phone might have a battery that needed to be recharged? Her father was always recharging batteries on the generator at home.

Anna knew she would need a phone to search for Jacob. Why not use this one? She was just putting the phone in her purse when Nadya walked into the bedroom.

"What are you doing?" Nadya asked with a perplexed expression.

Anna gave her a blank look.

Nadya came over and put her hand on Anna's forehead, the same way Anna's mother might do if she thought she was ill. "Are you all right, Miss Madison?"

"I need a phone," Anna confessed.

Nadya reached over Anna's shoulder and removed the phone from her purse. "Not this phone."

Anna held up Madison's purse phone. "I . . . uh . . . I need a charge—"

"You lost the charger cord again?" Nadya shook her head.

"Yes," Anna said. "I lost the charger cord again."

"I will find it." Nadya let out a sigh as she went directly to what Anna thought was a desk. She opened a small drawer and extracted a black cord with a box shape on one end. "Right where it always is." She handed it to Anna with a questioning look.

"Right where it always is," Anna echoed, hoping she didn't look too foolish. Of course, it wasn't much different than some of the cords her father used. Only smaller.

After Nadya left, Anna returned to the desk drawer to find not only another purse phone but also a small paperback book that seemed to have purse phone instructions. Thankfully, this book had simple diagrams that seemed to indicate that the charge cord must be attached to both the phone and an electrical outlet in the wall. Apparently the purse phone did have a battery inside that could be reenergized with electricity. She should have known this. Feeling like an Englisher, she plugged one end of the cord into the wall and the other into the phone.

With this accomplished, Anna dropped the other phone into her purse. Thankful to avoid Nadya, who probably knew Anna was an imposter, she hurried out the door and with no problems rode the elevator down to the lobby. Feeling as if she were risking her life, she crossed the busy street and went into the coffee shop called Viva. Realizing she was still hungry, she bought what was called a breakfast bagel as well as a small carton of milk. She sat down and began eating the bagel with eggs and ham and cream cheese. Strangely arranged perhaps, but at least it was real food.

She was almost done when Garret came to her table. "You're eating one of *those*?" He pointed to the last bit of her breakfast bagel with a questioning look.

She nodded and continued chewing.

"And drinking milk?" He looked slightly horrified as he sat down. "Whole milk?"

She wiped her mouth with the paper napkin. Obviously her food choices were not the same as Madison's. Oh well. "Change is good." She smiled.

"Unless it changes your weight." He frowned as he set what looked like a briefcase on the table, snapping it open. "Then you'll be singing a different tune."

She just shrugged as he removed what she suspected was a

computer, setting it on top of the briefcase. She watched with wide eyes as he opened it up, pushed a button, then scooted his chair closer to hers. "I've been doing some searching," he said as he pushed more buttons. "I've got some leads on this Jacob Glick."

Almost afraid to breathe, Anna waited as he pushed buttons, clicked things, and then produced a list of what looked like phone numbers, all with the name Jacob Glick next to them. "Did you bring your phone?" he asked.

She held up the phone she'd found in the drawer.

"So your Blackberry really is broken?"

"No. It's charging." She felt somewhat sophisticated to think she'd figured all the phone business out. However, Garret seemed unimpressed.

"Ready to start calling?" he asked as he pulled out his phone.

Now she was worried. What if she called a number and her Jacob actually answered? Would she be able to keep pretending she was Madison? Or would she be so excited she would turn back into Anna Fisher? Then the cat would be out of the bag.

"I will write the numbers down," Anna said.

"Write them down?"

"So I can call from the penthouse."

"Why not just call down here?"

Anna had no answer for that. They both began calling the phone numbers, and Anna imitated Garret by saying she was calling on behalf of Anna Fisher. She decided that, if by chance her Jacob answered, she would simply remember the phone number and call him back later—in private. But her plan seemed unnecessary because none of the Jacob Glicks who answered the phone were her Jacob.

"We need to get into the mind of Jacob Glick," Garret said after they finished calling. "If I were Jacob and I had just come to New York, where would I stay?"

"Jacob had little money." Anna rethought that. "Anyway, that's what Anna told me."

"The Y!" Garret exclaimed.

"Why?" Anna looked at him.

"You know, the YMCA."

She nodded, wondering what a YMCA was.

Garret was already punching keys on his computer again, and then he dialed a number on his phone and asked if Jacob Glick lived there. He listened for a moment, then frowned as he set his phone down. "The guy said he's not allowed to give out personal information about residents over the phone," he told her.

"Oh." She nodded. Residents—that seemed to suggest the YMCA was a place to reside. A house, perhaps?

"So it's pointless to try to call these places." He nodded at the computer, and she leaned over to see a fairly long list of addresses and phone numbers.

"What does YMCA stand for?" she asked, knowing she was at risk of sounding really stupid.

To her relief, Garret looked stumped too. "I'm not sure. I mean obviously it's a place where down-and-out guys stay."

"Right." She wondered what "down-and-out" meant. Perhaps an English term for *rumspringa*?

Garret punched some more keys on his computer, then pointed to the screen. "YMCA is an acronym for Young Men's Christian Association," he declared.

"Oh yes, that's right." She wanted to appear as if she knew that already but had forgotten. Still, it reassured her to imagine that Jacob might be involved in a young men's Christian group. "All those addresses," she said, "the ones listed by YMCA—they are places for young men to stay at?"

"Yeah. There's a bunch in New York."

"I can't call these places to find Jacob?"

"It doesn't sound like it." He closed his computer with a thoughtful expression. "I have an idea."

"Yes?" She looked hopefully at him.

"Why don't we head on over to Nantucket now? We can keep working on our Jacob search over there. It'll be more comfortable than sitting here. I got the house all stocked with food and everything." He ran his finger alongside her cheek and smiled. "Don't forget that you promised if I helped you with this, you would—"

"I said *if* we found Jacob," she reminded him. "We haven't found him yet."

Garret frowned.

"I am going to visit all those YMCA places," she declared. "I will find out if he is at one of them."

"No way. You can't do that."

She looked evenly at him now. "I can." He obviously had no idea how determined she was.

"There were like twenty or more, Madison. Do you realize how long that'd take to go to each one?"

She shrugged. "I don't care. I'm going to do it."

He rolled his eyes and let out a big sigh.

"I don't expect you to come with me." She picked up her purse and stood. She had no plan for how she would do this. Especially since she didn't even have a list of the YMCA places and had no idea how to best get around the city. But somehow she would figure it out.

Garret opened his computer again, and Anna stood watching over his shoulder as he started punching in the keys again. She wasn't sure if she was imagining it or not, but the more she watched, the more she thought she might be able to do what he was doing. That is, if she had a computer. Hadn't Madison mentioned a computer? Why hadn't Anna thought to search her room for one? Perhaps in the desk.

"Well, I guess we could start in Manhattan." He picked up his phone and pressed a number, asking whoever was on the other end to send a car. The next thing she knew, Anna was riding with Garret, being transported from one YMCA to the next, where she would go inside and ask whoever was at the front desk about Jacob Glick. But by the end of the day, she was completely discouraged. This really felt hopeless.

"I have to say that I admire how much energy you're putting into this search for Jacob," Garret told her after she asked to be dropped back at the penthouse. "I mean you barely met that Amish chick, and yet you give up a whole day of spring break just to help her. And that's cool. But seriously, don't you want to have some fun this week, Maddie?"

Unsure of how to answer, Anna simply shrugged. She wondered how Madison would've responded to that and whether or not she was having fun right now. Despite Madison's confidence that she could pass herself off as Anna—and have fun doing it—Anna knew better. Being stuck with Aunt Rachel and Uncle Daniel and those spoiled children couldn't be much fun for a pampered city girl. Anna would not be surprised if Madison was already regretting the switch. But, in all fairness, it had been Madison's idea. Hopefully she was putting her full effort into it.

Hopefully she was trustworthy too. Anna hated to consider

all the problems that could arise from this. Surely Madison wouldn't do anything to get Anna into so much trouble that she'd never be able to show her face there again. And what about Anna's own settlement? If Madison did something really terrible, Aunt Rachel would surely call Anna's parents. Anna did not want to think about that. More than ever, she knew she had to find Jacob! That seemed the only way out of this messed-up mix-up. The sooner the better.

10

For a "day of rest," Madison felt fairly exhausted by the time the sun went down. She'd helped with the cooking, where everything was made from scratch, followed by the never-ending tedium of cleaning up without the aid of any modern-day conveniences, including hot tap water. After running herd on Elizabeth and Jeremiah, breaking up fights between the twins, and finally helping the children get ready for bed, Madison was totally ready to crash. No wonder these people went to bed so early!

But instead of putting on her nightgown, which was still damp from being hand-washed in the bathroom sink, Madison got into bed with her dress on and just lay there, hoping she could stay awake. It had been Malachi's idea for them to meet out by the irrigation pond after everyone else was asleep . . . to look at the stars. Naturally, Madison had agreed. How could she not? Just the thought of those sky-blue eyes looking directly into hers sent a delicious shiver down her spine. But she could still hear the sounds of someone moving in the house. She would have to wait until all was quiet and still.

It was the sound of the rooster that woke Madison. She opened her eyes to see that night had vanished in an instant and the gray light of dawn was slipping in between the curtains again. She had fallen asleep and missed her clandestine meeting with Malachi!

"Mamm, Mamm!" Elizabeth called from her crib.

"Nicht Anna is comin'," Madison said as she climbed out of bed. Rachel had explained yesterday that if Elizabeth was taken to the toilet first thing in the morning, there would be no soggy nightgowns. Thankfully, Rachel was right. But after finishing in the bathroom, Elizabeth, now wide awake, could not be enticed to return to bed, which was what Madison had hoped. Not that this was a possibility since the rest of the household was coming to life as well.

With Elizabeth occupied with her odd-looking faceless rag doll, Madison closed the door and quickly removed her dress from yesterday, replacing it with a fresh one in a dull shade of blue. Mad at herself for missing her meeting with Malachi, she hung the wrinkled dress on a hook and just shook her head. So much for her big plans. Too exhausted to wake up, she'd slept straight through the night. She wondered how Malachi had felt to be stood up. Perhaps, like her, he had slept through their date too.

Today's morning routine wasn't much different than yesterday's. Except that after breakfast was finished and cleaned up, there was more housework to be done. Today was laundry day. Fortunately, the twins had school to attend, and Jeremiah begged to go with his father out to the field. The house was fairly quiet.

"It is true what they say," Rachel said as Madison cranked the wringer and Rachel caught the sheet. "Many hands make light work."

Light work? Madison bit her tongue. If this was light work, she didn't want to find out what heavy work was.

"It is so good to have you here." Rachel sat down on the wooden bench. She tried to lift Elizabeth onto her lap, but it was too small to accommodate the toddler. She sat her on the bench next to her instead.

Madison set the wet sheet on top of the others and turned to Rachel. She wanted to ask her how she did this day in and day out. How did she do all these chores, care for all these kids, cook all that food . . . and she was pregnant to boot? That reminded her of something Anna had said.

"Aunt Rachel?"

"*Ja?*" Rachel was playing a form of patty-cake with Elizabeth.

"I thought Mamm said you were not supposed to work too much." Madison patted her own slender midsection. "Because of the baby."

Rachel gave Madison a sly sideways glance. "*Ja*, that's what I told her."

Madison studied her. "You mean it's not true?"

Rachel smiled as she pushed herself to her feet. "It is time to fix lunch."

"Do you need help?"

"No. You peg sheets to dry and watch Elizabeth. Then you go and fetch Jeremiah back. Help him to clean up to eat."

Relieved not to be stuck in the kitchen again, Madison took Elizabeth's hand and went over to where the clothesline was. Hanging the wash was not as easy as she'd imagined.

116

Hanging the wash while keeping an eye on a toddler was even more challenging. But eventually the sheets were on the lines, not neat and straight like she'd wanted, but at least they were hanging.

Madison picked up Elizabeth and walked toward the field that was being planted. From a distance she could see a horse slowly moving along, pulling some kind of plow thing behind it. On the back of the horse sat Jeremiah, his straw hat bobbing with each step, and behind him walked Daniel. It made a pretty picture, but Madison wondered how safe it was. What if the boy fell?

When they were about ten feet away, she called out and waved to them, saying it was almost time for lunch. Daniel stopped the horse and lifted Jeremiah down. The small boy looked relieved as he came running toward them.

"Pferd Fahrt! Pferd Fahrt!" Elizabeth cried out for a horse ride.

Madison laughed, then reminded Elizabeth it was nearly lunchtime and that she was too little to ride a horse. But Daniel walked over, took Elizabeth out of Madison's arms, and placed her on the horse. Madison watched in horror. Surely he wasn't going to let the toddler ride on the horse by herself. To her relief, he walked alongside, holding onto Elizabeth as the horse slowly moved along.

Although it looked dangerous, Madison knew there was no point in questioning him. She walked Jeremiah back to the house, where she helped him scrub the dirt from his hands and face.

After their midday meal, Madison cleaned up the kitchen without any help from Rachel. While she still would not classify it as "light work," it was somewhat satisfying to do it unassisted. By the time she was finished, she found Rachel sitting on the porch with a sewing basket in her hands.

"Children are sleeping now."

Madison sat down on the other chair. "Good."

Rachel put her bare feet on a wooden crate, letting out a tired-sounding grunt.

Madison looked more closely at her now. Her eyes had dark circles beneath them and her feet looked swollen. "How are you feeling?"

She rubbed her big belly. "I will be better when baby comes."

Madison felt a strong surge of pity for this woman. "Can I get you anything? Water? Tea?"

Rachel sighed. "You know what I want?"

"What?"

"A bit of *wein*."

"Wine?" Madison was shocked. For one thing Rachel was pregnant, besides that she was Amish. Did Amish drink alcohol?

"*Ja*. Dandelion *wein*. You know, the kind your mamm makes."

"Oh, *ja, ja*." Madison nodded. So Anna's mother made dandelion wine. Who knew?

"It is in the baking cupboard," Rachel said softly. "Way in the back. A *flasche* of dandelion *wein*."

Madison wasn't sure what Rachel meant by this. "Oh?"

Rachel held up her thumb and forefinger a couple of inches apart. "Just a bit. I think it is all right."

"You want me to get you some wine?" Madison was getting more concerned now.

"Just a little." She waved her hand at her. "You go and get it, Anna."

Madison got up and went into the kitchen. She knew where the baking cupboard was, and sure enough, there behind a canister of flour and some other baking ingredients was a glass bottle of what appeared to be wine. The bottle was about half full with what was probably homemade wine. She pulled it out and swirled the golden liquid around, then uncorked it and sniffed. It was definitely wine. Should Rachel be drinking while pregnant? On the other hand, who was Madison to tell these people how to live?

She got a glass and poured a bit in it. Just to be on the safe side, she filled another glass with water. Then she went out and handed them both to Rachel. Rachel set the water aside and slowly sipped the wine. Madison picked up a ratty-looking knitted shawl, folded into a makeshift pillow, and slipped it beneath Rachel's swollen feet. "Better?"

"*Ja, ja. Denki.*"

"Can I ask you a question, Aunt Rachel?"

"*Ja, ja.* Sure."

"Did you love Uncle Daniel when you married him?"

Rachel laughed. "Oh, Anna, you know the answer to that question."

Madison laughed too. "*Ja.* I just wonder about love."

"You are thinking of Jacob?"

Madison was surprised. "You know about Jacob?"

"*Ja, ja.* You know yer mamm and I write letters, Anna. What do you think we write about?"

"How can you do all this?" Madison asked. "If you don't love Uncle Daniel?"

Rachel turned and looked curiously at Madison, and Madison worried she'd gone too far. Rachel just smiled. "Love is like a tree. You plant it, you water it . . . it grows."

Madison nodded. "You love Uncle Daniel now?"

"*Ja*. He is a good father to my children." She took another sip of wine and sighed. "He is a good man. Some say he is too good for Rachel."

"Too good for you?" Madison frowned. Daniel might be a nice enough guy by some Amish standards, but Madison didn't care much for the grouchy old grump.

"*Ja, ja*. Dey say Daniel is a hard worker and Rachel is lazy."

"You are *not* lazy!" Madison shook her head. Good grief, this woman rose at the crack of dawn, took care of her energetic children, cooked, cleaned, and did everything the hardest ways imaginable. Who would ever think she was lazy?

"Anna, you were *Yuchend*, but you can remember." She set the empty wine glass down. "No young man came for me when I was your age."

"Oh." Madison considered this. What would an Amish woman do if no one wanted to marry her? Their lives seemed centered around family, marriage, children—and lots of work.

"A friend told me of Daniel. As a young man, he married Lydia. She was a pretty young woman. Yellow hair, blue eyes." Rachel pointed to Madison. "Like you, Anna. But Lydia grew sickly . . . no children came . . . she died young. Daniel grieved for her." She waved her hand toward the field in front of them. "Working this farm, Daniel grieved and grieved. He was all alone. It was bad."

"That's sad." Madison imagined a younger Daniel plowing and planting, missing his bride. Maybe she'd been too quick to write him off.

"So Daniel married me." Rachel pointed to her ample chest. "We were happy in the beginning. Children came—not one but two baby *Yuchend*." She smiled. "Proud daed."

"And?"

"And . . ." She shook her head. "It is my fault."

"What is your fault?" Madison demanded.

"Other women see my house, my children, my cooking, my sewing—they see and they say that everything I do . . . is not good."

"Not good?" Madison so didn't get this.

"Not good enough."

"But you work so hard, Rachel."

Rachel looked at Madison and laughed. "You changed, Anna." She tapped the side of her head. "That fall on your head—when you knocked your noggin. It has changed you. Before, you worked hard, you looked at me like other women, you thought that Rachel was lazy too."

"No," Madison insisted. "I never thought you were lazy!"

Rachel laughed again, even louder. "*Ja, ja*. Maybe you cannot remember so well. But I remember." She reached over, patting Madison's arm with a smile. "You are different now, Anna. I like you better."

Madison chuckled.

"It is good that you are pretty, Anna."

"Why?"

She pointed to the clothesline, where the sheets were hanging all cockeyed and lopsided and one was actually dragging on the ground. "Because you are not so good at cookin' and cleanin' anymore. You will need a man to love you for other reasons."

This reminded Madison of Malachi and her missed "date" with him. She'd been keeping a lookout today, but so far she hadn't spotted him anywhere on the farm.

"Where does Malachi live?" she asked.

"He stays with Uncle Andrew. Andrew is Daniel's older brother. Malachi is helping him too." Rachel nodded in a knowing sort of way. "What do you think of Malachi?"

Madison just smiled.

"*Stattlicher . . . ja?*"

"*Ja.*" Madison chuckled. Rachel thought Malachi was handsome too.

"He can help you to forget Jacob?"

Madison wasn't sure how to respond. On one hand it sounded like a great idea, on the other hand . . . there was Anna to consider.

"Malachi is a good boy, a good young man, but he needs a good partner."

"You mean a wife?"

"*Ja*. But more'n that. He needs a good woman to bring him back."

"Bring him back?"

"*Ja*. Malachi is like me, Anna."

Madison frowned. "How so?"

"He is an outsider here too."

Madison did not get this. "You mean because what you said about the women saying you were lazy and all? Malachi did not seem lazy to me."

"There is more to the story. There is the Ordnung." She sighed. "And there is the bishop and the deacon. We are much more conservative here than where you live, Anna, where I grew up. It is different here."

"Oh." Madison thought she understood this—it was why Rachel wasn't fitting in. "Malachi grew up somewhere else?"

"*Ja*. His mamm is Daniel's sister. Daniel says she is like me, that she does not fit in here. She left her husband when

Malachi was *Yuchend*. Den Malachi grew up in the English world and made bad friends. His mamm was worried. She asked Daniel and Andrew to bring Malachi back here, to help him become a good man."

"He seems like a good man to me."

"*Ja*, I think so too." Rachel's eyes lit up. "You like Malachi?"

"*Ja*." Madison thought that compared to most of the guys she knew, Malachi seemed like a saint. Okay, maybe that was just her first impression. But sometimes first impressions were right.

"Oh no." Rachel shook her head.

"What is it?"

"Again I wasted too much time. Here come the twins, home from school, and I have done nothing."

Done nothing? Madison tried to remember all that Rachel had done since the sun came up, and the list alone exhausted her. In fact, Madison herself would just about kill for a nap right now.

Rachel rubbed her back and groaned as she went into the house. "It will be good when dis baby comes. Not a day too soon either."

Madison winced. It would not be good if this baby came while she was here. Especially if she was expected to help during childbirth. She remembered the famous line from *Gone with the Wind* and imagined herself using it, throwing up her hands in desperation and sobbing, "I don't know nothin' 'bout birthin' babies, Aunt Rachel."

Perhaps it was time to call Anna again.

11

On Sunday afternoon, after she returned to the penthouse, Anna made certain both of Madison's purse phones were charged or charging. After hearing Garret mention something about voice mail messages, she took the time to read through the little Blackberry manual until she learned that, yes indeed, these smart little phones were able to receive and hold many messages. But when she tried to listen to the message, the phone asked her for a password. Naturally she had none, so she gave up.

Feeling worried that Madison might need to reach her, Anna set one purse phone by the bed and kept the Blackberry with her. The more she thought about it, the more certain Anna became that Madison would want to switch back. It was insanity to think that a pampered city girl like Madison could cope with the demands of caring for four young children, cooking, cleaning . . . and helping an ailing and pregnant Aunt Rachel too. Anna knew she needed to be ready to switch back if necessary. Perhaps even tomorrow. She was tempted to call her uncle's phone but knew that was risky. Better to wait for Madison to call her.

Anna was ready to go back. Nothing about being in New

York City had gone how she'd hoped. She hadn't seen any of the things Jacob used to talk about—the Empire State Building or the Statue of Liberty. If she had seen them, she hadn't even realized it. With Garret sticking to her like jam on bread, she couldn't reveal her interest in such things. Not when Madison had probably seen them many times over. Garret already thought she was acting strangely. Acting like a tourist would make him even more suspicious.

This harebrained exchange had been disappointing on many levels. She had expected to experience a sense of freedom here. Yet it was impossible to feel that carefree abandon she had imagined. She was so consumed with acting and talking like Madison that she felt worn out. This was not fun—nothing like the books she used to read, where she would imagine she was a character in the midst of an exciting story, and where everything turned out just fine in the end. Anna had a strong feeling that her week in New York City would not end happily. If today were any indication, her chances of finding Jacob were minimal at best.

Besides all that, Anna was fed up with Madison's clingy boyfriend. Garret acted like he was trying to help, but he was far too pushy and his motives were disturbing. Of course, Madison had warned her about that. Anna understood now. After he'd finally grown weary of their "manhunt" this afternoon, she took the opportunity to inform him that she needed some time to herself. She said it had to do with some of the changes that she'd been making.

"I need to slow down," she said, "to think about my life."

He seemed a bit skeptical and perhaps bewildered, but thankfully, he didn't argue with her. She wondered if Jacob would be as understanding. She remembered times that, when he had gotten something into his head, Jacob could be stubborn as an old goat. Unless being out here in the English world had softened him—and she doubted that—he would probably never fit back into their community again. In fact, the more time Anna spent in this crazy, busy world, the more she wondered if she would ever fit here. Maybe she and Jacob were not meant to be together.

But maybe they were.

That was how her thoughts went all afternoon and into the evening. Round and round like a puppy trying to catch its tail.

By seven o'clock, Anna was hungry. She realized she had not seen or heard much from Nadya today. Thinking perhaps the housekeeper had the day off, Anna decided to fix herself some dinner. She was just taking things out of the giant-sized icebox when Nadya appeared. "What are you doing?" she demanded.

"I am fixing dinner." Anna held up what appeared to be cheese.

"No." Nadya took the cheese from her, set it on the countertop, and placed her hands on her hips.

Anna blinked.

Nadya shook her finger at Anna. "What is wrong with you?"

Anna sighed. Tired of this game, she felt ready to confess everything. Except that she didn't trust Nadya. What if the housekeeper thought the worst of her? What if she called the authorities? Or confiscated Madison's purse, money, phones, and credit cards and threw Anna out on the street?

Already Anna knew enough about this big city to realize it was a very scary place. She had seen some strange people today—Garret had used words like "druggies" or "lowlifes" or "homeless." While she didn't understand those things, a part of her felt sympathy for what seemed like lost souls, though another part of her was truly frightened. She had no idea what she would do if she were forced to fend for herself in a place like this. How would she get home? No, she decided, confessing to Nadya was a risk she could not afford to take.

"You are taking my job," Nadya continued.

"Taking your job?"

"You clean like there is no Nadya in the house. Now you want to cook?" She scowled at Anna.

"I am hungry."

"I am cook!" Nadya threw her hands in the air.

"You were gone—"

"What is wrong with you? Why you act this way?" Nadya leaned forward, peering curiously at Anna as if she could see right through her. Maybe she could.

Imagining herself out on the streets, Anna felt her knees growing weak. She had to pass herself off as Madison. But how? She thought hard, trying to recall a character in a book she'd read recently—a spoiled rich girl. How had she acted?

"Excuse me," Anna said in what she hoped was a haughty tone.

Nadya's eyebrows arched. "Yes?"

"You are a servant here, right?"

Nadya nodded.

"Yet you question me?"

Nadya looked uneasy.

"I am hungry." Anna looked her straight in the eyes. "If you are not here to fix me food, I will fix it myself."

"No, no, Miss Madison. I will fix you dinner."

"Good." Anna held her chin up. "Excuse me for cleaning up after myself for a change. I will be sure not to do it again!"

"Thank you, Miss Madison."

Although Anna felt guilty for treating Nadya like that, Nadya seemed pleased. Anna decided it might be wise to continue this little act. Turning on her heel, she marched out of the kitchen, went into the living room, and flopped down on the white leather couch. She put her feet on the blue velvet footstool, then reached for a sleek-looking magazine called *Vogue*. Imagining herself to be the spoiled character in a book, she lounged there in decadent comfort, flipping through the shiny pages of this bizarre magazine, blinking in surprise at the outlandish outfits these women were wearing, and trying not to feel foolish.

She turned another page and gasped at a woman practically naked. The next one looked like she'd been starved for months. Did English women really look like that? She'd seen some odd things in the city today, and some odd things on the television, but nothing quite as odd as this next woman with black hair that resembled a hedgehog and eyes that were so painted they looked frightening. The weirdest thing was the gown she had on. It appeared to be made of egg noodles and gold chains. Very strange indeed.

After a while, Nadya appeared. "You like your dinner in here?"

Anna shrugged, still playing the role of a spoiled princess. "Sure. Why not."

Before long, Nadya placed an attractive-looking tray of food on the glass table near the couch. "Anything else, Miss Madison?"

Anna tilted her nose in the air. "No. I think this is okay."

"Thank you." Nadya disappeared into the kitchen.

Anna thought perhaps this new attitude was working. Although the food wasn't nearly as tasty as it was pretty, and although it was nothing like what Anna normally ate at home, she ate every bite. When she finished, she resisted the urge to clean things up and return the tray to the kitchen. Instead she left it right there in the middle of the fancy room. She cringed to think what her mother would say if Anna did something like this at home. The English were such peculiar people!

Tonight Anna wanted to try out the luxurious bathtub, perhaps even use some of the fancy soaps and things. She didn't care that it was wasteful, she intended to fill the whole tub with hot, sudsy water and just sit in it for as long as she liked. Then she would pull the plug, or whatever it was, and let all that delightful water just go down the drain.

She tried not to think of her little sister Katie, and how she would appreciate having such fine secondhand water to use. At Anna's house, on bath nights, one tub of water was sufficient for the whole family. Of course, the water eventually turned gray and had to be warmed up, but the boys always went last anyway.

As Anna was trying to figure out how the drain stopper worked, she heard a ringing sound in the bedroom. Anna hurried to where the Blackberry was chiming and pushed the TALK button. Hopefully it was Madison. Unfortunately, it was Garret again. Did that boy never give up?

After a quick greeting, he asked her to go out with him "to go see a show."

"No thank you," she told him. "I plan to go to bed early tonight."

"What is wrong with you?" he demanded.

"I am tired." She sat in the chair by the window but didn't look out because it still made her dizzy.

"I'm tired too," he snapped back at her. "Tired of a girl-friend who acts more like an old woman than a seventeen-year-old."

Anna sat up straight. "An old woman?"

He laughed in a mean way. "Yeah—an old woman. In fact, I was beginning to wonder if that Anna chick you met might've actually been an Amish witch."

"*What?*"

"Maybe some Amish witch put a spell on you, changing you into one of them."

Anna felt anger bubbling inside of her. "One of them?"

"You know what I mean, Madison. One of those long-faced girls in their plain, homely dresses. Don't you think they all look and act like old women?"

"No, I do not."

"See, that proves my point."

"What point?"

"That Anna must've been an Amish witch and that she put a spell on you." He chuckled. "Hey, maybe I should pitch that premise to my uncle in Hollywood."

She wanted to defend herself as well as her community but realized that would only add fuel to his fire. Besides, for her entire life, she had heard how most of the outside world despised them. Why should she be so surprised that Garret would say such mean-spirited things?

"Thank you for expressing your opinion," she said in a chilly voice. "I need to go now."

"Hey, sorry if I stepped on your toes, Maddie."

"My toes are fine." She reached down to pull off a short boot that was actually pinching her big toe. Why did the English insist on comfort for everything except their shoes?

"I just don't get why you're so obsessed with this Anna and Jacob drama. It's like it's taken over your life. Seriously, I wouldn't be surprised if you were considering joining up with their cult."

"Cult?" Anna blinked.

"Cult, sect, faction—whatever they call their weird way of life."

"Is that how you perceive them—the Amish—as weird?"

"Isn't that how they want us to perceive them?"

"What do you mean?" She pulled off the other boot and leaned back.

"I mean they choose to live in this completely different world, cut off from the rest of us. They'd be fools if they didn't expect us to think they were weird."

"Maybe we think—" She paused, remembering she was supposed to be Madison. "Perhaps they think that we're the weird ones."

"I'm sure they do."

"Did you ever stop to consider—well, maybe we could learn something from them, Garret?"

"I suppose that's possible. I mean, in a way, they've got the right idea. Living off the land and off the grid is pretty cool. Having little or no dependence on fossil fuel sources is admirable too. Talk about leaving no carbon footprint."

"What?"

"You know, being totally green." He chuckled. "Well, except for all that methane gas they're producing."

"Methane gas?" All this was over her head.

"You know, from all those cows."

"Oh yes, right." His slang language was starting to hurt her head.

"I'll bet the Amish eat more healthfully than most Americans."

"I'm sure they do." She sighed to remember her less than satisfying dinner.

"But I don't get the whole clothes thing. What's up with the goofy straw hats the guys have to wear or those little white bonnets for the women? Why does everyone have to dress alike?"

Anna thought about her answer. "My understanding is that they don't want to draw attention to themselves because of their clothing."

"But isn't that all they do? I mean you see someone dressed like that in Manhattan and you can't help but look twice."

Anna remembered the strange outfits she'd seen in the *Vogue* magazine. Wouldn't a noodle dress draw some stares on the streets of New York? Maybe not.

"And what about individuality?" Garret persisted. "Why does everyone have to look and act the same? What's up with that?"

"I think it has to do with humility," she said. "No one is better than anyone else. The exterior appearance is supposed to represent the interior, and equality." Of course, even as she said this, she knew that it didn't always work that way. She knew more than one person in her settlement who, even if they looked like everyone else, might still act superior. But that was part of being human. No one was perfect.

"Now you're starting to worry me again."

"Why?"

"Because when you talk like that, explaining how they think, well, it works with my theory that you might be under a spell—or, worse yet, be thinking of joining up."

"What if I was?" she challenged him. "Would that be so terrible?"

He didn't respond.

"Maybe there is something to be said for a simple life." She looked around the fancy bedroom. "Do you ever wonder why people need so much . . . so much *stuff*, anyway? Wouldn't the world be a better place if everyone slowed down and lived more simply, more frugally, more spiritually?"

"Now it sounds like you're doing the recruiting."

"I'm only trying to show another way of thinking. I thought you wanted to discuss this since you are the one who brought it up."

"Okay. Then explain this to me, Maddie. How is it okay to stop education after the eighth grade?"

She didn't answer. She was already worried that she'd said too much.

"Maybe I stumped you with that one. See, I've been doing some research too. Did you know that they don't allow their children to attend high school or college? Did Anna tell you that she hasn't gone to school since eighth grade? Can you imagine, Maddie? Maybe the reason Jacob ran off like that was so he could finish his education. Maybe he wants the chance to go to college like you and me. What's your response to that?"

Anna very nearly pointed out that, despite Garret's so-called superior education, he did not seem one wit smarter than she. Oh, maybe he could work a computer, but she could probably do that too if given the chance. Of course, she probably would not get that chance—not at home. Even so, did she really care? How did it make his life better?

"I got you then. No smart answers for that?"

"Think about this," she said slowly and carefully. "How many young men do you know who can build a house all by themselves without using electricity? Do you think you could plant and harvest enough food to feed a community without using a drop of gasoline? And if you could do that, would you even know how to store it?"

He was quiet.

"Cat got your tongue?" she teased.

He laughed. "See, you go and say something like that, and I have to think that something very strange is going on in that pretty head of yours."

If only he knew! They continued bantering a bit more, and then he went back to his original reason for calling, trying to talk her into going out with him. But her resolution only grew stronger. He might think he was better educated, more modern, more sophisticated, but she was far more stubborn.

"I assume you're not backing down from your relentless search for the mysterious Jacob Glick," he said after she'd already told him good night twice.

"No, I am not."

"Well, if you need help, I'm still willing."

Now this surprised her. After the insults she'd just hurled at him, and he back at her, she assumed he would want to give their strained relationship a rest. A part of her hoped he would, but at the same time she knew she needed his help.

"You sure you want to help?"

"The truth is, I'm getting kind of curious," he said.

"Curious?"

"I actually hope we can find this dude, Maddie."

"Why is that?"

"I'm curious to see just what kind of a guy he really is."

She sighed. "So am I." As she set down the phone, she did wonder . . . what would Jacob be like? Would he be greatly changed? Would he be happy to see her?

12

It wasn't until evening that Madison discovered the real reason for Malachi's low profile around the farm today. She'd been discreetly looking for him off and on, but to no avail. She finally decided he was avoiding her. Why wouldn't he, after she'd stood him up last night? But just after she put the children to bed, Rachel mentioned that tomorrow would be a Malachi day.

"A Malachi day?" Madison asked.

"*Ja*. The brothers share Malachi. He works for Uncle Andrew on Monday, Wednesday, and Friday. He comes here on Tuesday, Thursday, and Saturday."

"Oh." Madison nodded.

Rachel gave her a sly look. "I thought you would want to know this."

"*Denki*."

"What else do you want to know?" Rachel said in a tempting way.

Madison just shrugged.

"He is nineteen. He is a hard worker. Good boy."

"*Ja, ja*." Madison waved her hand as if she didn't care. But Rachel laughed, almost as if she knew something.

Once again, although she suspected it was futile, Madison

went to bed with her dress still on. Tonight she made sure to stay awake until everyone in the house was silent and all she could hear was the sounds of crickets and what she assumed was the hooting of an owl. Fairly certain that everyone was asleep, she slipped out of bed, picked up her shoes, and tiptoed down the stairs, careful to avoid the squeaky treads. Softly closing the door behind her, she went outside, sat down on the porch steps, and put on her shoes. Knowing she was on a fool's mission, and with only a half moon to light her way, she walked through the hay field over to the pond.

Malachi was not there.

Madison decided she didn't care. Oh, perhaps she cared a little. But mostly she felt thrilled to be out here like this on her own, prowling around the farm after dark. Such independence! She looked over to the barn, remembering the phone, and decided there couldn't be a safer time to use it. Daniel should be fast asleep by now.

When the phone rang and rang, Madison wondered if perhaps Anna was sleeping too.

"Hello?" a groggy voice said.

"Anna!" Madison exclaimed. "It's me—Madison. How's it going?"

"Madison!" Anna shrieked.

"Shush," Madison warned her. "Remember Nadya."

"Yes, you're right. I'm just so glad to hear your voice. How *are* you?"

Madison gave her the quick lowdown of life on the farm. "Really, it's not too bad. I like your aunt."

"You like Aunt Rachel?" Anna sounded surprised.

"Yes. She's very sweet."

"Is she still lazy?"

"The poor woman works from dawn to dusk. You call that lazy?"

"Everyone works," Anna told her. "It's just that some work harder than others. Aunt Rachel's house is . . . well, it's not so efficient. You know?"

Madison wasn't sure. "Don't forget she's also very pregnant, Anna. That takes a lot out of her. Then there are her children. She spends a lot of time with them—"

"You mean playing?"

Madison felt surprisingly defensive of Rachel. "Hey, I happen to think it's pretty cool she plays with her kids. How can you fault her for that?" She decided to change the topic. "How is the hunt for Jacob going?"

"Not so good. It's like finding a needle in a haystack." Anna explained how Garret was helping her and all the places they had looked.

"Garret is helping you? Spending time with you?" Madison was shocked. "And he doesn't suspect anything?"

"Oh, I keep telling him that I—I mean you—have changed a lot."

Madison chuckled. "That's true."

"Oh, I almost forgot you had some phone calls too." She explained how her mom had called on Sunday and her best friend had called today.

"Did they believe you were me?" Madison twisted the phone cord nervously.

"I did my best. Your mother asked if I had a cold and I pretended I did. I used the same excuse with Vivian. She seemed to believe me."

"Good." Madison sighed. "By the way, did you get my message?"

"Oh, that is my question. I read the little book about your Blackberry, but I do not know the code for messages."

"That's right." Madison told her the number and explained how it worked. Then she thought she heard something—what if Daniel came out here to check on one of the pregnant cows? "I better go," she whispered.

"Yes. You don't want to get caught on the phone. I would be in trouble."

Madison hung up and waited for a long moment, listening intently for the sound of footsteps. Hearing only the sound of the cows rustling a bit, she decided it was just her imagination and slipped back out the door. Wishing that perhaps Malachi had come after all—was now sitting out there waiting for her—she hurried back to the pond. But it was exactly like before.

She picked her way through the tall grass, then sat down on a rough-hewn bench. She looked out over the black glossy surface of the pond, watching the trail of moonlight that sliced right through the middle, listening to the music of the crickets and the frogs and the occasional hoot of the owl. As odd as it seemed, she had never done anything like this before. Even when her family went to places like the Hamptons or the Adirondacks, she had never gone out into the dark of night to experience a piece of nature all by herself. For some reason she felt thoroughly refreshed and energized by this experience. It felt as if it had been missing from her life, and now here it was right in front of her. Amazing!

She leaned her head back and looked up at the sky, surprised to see how many stars were up there and wishing she knew more about constellations and the universe. Perhaps she should've paid more attention to seventh grade science.

As she gazed up, pondering the concept that many of the stars she was watching right now had already burned out, she began to wonder about God. She'd not given God much thought, not since childhood. In fact, she'd even begun to question the existence of a higher power. But something about being out here like this—smelling the fresh air, hearing the night sounds, looking at the starry sky—made her suspect there must be a Creator. For some unexplainable reason, more than ever before, Madison wished she knew him. She felt a deep need to pray—a yearning down inside of her. But remembering how long Daniel prayed before each meal, and how long the deacon and minister at meeting had prayed on Sunday, Madison felt fairly certain she would not get it right. So she simply said, "Hello, God. Are you up there?"

On Tuesday morning, Madison awoke to what almost seemed familiar sounds: Elizabeth calling for her mamm, the rooster crowing, and birds singing. The surprising thing was that today, her third day here, Madison felt ready to rise and shine. As incredible as it seemed, it was like she was looking forward to the challenges before her. Maybe she was just looking forward to seeing Malachi again. But as she helped get Elizabeth ready for the day, giving her a quick cleanup in the spartan bathroom, Madison longed to wash her own hair. With real shampoo and conditioner, which was not an option. After her evening walk last night, she had taken a sponge bath, but the truth was she hadn't felt much cleaner by the time she finished. Just colder.

There were a few things Madison was starting to appreciate about the Amish lifestyle. Simple things like fresh air, quietness, green growing things, flowers, farm animals, sunshine . . . She could actually see some positive aspects of being disconnected from electricity, phones, TV, the internet—it slowed life down in a surprisingly refreshing way. Although she didn't think she could really live like this—not for more than a few days, anyway.

Sweet simplicity aside, there were a lot of other things that she totally did not get about these people. Like what was wrong with a little comfort? Why did every chair, bed, and bench have to be so hard? Would it be a sin to have a pillow here and there? Some softer sheets? A hot water heater? A dishwasher?

Still, those things were small compared to her biggest complaint. The thing she could not wrap her head around was related to personal hygiene, or rather the lack of it. It wasn't that these people were filthy—she understood that living and working on a farm brought some dirt with it—but seriously, did Aunt Rachel have no sense of smell? There was obviously no such thing as deodorant in this house. No scented soaps or cologne or air fresheners either. Thankfully, Rachel liked opening the windows to air out the house in the morning, but still Madison longed for a little squirt of perfume to give her nose some relief.

Madison didn't really mind the low-maintenance hairstyle. All she had to do was comb, part, and pin up her hair. But after three days, her scalp was feeling a little creepy. Still, the thought of washing her hair with that frightening substance Rachel referred to as soap was equally creepy. She sniffed the greasy gray lump, then set it back by the sink. No way. She was not that desperate yet.

Besides, she could hear the boys getting up now, and when

a family of six (plus a guest) all shared one bathroom, there was no time to waste. Her hair would have to wait.

After breakfast was cooked and cleaned and the twins were off to school, which Madison now knew was a one-room building where a girl about her age taught, she asked Rachel about washing her hair.

"What?" Rachel frowned like she hadn't heard her correctly. "It is not *Saturday*, you know?"

Madison made a face and pointed to her head. "Remember, Aunt Rachel, when I hurt my head?"

Rachel looked up from where she was kneading dough. "*Ja, ja.* I remember." She stared at Madison's hair. "Your hair is clean, Anna."

Madison pointed out the window toward the field being planted. "But Malachi is here today, no?"

Rachel threw back her head and laughed. "Oh, *ja, ja.* I know what you mean now. You want your hair to be *very good*."

"*Ja.* Very good."

"I have something you will like, Anna." Rachel chuckled as she wiped the flour from her hands onto her apron. "You keep working this dough and I will get it."

Madison wasn't quite sure how to knead dough, but imagining she was Rachel, she pushed up her sleeves and jumped in, rolling her fists into the soft mound. She was surprised at the silky smoothness of the dough, and it smelled good too.

"Oh, that is enough," Rachel said as she returned with a bottle of something. "You not want to work the dough too hard." She handed Madison the bottle, then began shaping the dough into a ball, which she tossed back into the bowl with a dull thud. "Now we must let it rest."

Madison opened the bottle of yellow liquid and was surprised that it actually smelled okay. Not great. But much better than that gray lump of soap that they used for everything.

"When I first came here," Rachel told her as she placed a dish towel over the bowl of dough and set it back behind the stove, "I used this soap to wash my hair. A friend from home makes it. But here—" She shook her head with a sour expression. "It is not allowed."

"Not allowed?"

She waved her hand under her nose as if smelling something. "You cannot smell like flowers here. It is forbidden."

Madison nodded. "Oh, *ja*."

Rachel pointed to the bottle. "One more way Aunt Rachel makes trouble. You keep the hair soap, Anna. Do not let anyone but Malachi smell your hair." She pointed to the kettle on the stove. "You can use hot water. Remember to refill it dis time."

Madison lugged the heavy kettle and the bottle of soap up to the bathroom, where she used a water pitcher to mix warm water. Leaning over the bathtub, she did the best she could to wash and rinse her hair. What a chore! But when she was finished, she did feel a bit better. If only she had some conditioner. Although Anna's hair was naturally blonde, Madison got help for hers every few weeks at the salon.

She used the limp towel to blot her hair, trying not to lament over the lack of a hair dryer. But it was still dripping when she returned to the kitchen.

"Is it good?" Rachel reached over to touch Madison's damp hair, then frowned as if something was wrong. "Your hair is so stiff, Anna. Like straw. Has the hair soap gone bad?"

To avoid having to concoct an explanation for her

143

chemically lightened hair and lack of conditioner, Madison offered to take Elizabeth and Jeremiah outside to play until lunch, suggesting that Aunt Rachel might like to put her feet up for a bit. Madison hoped to wear the kids out as well as to dry her hair in the sun. Then perhaps while they were napping, she might take a walk and run into Malachi.

She had to question why she was so interested in Malachi. It made no sense. Well, other than the fact that he was absolutely gorgeous. But seriously, what kind of future would she have with someone like him? As unique and challenging as this experience was, she wouldn't be here after Saturday.

13

By Tuesday afternoon, Anna was ready to give up. She was wrong—searching for Jacob wasn't like looking for a needle in a haystack, it was like looking for a needle in a freshly cut hay field of a hundred acres.

Although Garret was trying to be helpful, he was also aggravating. She could understand why Madison had been put out with him. The boy did not give up.

"Thank you for your help," she said in front of her building. "But I'm taking a break from this."

"All right!" Garret nodded. "That's what I'm talking about. You run up and get some things and we'll be in Nantucket in time for dinner."

"No. That's not the kind of break I meant."

He reached for her hand, making those sad puppy dog eyes at her. She wondered if that had worked on Madison. Well, it certainly was not going to work on her. Besides the fact that he was not Anna's boyfriend, he was not her type.

She pulled her hand from his and shook her head. "Goodbye, Garret," she said. She stepped away and hurried to where Henry the doorman already had the door open. He gave her a somewhat sympathetic glance.

In her rush to escape Garret, Anna ran smack into the girl from the elevator. What was her name?

"Hey, Madison, where's the fire?"

"I'm sorry . . . Lucinda." Anna forced a smile. "I was trying to get away from Garret."

"Glad to see you've come to your senses." Lucinda turned around, walking with Anna through the lobby. "Now about Fashion Fling . . ." She smiled in a funny way. "Can I sign you up?"

"What is it you want me to do?" Anna asked.

"You know, the usual thing." Lucinda held her hand up as if to point out Anna's height, something Anna tried to forget. It wasn't easy being one of the tallest girls in her community. Just one more reason she missed Jacob—he was taller than her.

"The usual thing . . ." Anna echoed her as if it made sense. What was the usual thing?

"So you're in?" Lucinda's dark eyes lit up.

"When is it again?"

"The second Saturday in April."

Anna knew she shouldn't commit Madison to something without speaking to her first, but this Fashion Fling thing seemed to be for a good cause. Besides, Madison could un-commit herself later. "Sure," Anna told Lucinda. "I'll do it."

"Fantastic!" As they waited for the elevator, Lucinda pulled out a phone that was very similar to Anna's (rather, Madison's) and was soon talking to someone who sounded like her mother, explaining that Madison had decided to participate after all. "Hang on, Mom. I'll find out." Lucinda turned to Anna. "Are you busy right now?"

Anna shrugged as they went inside the elevator. "No. Not really."

"Mom wants to know if you can pop in for a fitting." Lucinda pushed the button with a 7 on it.

Pop in for a fitting? Anna frowned as the elevator went up. What kind of slang was that?

"It'll only take a few minutes." As the elevator doors opened, Lucinda gave Anna a hopeful look, as if she expected Anna to follow her out.

"Okay." Anna braced herself as she emerged from the elevator. A sign said SEVENTH FLOOR, and Lucinda turned to the right. Anna had no idea what she'd just gotten herself, or Madison, into. But there seemed no gracious way to get out.

Lucinda walked down the hallway past a number of doors, finally stopping at a door with the number 756 on it. She pulled out a key and let herself in. "Mom is downtown right now, but she told me which outfit you'll be wearing. She's so excited that you're going to model."

What was Lucinda talking about? Anna just nodded, trying to act normal as Lucinda started going through a rack of dresses. Anna glanced around the room to see more racks of clothing, almost like a store. There were also big tables with bolts of colorful cloth and baskets with all sorts of sewing notions.

What really caught Anna's eye was what appeared to be some modern sewing machines. Anna put her hand on a sleek-looking silver one. It had all kinds of buttons and gadgets and a large spool of red thread. The electric machine reminded Anna of a fancy car—the kind that zipped past her family on their way to town in the wagon. Anna had heard of such sewing machines, had wished for such a sewing machine, but this was the first time she'd seen one.

"Sorry it's taking so long," Lucinda called from where she was still searching through a rack.

"It's all right." Anna wanted to study everything in this amazing room. It was like a seamstress's dream come true. Except that the fabric and colors were wrong. Anna paused to admire a board with every color of thread imaginable displayed on it. All that thread—pretty as a rainbow! Anna had been responsible for most of the sewing in her household for a few years now. She loved to sew, but sometimes the treadle machine took so long, and even when her feet were moving as fast as they could, she sometimes felt impatient at the speed of the needle. Although it was much better than hand sewing. Still, to have a machine like this.

"Here it is," Lucinda said as she came over with a dress in her arms.

Anna tried not to blink at the bright-colored fabric. Red, purple, pink—the colors seemed to clash into each other with an intensity that made her eyes burn. "Oh."

"You don't like it?" Lucinda frowned. "This is one of Mom's favorites."

"It reminds me of a flower garden." Anna tried to sound gracious.

Lucinda laughed, then peered curiously at her. "No offense, Madison, but you sound kind of weird."

"Sorry." Anna looked away.

"Anyway, go ahead and put it on and I'll do the fitting." Lucinda pointed to an area that was draped off. Anna assumed that was where she was supposed to change.

"Did you say the Fashion Fling is in April?" Anna said as she unbuttoned her shirt.

"Sure. Just like always. Mom's got a lot of dresses to finish by then."

Like a seamstress, Anna was piecing the facts together as she pulled off the trousers that she'd opted to wear today. Lucinda's mother must be a dressmaker, and for some reason she wanted Anna—rather, Madison—to wear one of her dresses. As she slipped into the dress, she realized that it wasn't finished yet. That was why she needed to fit it to Anna.

"I'm ready," Anna said as she emerged from behind the curtain. "I think it fits me good."

Lucinda frowned. "I think it looks about two sizes too big. Mom had been getting this dress ready for Brianna McCluskey to wear. Really, it looks much better on you." She stepped forward with pins. "Just let me take it in here and there."

Anna cooperated with her, holding her hands up, turning from side to side. She controlled herself from saying that Lucinda was pinning the dress too tightly. After all, this was an English dress, and they all seemed to be tight. Again the irony of it hit Anna. The English liked their beds and furniture to be soft and comfortable, but their shoes and clothing had to be tight and constricting. It just made no sense.

"Now step on that stool and I'll set the hem."

Anna stepped up. She was still admiring this amazing sewing room. She would have such fun in a place like this.

"What's up with the hairy legs?" Lucinda asked. "Don't tell me you're turning into an earth muffin."

"Earth muffin?" Anna frowned.

Lucinda laughed. "That's what my mom calls hippies."

Anna was about to question the meaning of the word *hippy*

but decided that might draw more suspicion. As it was, she hadn't even considered the hair on her legs. She knew English girls shaved their legs—which was very strange—but she had no intention of doing such a thing.

"Madison?" Lucinda's voice had a surprisingly sharp tone now. "What is going on with you?"

"What?" Anna turned back around to look at her.

Lucinda's eyes were narrowed and her jaw was firm. "What is going on?"

"I don't know what you mean." Anna bit her lip, trying to think.

"I mean—*who are you?*"

Anna stepped down from the stool and tried to make an expression that she thought Madison might make. "What are you talking about?"

"I'm talking about you."

"I'm going to change back into my clothes," Anna said.

"No, you are not." Lucinda stood in front of her now. "Not until you tell me who you really are."

"I do not understand." Fear rushed through Anna.

Lucinda pointed a finger at her. "That's another thing. You talk weird. I thought maybe you had a sore throat, but your voice and your words are different." Lucinda reached up to touch Anna's hair. "Your hair is different too. I thought so the other day, but I figured you'd just found someone really good. But today when I saw your hairy legs—"

"I gave up shaving," Anna said quickly. "Just to try it."

"Well, how about that scar?"

Anna glanced over to the curtain where her things were, wondering if she could dash over, get them, and make a run for it.

"What happened to it, *Madison?*"

"What?" She inched toward the curtain.

"The scar."

"What scar?" Anna knew it was futile to pretend.

"The scar where Bobby bit you."

"Bobby?" Anna imagined some guy sinking his teeth into her.

"Your grandma's schnauzer." Lucinda reached over and grasped Anna's forearm. For a small girl, she had a tight grip. "Who are you? And what have you done to Madison?"

"I don't know what you're—"

"I know you're not Madison." Her dark eyes were penetrating. "Madison and I were best friends for seven years. You can't fool me."

"I just want to get dressed," Anna said. "And leave."

"You are going nowhere until you fess up." Lucinda pulled her phone out. "Or else I'll just call the police and that will—"

"No," Anna said quickly. "Please do not do that."

Lucinda held out her phone almost as if it were a weapon. "Tell me the truth—who are you?"

Through tears, Anna told Lucinda the whole unbelievable story.

"No way." Lucinda paced back and forth, still waving her phone as if she planned to use it. "There is no way Madison would do something that crazy. I don't believe you."

"It's true," Anna pleaded. "I promise you it is true."

Lucinda stopped pacing now. She came closer and peered into Anna's eyes. "I suppose you don't know that Madison Van Buren is a member of one of the wealthiest families in New York—in the world, for that matter."

"I—I don't know what you mean." Anna shook her head. "I know she is rich. What are you saying?"

"I'm saying that between Madison's mother's family and

her father's family—we're talking old money and a lot of it—they are worth more than a billion."

Anna was trying to understand this. Was Lucinda suggesting that Anna was here to steal? "I have taken nothing," she said. "Nothing that Madison didn't tell me to use. That is all." The truth was Anna had been quite frugal with Madison's money and credit cards.

"How am I supposed to believe you aren't part of some kidnapping crime ring? Maybe you've got Madison stashed off somewhere while you bilk her family for millions."

Anna blinked. "What?"

Lucinda held up her phone again. "I'm calling my mom."

"Please don't."

"Then prove to me you're not a criminal, and that the insane story you told me is really true." Lucinda was starting to dial.

"I have a message from Madison," Anna said suddenly. "It's on her phone." Anna started to go back to get her purse, but Lucinda stopped her.

"I'll get it," Lucinda said. "You stay put."

When Lucinda returned with Madison's purse, she pulled out the Blackberry and turned it on, waiting as Anna told her the code numbers. It felt like an eternity as Anna waited for Lucinda to push the right buttons and listen. Finally she dropped the phone back into the purse and looked curiously at Anna. "That first message sounded like Madison. It also sounded like she wanted to switch places with you."

"She did." Anna nodded. "I wanted to switch with her also. But then, by the time we spoke on the phone together, Madison had changed her mind." Anna shrugged. "I was very surprised. I still cannot believe she would want to stay with my aunt Rachel for a whole week. Even I did not want to stay with her."

Lucinda's features softened. "So, really, you're telling the truth?"

"I promise you, I am." She glanced toward the curtain. "I want to change my clothes now, please."

"Go ahead." Lucinda set Madison's purse on a table and laughed. "Yeah, I knew something was fishy about you when I saw you wearing that outfit in the elevator the other day. Madison never dressed like that."

"You said you liked it." Anna carefully removed the bright-colored dress, trying not to get stuck with the pins.

"I did like it. You have a fun sense of style—especially for an Amish girl."

"I would never dress like that at home. Never!" As Anna pulled on the trousers, she realized she would never dress like this either. So many things to feel guilty for.

"What's your real name?"

"Anna Fisher." As she buttoned her shirt, she explained about how she'd been looking for Jacob. "That is why Garret has been with me so much. He wanted to help me."

Lucinda laughed. "Or wanted to help himself *to* you."

Anna emerged from behind the curtain. "I can make him mind his manners."

"Maybe so."

"I am sorry, Lucinda." Anna handed her back the bright dress. "I should not have promised you that Madison would wear your mother's dress for the Fashion Fling."

Lucinda rolled her eyes. "I should've known it was too good to be true."

"Can I ask you something?"

Lucinda nodded as she hung the dress back up.

"Why are you and Madison no longer friends?"

"It's a long story."

"I have time."

Lucinda glanced up at the big wall clock. "Unfortunately, I do not. I'm supposed to meet my mother in half an hour. I'm going to be a designer someday too. I work with my mom, learning the ropes of the business."

Anna nodded. "That is how it is in my community too. Children learn from their parents." She ran her hand over one of the sleek sewing machines again. "Do these sew fast?"

"Fast enough." Lucinda turned off the lights. "Do you sew?"

As they went to the elevator, Anna told about the treadle machine she used at home. "It is not so fast. But like you said, fast enough."

"Hey, maybe you can come over here tomorrow," Lucinda offered. "You can try out a machine if you like."

"Really?"

Lucinda nodded as she pushed the down button. "Then we can talk some more. Maybe I can tell you about Madison and me."

"I would like that." Anna smiled.

Riding back down to the lobby with Lucinda, Anna felt even more curious. Why would Madison give up a nice friend like her? Lucinda seemed like a genuine person—and a hard worker too. As Anna rode the elevator back up to the penthouse, she hoped she might solve the Lucinda and Madison mystery tomorrow. As for the missing boyfriend mystery . . . maybe she would never get to the bottom of it.

14

Madison was just ladling herself a bowl of creamy potato soup when Malachi walked into the kitchen.

"Any more of that left?" Malachi asked as he went over to the sink to wash his hands.

"*Ja, ja,*" Madison said, trying to imitate Rachel. "There is plenty."

"Where is everyone?" He rubbed the gray block of soap so vigorously that it almost began to lather. Was he angry or just energetic?

"Uncle Daniel came early to eat," she explained as she filled another bowl. "He had to drive over to the Vorschke farm to get something for his plow."

"*Ja.* He broke down this morning. He thought he could fix it himself."

"Maybe not." She sliced a few more pieces of the whole wheat bread, setting them on the table next to the homemade butter. Yesterday afternoon Madison had cranked the handle of that butter churn herself, watching in wonder as the cream went from liquid to solid. Who knew?

As Malachi dried his hands, she explained that she had just

fed Jeremiah and Elizabeth their lunch, and that Aunt Rachel was putting them down for naps. "Then she will rest too."

"So we are alone?" His blue eyes lit up with mischief.

"*Ja.*" She smiled boldly at him. "Just the two of us." She wondered if he would mention the missed meeting by the pond. Or perhaps he had missed it as well. But he just sat down on the bench and rubbed his hands together.

"Some of the women say Aunt Rachel is not so good in the kitchen," he said quietly. "But I say no one makes potato soup as good as her." He picked up his spoon and dipped it in without bothering to pray, to Madison's surprise.

"You don't pray before eating?" she whispered.

Looking embarrassed, he left his spoon in the soup and bowed his head. He did seem sincere. "Sorry about that. I was too hungry."

"It's all right." She picked up her spoon. "You were saying . . . other women say mean things about Aunt Rachel?"

He nodded and took another bite.

"Why do you think that is?"

He shrugged. "It's just the way it is."

"It seems wrong and mean."

"It is wrong and mean. Some people are like that."

She thought about this. It was somewhat reassuring that Rachel had been telling the truth about how she was treated. Certainly she had no reason to lie about something as unflattering as being called lazy. Although that seemed unfair. Rachel worked hard.

It was disturbing to think that "godly" women thought it acceptable to gossip and slander each other. And what was up with the shunning business? Rachel had said that Malachi and his mother had experienced something like that too.

Madison wished she had the nerve to ask Malachi about this, but for now his attention seemed primarily on his food.

She discreetly watched him eat. Focused intently on each bite, he seemed ravenous, yet he moved the spoon gracefully up and down, not spilling a drop. He even tore his bread in half, buttering it with care. Almost as if he'd had some kind of etiquette training. Anna's uncle, who slurped his soup and belched on occasion, must've slept in on that day.

"I know you're watching me." Malachi suddenly looked up, catching her staring.

"I'm sorry." She looked down at her barely touched soup.

"You aren't hungry?"

She chuckled. "Yes. Just distracted."

"What has you so distracted?" Again he flashed that killer smile—like he knew he was the reason for her anxiety.

"Oh, you know . . ." She tried to think of something harmless and believable. "Aunt Rachel is so pregnant. I'm thinking she could have that baby any day now."

"*Ja*, for sure." He looked dismayed. "I hope not too soon, Anna."

"Why is that?"

He smiled sheepishly. "Because after you help Aunt Rachel, would you go back to your family?"

"*Ja*. After a while I have to go home." She wanted to confide in him that she had only a few more days here. She wanted to admit that she was not Anna, that she'd never lived like this before, and that she knew nothing about birthing babies. Instead she decided to see what she could learn about him. "Aunt Rachel tells me you're not from here, Malachi. Is that right?"

He nodded, wiping his mouth with the back of his hand, reminding her that there seemed to be no napkins in this house. Whether it was just Rachel's way or something Amish, Madison didn't know.

"And you work for your other uncle part of the time."

"*Ja*. I work in his wood shop. He is teaching me how to make furniture."

"Furniture?"

"*Ja*. I am working on a table now."

A handsome young man who was capable of working a farm and making tables? Perhaps she had been too hasty in writing him off. She tried to imagine the two of them as a couple, living plainly, working hard, being together. On some levels it had allure. Then she remembered all the little—and the not so little—inconveniences of this so-called simple life, and she knew it was nothing more than a fantasy. At least for her.

"Do you want to walk outside?" Malachi asked as he stood. "There's something I can show you."

She stood and smoothed her apron. "*Ja*. I would like to come."

"It's at the pond," he said as he led the way through the planted field, stepping carefully between the rows of young corn plants.

"The pond?" She remembered their planned meeting. Should she mention it?

But he didn't say anything more as they cut through the tall grass and reeds right near the pond. He stopped and put one forefinger to his lips, then pointed with the other to a shady corner on the far side of the pond. "See?" he said.

Shielding her eyes from the sun overhead, Madison peered into the shadows, curious as to what he was looking at. Then she saw them—a mama duck with five or six baby ducklings paddling along the edge of the pond. "Oh, that is so sweet," she whispered.

"I spotted them this morning." He led her over to the bench, turning to look into her face. "I was here Sunday night, Anna. But you were not."

"Oh." She sighed. "I'm so sorry. I was so tired that night, I fell asleep."

He chuckled. "That is better than saying you forgot, or that you didn't care."

She looked into those sincere blue eyes. "I came here last night."

He seemed surprised. "You did?"

She nodded. "I did. It was so beautiful. I did not even mind that you weren't here."

He frowned. "You didn't miss me at all?"

She laughed. "Oh, *ja*, I missed you. But I enjoyed just being here, even by myself."

"I know." He sat on the bench, patting the spot beside him.

"I looked at the stars," she admitted as she sat. "And I thought about God. It felt like he was near."

"That is amazing."

"I know." She nodded. "I didn't expect that."

"Do you know that is exactly what I did, Anna, when you never came on Sunday night? At first I was disappointed. Then I sat here and I thought about God too. And then I prayed. For the first time since I was a boy, I prayed. I have to say it felt good."

"It was the first time you'd prayed since you were a boy?"

"*Ja*. When my mother and me left here, I was hurt and angry. I know now I was hurt and angry at some people, but back then I thought it was at God."

"You're all right with God now?"

"I am all right with God now, Anna." He looked directly into her eyes. "I am so all right with God that I told Uncle Andrew I want to be baptized."

"Baptized?"

"*Ja*." He reached over and took her hand in his. "You know why, Anna."

All this was over her head. What was he saying? What did it mean to be baptized, and what did it have to do with her?

"How about you, Anna? Will you be baptized too?"

"I, uh, I don't know."

Disappointment washed over his face. "You don't know?"

"It is much to think about." She stood.

"*Ja, ja*. You are right, Anna. It is much to think about." His smile returned. "And if Uncle Daniel finds me sitting around like this, I will have much to think about too."

Madison nodded. "*Ja, ja*. I will talk with you later, Malachi."

His eyes twinkled. "*Ja*, you sure will."

As Madison hurried back to the house, she was seriously worried. This game had gone too far. It was time to tell Malachi the truth. He trusted her. He deserved her honesty. But what if he was hurt or angry? What if he told his uncles? Then Anna would be in a lot of trouble. Yet by being here, being with him, talking like that—even if no one ever guessed about the switch—she had probably gotten Anna into trouble. The kind of trouble that would catch up with her eventually.

Madison worked hard to clean up the lunch things in the kitchen. Strangely enough, she was taking some of these chores in stride now, like washing the dishes. She had come a long way in a few days.

"You were with Malachi," Rachel said as she came in the kitchen, pausing to rub her lower back.

"How did you know?"

Rachel laughed. "Our bedroom window. It looks out to pond."

"Oh." Madison put the last plate away, then wiped the water off the countertop. "Malachi told me something, Aunt Rachel. You must keep it a secret." She wasn't even sure why she was saying to keep it secret, but it seemed necessary.

Rachel's eyebrows arched. "What is it? Do tell."

Madison repeated what Malachi had said about asking to be baptized. Rachel's hand flew up over her mouth and she began to giggle.

"Why is it funny?" Madison asked.

"Oh, you know why. Silly girl."

Madison already had a bad feeling about this, but it was growing worse by the minute. "Why?"

"You know, Anna." Rachel gave her a sly look. "A boy must baptize when he wants to marry."

Madison took in a quick breath. "But not *only* to get married." Of course, she wasn't sure about this assumption, but it seemed plausible.

"*Ja*, sure. Malachi tell you this, Anna, because he wants to marry—"

"I can't—"

"Oh, Anna, I know you grieve Jacob. But in time, your heart . . . it will change. You see."

Madison shook her head, then dashed out the door. She didn't want to hear another word about this. Rachel would think she was acting like a drama queen, if there was such a thing in the Amish community. But it was all Madison could come up with at the moment.

She went out to the vegetable garden, bending here and there to pull a weed that Noah must've missed, since weeding this garden was one of his chores. This garden amazed Madison. Everything growing in tidy rows—young plants, fresh and green, full of promise. It felt contained and controllable. She would miss it back in Manhattan.

Madison wondered what Anna was doing right now. Had she found her beloved Jacob? If she did find him, what would that mean? Would she entice him to return with her . . . to marry? And what about Malachi? How would he handle it when "Anna" disappeared from his life? Would he regret his baptism? What if he tried to track Anna down, found where she lived, and demanded an explanation? It all made Madison's head hurt.

This was Anna's world. Anna would have to deal with this Malachi development later. Maybe she could right now.

Madison glanced over at the barn, wondering if it was too risky. Seeing no one, she decided to take a chance. She would use the phone and call Anna, demanding that they switch places immediately. But when she was almost to the barn, she heard the sound of the horse and buggy. She peeked around to the driveway and saw that Daniel was coming. She would have to call Anna later.

Back in the house, she found Rachel spreading some light blue fabric on the kitchen table. At first she thought it was a tablecloth and was about to ask what the special occasion was since she had never seen anything like that before. Then Rachel laid what appeared to be pattern pieces on the fabric.

"What are you making?" Madison asked.

"You are better now?" Rachel gave her a questioning look.

"*Ja*. I will be all right."

"It is for Elizabeth." Rachel stood straight now, rubbing her back. "I wanted to make it before baby comes. Elizabeth is getting big, you know."

"Want any help?" Madison realized this was a somewhat deranged offer since her sewing skills were sketchy at best. Her old friend Lucinda had taught her to sew when they were in grade school. The goal had been to make designer clothes for their Barbie dolls. Since Lucinda's mom was just starting her own line of clothing, it seemed feasible. Madison loved picking out the fabrics and dreaming up dresses, but she soon discovered she hadn't cared for the sewing part. It was painstakingly slow and she usually made mistakes.

With a relieved expression, Rachel handed Madison the scissors. "*Ja*, sure, Anna. You were always better at sewing than me."

Madison suddenly remembered her supposed brain injury. "I might mess it up."

"It is all right." Rachel sat in a chair, leaning back and rubbing her tummy. "I will watch. If you make mistakes, I will tell you."

With Rachel coaching her along, Madison arranged the pattern pieces. Using table knives as weights to hold the pieces in place, she carefully started to cut out the skirt, sleeves, bodice back, and bodice front. One by one, she set them in a neat pile.

Rachel peered curiously at Madison as she set the scissors aside. "You are much slower than before, Anna."

"Sorry." Madison pointed to the side of her head and shrugged.

"It is all right." Rachel smiled. "You make me feel good—I am not as slow as you."

Madison chuckled as she followed Rachel into the other room, where she opened up a cabinet containing what appeared to be an ancient sewing machine. Again Madison had to plead loss of memory. She watched as Rachel threaded the machine, paying close attention as she demonstrated how it worked by tapping one's toes on the rocking foot paddle. This caused the wheel to turn, making the needle go up and down and moving the fabric along. "You remember now?"

Madison nodded. Thankfully, this machine seemed much slower than the state-of-the-art one Lucinda's mother had let them use. Perhaps Madison could do this.

"All right. You sew and I will be in the kitchen with the children."

Madison had no idea where to start. She unfolded the piece marked "front bodice," opened it up, and laid it out, then placed one of the sleeves alongside it. She set the skirt in place, picturing how the finished garment might look. It seemed simple enough, so she began sewing.

For a while she thought she was doing it right. Then she discovered that she'd sewn the bodice fabric wrong. The outside of the fabric was now on the inside of the dress. Although someone like Madison might not notice the difference, she suspected the women in Rachel's community would. Poor Rachel already had a reputation for being slovenly. It wouldn't help matters to see young Elizabeth running around in a messed-up dress. So she began to pick out the threads where she had attached the sleeves. Talk about tedious—this was grueling.

So much so that she was happy to hear the sound of the twins' voices as they came bursting into the house. She could almost understand how Rachel could prefer playing with her children to things like sewing and cooking. Who could blame her?

But it seemed that Rachel had no energy to play with her children today. She simply sat on a kitchen chair, rubbing her big tummy and looking flushed and extremely uncomfortable.

"Is your baby coming?" Madison tried not to appear as nervous as she felt. What if Rachel did go into labor before Anna and Madison switched back? What would she do?

"No, no." Rachel shook her head. "It is too soon. This does not feel anything like before."

"What *does* it feel like?" Madison asked. Before Rachel could answer, Jeremiah began wailing loudly, claiming that Ezra had slammed his fingers in the door—on purpose. Naturally Ezra insisted that was not true. The volume started to go up.

"I will take them all outside," Madison told Rachel.

"Denki." She nodded with tired eyes. "You are a good girl, Anna."

Madison couldn't help but question that compliment as she lured the children out into the yard with the promise of a quick game of tag. *A good girl?* She was actually lying to everyone here, pretending to be what she was not, and worst of all, leading on a perfectly nice young man. Really, how could she keep this up another day?

As she and the children were running around, screaming and shrieking and acting like wild things, Malachi came over and joined in, and the game got totally crazy and boisterous. But the kids were having so much fun. As the game wound down, Malachi continued to play with the children, giving them piggyback rides, flying them like planes, or spinning them around like rag dolls. His energy seemed limitless, and his little cousins were eating up his attention.

Madison sat on the porch step watching. It was sweet to see this handsome young man, only two years older than her, displaying such fatherly attributes. Not many nineteen-year-old men would act this way. And yet . . . if Malachi married (like he seemed inclined to do), he might possibly be a father before he turned twenty. According to something Rachel had said, Madison was pretty sure the Amish did not believe in birth control. One family in this community had sixteen children!

Finally it was time for the twins to do their afternoon chores. Malachi invited Jeremiah to help him with the horses, and Madison took Elizabeth back into the house. She did not miss the longing glance Malachi tossed her way as they parted. Maybe it was her imagination . . . or maybe not . . . but she strongly suspected he was falling, or possibly had already fallen, for her. Normally Madison was flattered when a guy showed this kind of interest. But this time she was seriously disturbed.

As she went into the house, she reminded herself that it was not actually Madison Van Buren he was falling for. He didn't even know the girl from Manhattan. Malachi was falling for who he thought she was—Anna Fisher, a nice Amish girl. Oh, what a mess she had made!

15

Anna felt somewhat relieved that Lucinda knew her true identity, and she was fairly sure she could trust her with this secret. Lucinda seemed like a nice, sensible girl. On Wednesday morning, as Anna rode the elevator down to the seventh floor, she looked forward to seeing Lucinda again.

"Come in, *Madison*." Lucinda winked at Anna as if to send a message. "My mom's here this morning too."

Anna nodded. Lucinda was hinting that she had not revealed Anna's secret to her mother. Which probably meant that Anna needed to continue with her Madison act as Lucinda's mom greeted her.

"I'm so glad you decided to model for us this year, Madison. It will make the show so much better. Maybe you could get Vivian Richards to come on board too."

"Maybe." Anna forced a smile. "The dress was pretty. Very bright."

"Too bright?"

Anna shrugged.

"Well, I don't have time to chat now. I need to run over to Mood to check on some new fabrics and run a bunch of errands." She waved. "Later, girls!"

After she was gone, Lucinda told Anna how pleased her mom was to have Madison in the fashion show. "She's certain this will get the media attention she's been wanting."

Anna frowned. "What is media?"

Lucinda explained the basics of publicity to Anna. "Newspapers and tabloids always get more interested when rich or famous people are involved. Madison Van Buren falls into that category."

"So if you are rich, you are famous?"

Lucinda's mouth twisted to one side. "Yeah, I guess so."

Anna looked eagerly toward the sewing machine. "It's really all right for me to sew on that?"

"Absolutely." Lucinda went over and began to explain how it worked. She secured a long strip of fabric under the pressure foot, then showed how to push a pedal with one foot—and just like that, the machine stitched, and not just a straight stitch either. It had a little blue box, similar to a phone, where one could select all kinds of stitches and just push a button, and like magic the machine would stitch it. Anna was amazed.

"Would you use a machine like this at home?" Lucinda asked.

Anna laughed. "Only in my dreams. In real life it would not work."

"You mean because of no electricity?"

"For sure, that would be a problem." Anna tried to explain why her people chose to live simply for many reasons. "We are made to be equal," she said. "No one is better than another. Both in God's eyes and in one another's. If I had a fancy sewing machine like this, I might think I was better. Or someone might be jealous. It would bring trouble into our community." She looked at the stitch pattern that resembled a row of butterflies and flowers. "All these fancy stitches . . ." She shook her head. "They would not do at all for our style of sewing. Our clothing must be simple. Straight seams, no fancy stitches. Some districts do not even allow buttons."

"Seriously? No buttons?"

"Because we oppose war."

"So do I." Lucinda looked confused. "But I don't oppose buttons."

"In old days, buttons resembled a soldier's uniform—it was unacceptable to dress like a soldier."

Lucinda held up a big pink button. "No soldier's uniform would have buttons like this."

Anna looked at what Lucinda was working on, and to her amazement, Lucinda was sewing those pink buttons to a garment, using the machine. "Oh my! The machine can sew on buttons too?"

Lucinda laughed. "You can do anything on a machine. But my mother still hires people to hand-sew some things." She groaned. "Like hems. In fact, that's what I'll be working on most of the day."

"I can help."

Lucinda blinked. "Really?"

Anna nodded. "I want to."

"My mom will pay you."

Anna shrugged. The truth was she was happy to do it for free. The thought of spending the day in here, just sewing . . . well, it was lovely.

As they worked together, Lucinda's story unfolded. She told about how her friendship with Madison had gone awry a couple of years ago. "We became best friends in the summer before third grade, right after my parents moved into this building," Lucinda explained. "We weren't wealthy like the Van Burens, but our families hit it off anyway. Our dads both worked on the stock market. Although, as my dad used to say, he actually worked. Mr. Van Buren just managed the family fortune."

"I thought Madison's father lived somewhere else."

"Yeah. Madison's parents divorced in our freshman year. It was an amicable split. Or so Madison claimed. I wouldn't know."

Anna couldn't quite grasp all this, but she pretended she was reading one of her English novels—they didn't always make sense either.

"Anyway, back then our moms got along too. Throughout grade school and middle school, our families vacationed together and stuff. The Van Burens have this really cool house in the Hamptons and a home in the Adirondacks and several other places too."

"They have more than one home?"

"Sure. Like I said, they are really rich."

"Yes." Anna slipped the needle through the silky fabric, pulling it through, making sure the stitch was perfect. "I know that."

"Anyway, we were tight."

"Tight?"

"Really close. Madison and I were, like, inseparable." Lucinda frowned as she turned around the garment she was working on. "Until a boy came between us."

"A boy came *between* you?"

Lucinda nodded. "Actually, it was a boy *and* a girl." She told Anna about becoming good friends with a boy named Alistair one summer. "Alistair's family was from London.

They moved into our building shortly after Madison went to Europe with her grandmother. I guess I was lonely, and so was Alistair. As a result we got really close. So close I think I had a serious crush on him. I even wrote Madison about it, although she claimed she never got my letters." Lucinda sighed. "Alistair was so cool."

"What happened?"

"What happened is that Madison came home and the next thing I knew she and Alistair were together."

"Oh." Anna remembered the time Leah Riehl had tried to steal Jacob from her. Fortunately for Anna, Jacob had remained true.

"Anyway, I was so mad. I mean what kind of best friend steals your boyfriend?"

"That is hard."

"Yeah. Madison and I weren't talking when school started. She and Alistair were still together, and this new girl—Vivian Richards—started going to our school. She glommed onto Madison." Lucinda let out a shriek.

"What?"

She held up a bleeding finger. "I stabbed myself with the needle."

"Oh." Anna gave her a sympathetic look.

Lucinda stuck her finger in her mouth.

"So you lost your best friend and your boyfriend?" Anna asked.

With her finger still in her mouth, Lucinda nodded.

"I'm sorry."

"Now, if Madison told you that story, she would probably make me out to be the villain. She would say that I later stole Alistair from her."

"Did you?"

"Not really. Madison was starting to get interested in Garret by then. I just picked up where Alistair and I left off."

"So Alistair is . . . he is your boyfriend now?"

Lucinda shook her head. "No. He moved back to London last summer."

"You and Madison never restored your friendship?"

"We don't even speak."

"But you spoke to me in the elevator," Anna reminded her.

"Because you were acting like a doofus."

"A doofus?"

"Remember, you didn't even know how to operate an elevator."

Anna chuckled. "I remember."

"I should've known then you were an imposter. I thought maybe you had a hangover."

"A hangover?"

"From drinking too much alcohol the night before." Lucinda held her head between her hands and made a face. "You know?"

"*Ja, ja.*" Anna laughed. "We have a neighbor who sometimes drinks too much dandelion wine. Next day he is *kranker.*"

"Yeah. I thought maybe you—or Madison—were *kranker.* Then you smiled at me and I was caught off guard. That's why I was nice to you."

"Just because I smiled?"

Lucinda shrugged. "Hey, it doesn't take much. Then you said you were meeting Garret and I figured you hadn't really changed."

"You don't like Garret?"

"More like he doesn't like me. Both Garret and Vivian treat me like dirt."

"Why?"

Lucinda laughed, but she did not sound happy. "Why? Because I, unlike them, am not filthy rich. My parents both *work* for a living."

"Oh." Anna nodded. "So do mine."

"Yes. But that is different."

"That is true. We are very different."

"What I want to know, Anna, is why did you agree to do this switch?"

Anna explained about Jacob, confessing that she was certain they were going to marry, but then he'd left. "I believe if I can find him, my future will be good."

"You'd get married?" Lucinda looked shocked. "Now? At your age?"

"Maybe not right now. Jacob would have to prove himself, get baptized . . . but maybe by winter."

"And you're seventeen?"

Anna nodded. "Many girls get married at my age. By twenty you are old maid."

Lucinda laughed. "That is so twisted."

"Twisted?"

"Never mind. I don't want to sound disrespectful. But seriously, I so would not want to be married before I was twenty. I have too much to do."

"What?" Anna asked. "What do you have to do?"

"Get into a good design school. Become a famous designer. Travel the globe. Have some interesting experiences. Some romances. Then, if I feel like it and if I meet someone incredibly special—when I'm, say, around thirty—then I'll consider marriage."

"Thirty?" Anna blinked. Her own mother was in her thirties. She might be a grandmother before long. *Thirty?*

"Back to your guy," Lucinda said as she measured off a length of thread, cut it, and threaded a needle. "Do you really think you can find him?"

Anna frowned. "I do not know. So far it is impossible. I think Garret has given up helping me. Maybe I will give up too."

"What about the police?"

Anna gasped. "The police?" She did not want anything to do with the police. That was too frightening.

"I mean they have access to all kinds of records of things. My aunt works for a precinct nearby."

"Your aunt is a police?"

"She works in the office. She might help us."

"She could do that?"

"Maybe." Lucinda slid a small notebook toward Anna. "Write down everything you know about Jacob. You know, birth date, where he was born, anything that could be used to identify him."

Anna was unsure. But she was also desperate. She had less than three days to find Jacob now. She wrote down all she could think of, then handed the notebook back to Lucinda. "You will not tell your aunt my name?"

"No reason to."

"And Jacob will not get into trouble?"

"Why should he?"

Anna shrugged. Lucinda picked up her phone and dialed, then told someone named Danielle all the information.

"Thanks," Lucinda said finally. "It's for a good friend. She's only in the city for a few days, but she'd really like to see this guy. Yeah. I really appreciate it." She turned off the phone and grinned.

"Did you find him?"

"No. Not yet. But my aunt is on it. She'll call back."

For the rest of the afternoon, Anna was not only working with pins and needles, she felt as if she were sitting on them too. She wished Lucinda's aunt would call. And soon. But finally it was time to quit.

"Do you think your aunt will still call?" Anna asked as she was about to leave.

"If she finds out something."

"You will call me?"

"Absolutely."

"Thank you!" Anna smiled.

"Hey, thank you. You're a great seamstress. My mom's going to be pleased at the quality of your work."

Anna chuckled. "Surprised too? She might not think Madison can sew like that."

Lucinda nodded. "That's true. Madison can't."

Speaking of Madison made Anna wish she would call. Then Anna realized she had forgotten to bring the phone with her. What if Madison had called?

Anna pushed the elevator button, tapping her toe as she waited. She wanted to get up there to check the phones. *I am acting just like an Englisher*, she thought as she got on the elevator. Impatient, relying on all these "conveniences," checking messages on phones. Wouldn't her family be appalled if they could see her now!

16

On Wednesday morning, while cleaning up the breakfast dishes, Madison kept a close watch on the north field. After Daniel and his horse, with Jeremiah seated on top, were a long way out, she set down the dish towel and slipped out the door. She ran over to the barn, picked up the phone, and quickly dialed. When Anna didn't answer, Madison wanted to scream. Instead she left a message.

"Anna, I'm getting worried. I think we need to switch back before Saturday after all. Something is happening here that makes me uncomfortable. If you get this message, make sure you keep your phone with you—and answer it. I'll try to call you back this evening, after everyone is asleep. You better be there!" She hung up and hurried back to the house.

"Where were you?" Rachel asked as Madison came inside.

"Just getting some air."

"*Ja*, it is nice out there." Rachel rubbed her back and moaned. "Dis baby is restless."

"Kicking again?"

"*Ja, ja*. Kicking and moving. Must be another boy."

Madison smiled. "Girls can be restless too."

"*Ja, ja.* Tell me about it." She nodded over to where Elizabeth had pulled the pots and pans out onto the floor again. She was banging a wooden spoon on an overturned pot like she thought she was going to be the drummer in a rock band someday.

Rachel sighed as she sat down. "How is the dress coming?"

Madison grimaced. "Slowly."

"Not done yet?"

"I had to rip something out."

Rachel shook her head in disappointment. "Anna, Anna."

"I'm sorry. I'll fix it."

"You bring it here for me to see."

Madison went into the other room and opened the basket on top of the sewing machine cabinet, where she had stowed the sad little pieces of the dress. Not only was it not finished and messed up, now it was all wrinkled. She carried it into the kitchen and set it on the table in front of Rachel.

Rachel looked down at the mess and laughed. "Oh, Anna. You are not yourself."

"I know."

"Go get my sewing basket. We will work together."

As Madison went back for the basket, she wished she'd paid better attention when Lucinda had tried to teach her to sew. She sat down across from Rachel at the table, and as Elizabeth banged pan lids together, the two women undid the bad seams of the little dress.

"You are making me wonder, Anna."

"Wonder?" Madison kept her eyes downward.

"Do you act like this to make poor Aunt Rachel feel good?"

"What do you mean?"

"You know. This thing with your head . . . you cannot

177

remember how to cook and clean and sew. Is it to make me feel better?"

Madison smiled. "No. I am not pretending to be bad at these things. I just am."

Rachel shook her head. "It is very strange indeed."

"Tell me about it." Madison jumped when she stuck her finger with the seam ripper.

"Tell you about what?" Rachel looked even more perplexed.

But instead of explaining her vernacular faux pas or telling Rachel about anything, Madison listened as Rachel told story after story about how certain older women had made her life miserable. Nitpicking her sewing skills, criticizing her cooking, pointing out flaws in her children. Madison suspected this was Rachel's way of warning her—that this is how it would go with her if she didn't improve her domestic skills.

"Those women sound just plain mean," Madison said finally.

"Dey say it is to help me." Rachel sighed. "When I say I don't want help, I am chastised. I am told I must repent. When I say I don't want to repent, I am warned . . . I may be shunned someday." She gave a small smile. "I do not mind that so much. Now the women do not trouble me. They stay away. I can do as I like."

"Are you lonely?"

Rachel nodded. "*Ja*. Daniel is not pleased with me. He does not say much, but is he unhappy. I know this."

Madison wished she had something encouraging to say, something to make this better. Mostly she felt sorry for Rachel—like this poor woman was caught in a horrible trap that she would never escape. Yet most of the time, Rachel seemed fairly happy. She loved her children. She didn't complain about all the hard work. Maybe her house wasn't as clean as her neighbors', but it wasn't that bad.

"Having you here, Anna, is like sunshine after the rain." Rachel reached across the table and clasped Madison's hand. "*Ja*, you are changed, for sure. But it is a good change." She chuckled. "You just be sure to marry the right man. A man who loves you no matter what. I think Malachi is like that. He has a good heart and understanding eyes."

Madison cringed inwardly. Yesterday she had declined Malachi's invitation to meet him at the pond after bedtime. He had seemed hurt, but he had bounced back and promised, "Anna or no Anna, I will be there." Thanks to that, she'd been afraid to sneak out and use the phone after everyone was asleep. Afraid she'd bump into him . . . afraid that he might actually sweep her off her feet . . . afraid that she might actually break his heart. She wanted out of here. Now.

"Oh, Anna!"

Madison jumped, looking up to see Rachel's eyes wide. "What?"

Rachel scooted her chair back, pointing down at the floor, staring in horror at a puddle of water.

"What is it?" Madison asked. "Did you spill something?"

"My water." Rachel groaned loudly.

Madison looked around for a water glass, trying to figure out why this was so upsetting. "Did the glass break? Do you want another drink?"

"Oh, oh!" Rachel grabbed her belly. "It is time!"

"What time?"

"The baby! It is coming!"

Madison jumped to her feet, horrified. "It's coming? *Now?*"

"Help me." Rachel stood too.

"What? What do I do?"

"Help me to my room. Hasten—before the next one."

"The next what?"

"Birth pain."

Madison walked next to Rachel, holding her arm, guiding her toward the stairs. When they were halfway up, Rachel doubled over in pain. "Too late. Here it comes."

Madison didn't know what to do as Rachel squatted right there on the stairs, moaning and groaning and clinging to Madison's hand so tightly that her fingers grew numb. Everything in Madison told her to run to the phone and dial 9-1-1 and demand that an ambulance be sent out.

"It is enough." Rachel stood up straight. "Help me, Anna. Hasten."

Madison was thankful for her height as she partially led, partially dragged Rachel to her room, getting her settled on her bed just in time for another contraction. Madison watched helplessly as Rachel tossed and turned, crying out in pain, and then she grew quiet, beads of perspiration glistening on her forehead.

"Are you all right?" Madison asked.

"Baby is coming fast, Anna. The pains—are close."

"What do I do?" Madison asked in desperation. "Is there someone I can call?"

Rachel told her a number and name. "Make sure the kettle is on." Madison was about to go when Rachel shrieked that another pain was coming. Madison didn't know what to do—whether to run to the barn and call the number or stay here to make sure Rachel was okay. What if Rachel died while she was gone?

Finally Rachel stopped moaning and looked up at Madison with frightened eyes. "Go, Anna! Run and call Sarah. *Schnell!* And watch Elizabeth!"

Madison nodded, streaking down the stairs. She looked for Elizabeth, who was no longer in the kitchen.

"Elizabeth!" she shouted. "Where are you?" No answer. "Elizabeth," Madison called again. "You want bread and jam?" She waited, listening, and Elizabeth came running, holding up her chubby hands.

"*Ja, ja,*" she said. "Jam!"

"Not right now." Madison swept the toddler up, set her on a hip, and headed out the door.

"Jam! Jam!" Elizabeth cried as Madison ran toward the barn.

"Horsey ride," Madison said as she paused to hoist Elizabeth onto her shoulders.

"Giddyup!" Elizabeth cried.

Madison ran as fast as she could, then breathlessly picked up the phone, hoping she had remembered the number correctly. She'd always been good at memorizing numbers, but this was the one time when it really counted. She dialed and waited . . . and waited . . . and waited. Elizabeth was yelling in her ear for jam when a man's voice finally answered.

"I need Sarah Hostetler now!"

The man spoke in German, asking her who she was and why she was calling.

"Frau Rachel Bender is having baby now!" she shouted. "Sarah Hostetler must come now! Hasten!"

Fortunately, he understood her. The best Madison could make out as he spoke in fast German was that he would bring his wife in the wagon.

"Hold on," Madison told Elizabeth as she hung up the phone and started running back to the house. She looked out to the field where Daniel was working, but couldn't see him. He probably wouldn't come in for lunch for another hour.

"Jam!" Elizabeth shouted, struggling to get down as Madison ran through the kitchen.

"Not now." Madison paused to make sure the kettle was full and hot, opened the front of the stove, and tossed in a few pieces of wood. "Come, Elizabeth," she yelled as she ran out. "We need to go to Mamm."

She could hear Elizabeth's footsteps running behind her. She probably thought they were playing some kind of game, which was fine. What would Elizabeth think to see her mother in such pain?

When Madison burst into the bedroom, it was quiet and Rachel was not moving. Elizabeth started to climb onto the bed, but Madison picked her up. Rachel's face was white and her eyes were closed.

With pounding heart, Madison touched her arm. "Rachel?"

"*Ja,*" Rachel answered in a hoarse voice.

"Sarah is coming now."

"Good."

"The kettle is on. Elizabeth is here with me."

"Good." Rachel opened her eyes and looked up at them, giving Elizabeth a weak smile. Her eyes were bloodshot and her hair was wet from perspiration. "When the birth pain comes, Anna, you must take her out of here."

"I will." Madison took in a quick breath. "Is there anything I can do for you?"

"You can pray."

"*Ja.*" Madison nodded. "I will do that."

"Dis baby is not like the others, Anna. Something feels wrong."

Madison reached down and took Rachel's hand. It was clammy. "It's going to be all right, Aunt Rachel. You will be all right. Baby will be all right."

Rachel's face twisted in pain, and Madison knew another contraction was coming. "Let's go, Elizabeth," she said. They quickly exited the room, closing the door behind them. She carried Elizabeth to their room, closed that door, and sang loudly to cover up the sounds coming from Rachel's room.

"Blacks and bays, dapples and grays," she practically shouted, "all the pretty little horses." She had no idea where that song came from, but thought perhaps her grandmother used to sing it to her. Elizabeth seemed to like it because she was clapping her hands. Madison paused and realized it was quiet again.

"More!" Elizabeth demanded.

"More later." Madison went back to Rachel's room to see, again, that she was still and white as death. "I'm here," she said. "Tell me if there's anything I can do."

"Just pray."

"*Ja.*" Madison nodded, and although she had no idea how to do this, she began to pray. "Dear God, please help Aunt Rachel. Please keep her baby safe and healthy. Keep Rachel safe and healthy. Help this baby to come soon. Take good care of both of them." She rambled on until Rachel's grimace returned. Then, as fast as she could go with Elizabeth still in her arms, Madison ran out of there and back to her room, where she continued to sing loudly.

Fortunately, Elizabeth began to think this was a game. Although it was tiring and Madison could feel her dress growing damp with perspiration, she knew that her exhaustion was nothing compared to how Rachel must be feeling. In fact, each time Madison went into the bedroom, she was worried that Rachel might really be dead. How did women survive this? What if she really did need a doctor? Rachel had told Madison that doctors were both expensive and unnecessary for something as common as childbirth—especially when it was a fifth child. Daniel would never hear of it.

Madison wasn't sure if this was an Amish thing or a Daniel thing. Would he change his way of thinking if a life—perhaps two lives—were in danger? She was tempted to go down and call 9-1-1 for real now. She would simply confess to everyone that she was not Anna Fisher but was an Englisher girl, and that was what Englisher girls did in emergencies. But before she could do this, a tall, gray-haired woman and two younger women burst into the bedroom. The older one started barking directions and the other two sprang into action. The older woman told Madison to go—to take the child outside until this was over.

With mixed feelings, Madison did as she was told. On the one hand, she was relieved to finally have someone here who knew what to do. On the other hand, she felt as if Rachel needed her there too. But the woman was right, it was better to get Elizabeth out of there. The poor child might be damaged for life after seeing her mother like that. Madison doubted that there would be any Amish therapy groups to help her when she was older.

It wasn't long before more buggies started to arrive. It seemed that bringing a baby into the world was an event that others felt entitled to participate in. Oh, not the actual birthing. Thankfully for Rachel's sake, that was restricted to

Sarah and her helpers. But other women came, bringing food and things, bustling about in the kitchen and in the house, taking over as if they lived there.

Madison tried to stay out of their way, but she couldn't help overhearing some of their comments. It was just like Rachel had said. A couple of the women—not all, thankfully—began to make mean comments about Rachel's domestic skills, or rather her lack of them. It really irked Madison. So much so that she decided to say something to the woman with the sharpest tongue. Madison thought the dark-haired woman's name was Berta. She had the face of a bulldog and reminded Madison of an army sergeant.

In her best German, mixed with English, Madison introduced herself as Anna Fisher, Rachel's niece. She told Berta that she had been brought up in a different community, and where she came from, friends did not speak about friends like that. She said that a person who used cruel words like that suggested that they must be an enemy. She asked Berta if she was Rachel's enemy, and if so, why was she here in Rachel's house? Then, remembering a bracelet that a friend used to wear in grade school, Madison asked Berta if that was what Jesus would do.

Two bright red spots appeared on Berta's cheeks, and she glared at Madison as she opened her mouth. Before she could speak, a short, plump woman came over and stood next to Madison. "Anna is right," she said loudly.

To Madison's surprise, another middle-aged woman came over and stood on her other side, nodding her head. "*Ja*. Anna is right," she said. "That is enough."

Berta looked like she was about to shoot steam out of her ears, but instead she spun around and stomped out of the house. To Madison's relief, another woman, the one who'd been agreeing with Berta about Rachel's slovenly ways, left as well. When both of them stopped in the yard and made quite a display of shaking their feet, Madison asked a young woman what they were doing. The girl, who probably wasn't much older than Madison, giggled, explaining that they were shaking the dust from their feet. When Madison looked confused, an older woman reminded her that it was in the Bible. Maybe so, but Madison still didn't get it.

However, she did understand that something in the house changed dramatically after the two grumpy fraus were gone. The remaining women seemed less uptight and the atmosphere in the house grew much more pleasant. Even though they were still bustling about the kitchen, getting lunch ready and scrubbing here and there, it wasn't in the mean, condescending way Berta and her friend had. These women seemed to genuinely enjoy helping. Madison began to think the neighbors weren't quite as bad as she'd thought. At least not all of them.

Madison glanced up the stairs, wondering how Rachel was holding up and if she was okay. Why was it so quiet up there now?

Elizabeth was happily occupied by a girl who appeared to be about five, and suddenly Madison felt unnecessary and wished there was something she could do to help. Then she remembered what Rachel had asked her to do. She slipped outside, and as she walked around the garden, she prayed for Rachel and the baby. She had no idea whether or not she was doing it right. Maybe what mattered most was that she was doing it.

17

For no explainable reason, Anna felt very tired on Wednesday afternoon. It wasn't as if she'd worn herself out helping Lucinda. The sewing had actually been fun—almost like a small frolic. Anna suspected her tiredness came from a different source. She felt like she was weary deep down in her soul. Weary and unhappy. Perhaps even a bit homesick.

She felt she had come on a fool's mission. Her grand plan to search and find Jacob was truly madness. Now she knew that if Jacob had wanted to be found, if he had wanted to be part of her life, he would have written to her back at home. He'd had more than three months to communicate . . . and yet he had not. Unless something bad had happened to him—and Anna hated to even think about that—it seemed clear that Jacob was finished with her.

Avoiding the big windows, which still paralyzed her, Anna paced restlessly around the lavishly appointed penthouse. More than ever, she felt as if she were trapped in a luxurious prison cell. How did people live like this? Didn't they know that idle hands were the devil's workshop? As badly as Anna wanted to do something useful in here, there really was nothing that needed doing. Furthermore, if she did lift a finger to help, the wrath of Nadya would fall on her.

Finally, Anna gave in to the decadence and took a nap. When she woke, she felt even more glum. Why had she ever agreed to this senseless switch? Oh, she had tried to convince herself she was doing it for all the right reasons. Finding Jacob seemed a romantically noble cause. Allowing Madison a chance to sample a simpler life seemed admirable too. But the truth was Anna had agreed to this life swap out of pure selfishness. There was no denying it now. And the price she was paying for her selfishness was pure misery.

Anna looked at the clock. Still three hours until Madison would call. She picked up Madison's phone and stared at it. She could call the phone in her father's barn, confess everything, and apologize. Her parents would have to forgive her, but they would be angry. The pressure to marry Aaron Zook would become extreme. Anna had placed herself in a poor position to protest such a match. Being stuck for life with someone like Aaron Zook was probably exactly what she deserved. Aaron was a good man and many girls would feel lucky to get him, but he had an obnoxious habit of clearing his throat and spitting. Just thinking of his beady eyes and scrawny neck made her skin crawl. How would she ever learn to love him?

Just one week ago, Anna would have firmly put her foot down. She would have proclaimed that she would rather be an old maid than marry a man she did not love. Just one week ago, her parents might have listened. But they would not listen now. Not if they knew where she was and what she had done.

If she weren't so homesick, and if she weren't so disenchanted with the English lifestyle, she might have considered never going back at all. But the truth was Anna could not bear the idea of never going home again. She missed everyone in her family—even her little brothers. She missed the smell of the barn. She missed gathering eggs. She missed the open sky and the fields. She even missed pegging the wash on the line.

Oh, why did she risk everything—and for what? She frowned at Madison's fancy bedroom. A week of being stuck here? What an idiotic exchange. If only she could undo it.

Anna had heard about God for her whole life. There had been many times when she felt she'd been on good terms with him. Not so much in the past couple of years. Her parents had blamed Jacob's rebellious influence for Anna's loss of interest in spiritual matters. Her mother had been nagging her for quite some time—telling Anna it was time to come to her senses, be baptized, take her place in the community, marry, have children. But Anna had been dragging her heels. Now she wondered if God would even listen to her prayers.

Just the same, Anna went into Madison's enormous closet, closed the door, turned off the light, and got down on her knees. With tears streaming down her cheeks, she told God she was very, very sorry. She confessed that she'd been selfish and that she had lied and that she was not worthy to belong to him . . . or to her family or her community. She asked God to forgive her, and she promised she would do better. She asked him to help her out of this mess that she had willingly jumped into.

Finally she could think of nothing more to say, so she just waited in silence. Slowly but surely, her frantic fear seemed to be replaced with a sense of calm and peace. Nothing like she'd felt before. She took in a long, deep breath and thanked

God for listening. She truly believed now that he had listened to her and that he was answering her prayers. As she exited the closet, she had no idea how he could salvage anything from the wreckage of her life, but she felt certain he would.

Suddenly she felt a strong urge to call her father. Was it coming from God? If it was, she did not want to risk this sense of peace by not obeying. She picked up Madison's phone and dialed the number. As it rang, she realized that it was unlikely that her father would answer. But to her surprise, he did.

"Daed?" she said with a slightly trembling voice.

"Anna?"

"*Ja*, it is me."

"What is wrong, Anna?"

"I just wanted to tell you I am sorry, Daed."

"Sorry for what?"

"I am sorry I have not been a better daughter."

"What have you done, Anna?"

"I have not been obedient and I am sorry. I am going to live differently now. And I want to be baptized."

"You do?"

"Yes. I have just been talking to God about it. I want to be baptized. I am ready to take this important step now. I want to obey God and I want to obey my parents."

"That is very good to hear."

"*Ja*. I just wanted you to know, Daed. I'm sorry to call when it's not a real emergency."

"No, Anna. It's all right. It is good to hear your voice. I am happy about your news. Mamm will be happy too."

"I love you, Daed."

"I love you too, Anna."

"Tell Mamm I love her too."

"I will do that."

They said goodbye. Anna sighed happily as she set the phone down. She realized that she hadn't told her father everything, but she felt she had told him enough . . . for now. To have told him more—to reveal where she was right now—would have only worried him. She was too far away for him to come and get her. Perhaps when Madison called tonight, she would tell Anna to meet her in town tomorrow and that they would be back in their own worlds before sunset. Even being at Aunt Rachel's would be much better than being here.

Anna had dozed off and was startled awake at the ringing of the phone. To her relief, it was Madison and she sounded very excited. "Anna?"

"Yes!"

"Oh, good. I have so much to tell you."

"We will switch back tomorrow?"

"No, not tomorrow. But I have news, Anna. Your aunt had her baby and—"

"Aunt Rachel had her baby?"

"Yes. It's been so exciting here." Madison launched into a detailed story about how Rachel had gone into labor and only Madison was there and it was hard and stressful, but she had managed to handle it. She explained about the midwife and the neighbor women coming, and how the baby was breech and Rachel wasn't doing very well and it took a long time.

"I was really praying hard for her," Madison said breathlessly. "Rachel had asked me to do that. Then God did a real miracle, Anna. It was truly amazing. The baby turned around and Rachel gave birth about an hour ago to a girl. I'm just so happy. It was an incredible day!"

"Aunt Rachel is all right? The baby is all right?"

"Yes. The baby is fine. Rachel is exhausted, but fine. She is such a good person, Anna. I really love her."

"I am glad you were there for her, Madison."

"Are you okay?"

"I am fine. But I am eager to trade back with you."

"Did you find Jacob?"

Anna sighed. "I think perhaps Jacob does not want to be found."

"I'm sorry. Are you okay with that?"

Anna felt a lump in her throat. "Yes. I am fine."

"And you'll be okay there until Saturday? I don't think I can get to town any sooner than Saturday, Anna. Especially now that the baby is here."

"Yes. I am all right until Saturday." Anna could not imagine how she would pass the next two days.

"Great. We'll meet in the same coffee shop, okay?"

"In the morning?" Anna asked.

"I think so."

"I will be there."

"Thanks, Anna. I mean thanks for letting me do this. I can't really explain it, but I feel it has changed my life completely. I'm so happy."

"I am happy for you." Anna tried to sound happier than she felt.

Madison explained that she'd told Daniel she was calling Anna's parents to inform them of the good news. "You better call them, Anna."

"Yes. I will do that in the morning."

"Okay. See you on Saturday then."

"Yes. See you then."

After Anna turned off the phone, she felt discouraged. She knew it was probably selfishness again. Perhaps envy too. Neither of those were particularly admirable qualities. But it was painful to hear Madison sounding so thrilled about doing what Anna should have been doing.

More than ever, Anna wished she had never agreed to this switch. Perhaps this was her punishment—feeling completely left out while Madison lived Anna's life. Or maybe it was discipline. Maybe God was trying to teach her a good lesson. Anna could only hope.

18

On Thursday morning, Madison had her hands full. Attempting to make breakfast for Daniel and the four children, keeping Elizabeth out of harm's way, and tending to Rachel and the baby felt like participating in a weird triathlon. When someone knocked on the kitchen door just as the oatmeal boiled over, Madison felt tempted to throw something.

"Hello?" A young woman stuck her head in the door.

Madison frowned. "What?"

"I came to help." The woman opened the door a bit wider.

Madison brightened. "*Ja, ja*. Come in. Welcome!"

"I am Rebekah Lapp," she said as she came in.

"I am Anna." Madison grabbed a singed pot holder, using it to move the oatmeal to a cooler part of the stove, and put the lid on halfway like she'd seen Rachel do.

"I know who you are." Rebekah smiled as she picked up Elizabeth. "You are Rachel's niece. You speak English."

"*Ja, ja*. And some German also."

"You are the one who spoke to Berta."

Madison made a face as she set the bowls on the table with a thud. "Berta was unkind to my aunt."

"Berta is good at faultfinding."

"*Ja*, that's for sure."

Rebekah moved effortlessly through the kitchen, helping and doing things without being told. Madison felt a bit envious but reminded herself that Rebekah had probably been doing this most of her life. Madison had been here less than a week. Besides that, Madison felt certain she could not have gotten breakfast served without her. Finally, the twins headed off to school and Daniel once again offered to take Jeremiah with him for the morning. Then it was only females left in the house.

"My mamm is bringin' my sister Lydia today," Rebekah said as they finished cleaning the dishes.

"Why?"

"They want to help Rachel and you."

"*Denki*." Madison smiled. "Aunt Rachel has not got many friends."

"I know."

"I think she is lonely."

"*Ja*. My mamm says is time to be friends."

"Good."

By midmorning, Rebekah and her mother and sister had rolled up their sleeves and done some serious spring cleaning. Madison was surprised to see how much grime was removed from the wood floors and how the windows sparkled. Even the curtains got washed and pressed. This three-woman cleaning team was impressive!

While Madison tried to make herself useful downstairs, it seemed her most important role was seeing to Rachel and the baby. Rachel was still worn out from yesterday, but her smile had returned and she looked happy and peaceful with the baby at her breast.

"What is her name?" Madison asked as she tucked the sleeping infant back into the wooden cradle near the bed.

"I think I call her Anna." Rachel gave a funny grin. "For you."

Madison felt a little uneasy now. "*Ja*. Anna is good name."

"But not your name." Rachel's eyes locked on her.

Madison took in a quick breath, then turned away. What was going on?

"I know you are not Anna."

"Of course I am Anna," Madison said with her back to Rachel. She pretended to fold a diaper, something she had no idea how to do.

"Who are you?" Rachel asked quietly.

Madison turned back around. Rachel didn't look angry, just confused.

"What do you mean?" Madison held up her hands in a helpless gesture. "You know I am Anna."

"Close the door," Rachel told her.

Madison did so.

"Come here." Rachel pointed to a chair by the bed. "And sit."

Madison complied.

"Tell me who you are. Tell me where is Anna."

"What makes you think I am not Anna?"

Rachel chuckled. "When I first saw you . . . I knew something was not right." She frowned, tapping the side of her head. "Then I think I must be daft. Sure, you are Anna. You must be Anna."

"*Ja*." Madison nodded.

"Then yesterday . . . such pain . . . and it came to me so plain and clear—you are not Anna." Her brows drew together.

"I cannot explain how I know it is true. I just know it is. Now, tell me *who you are*."

"I am sorry." Madison choked up. "You're right. I'm not Anna."

Rachel smiled. "*Ja!* I knew that."

Madison told her the whole story, and the entire time Rachel just listened with wide eyes until Madison finished. Then she clapped her hands. "Good for you. Good for Anna also."

"Really?" Madison felt confused. "You're not angry?"

"No." She reached for Madison's hand. "You are a good girl. Anna is blessed to have you for a friend."

"I'm your friend too, Rachel."

"*Denki.*" She smiled. "You are a good friend. Now, tell me, what is your name?"

"Madison Van Buren."

"Madison?" Rachel frowned. "It is a girl's name?"

Madison shrugged. "It is for me."

Rachel pointed to her sleeping baby. "Her name—it is Madison too."

Madison felt her jaw drop. "No way."

Rachel chuckled. "*Ja.* Baby Madison."

Madison wondered what Daniel would have to say about that but decided not to spoil this moment by bringing it up. "*Denki*, Rachel."

"*Denki*, Madison."

"Some of my friends call me Maddie."

Rachel smiled. "I will call you Maddie too. But only inside my head. For everyone else you are still Anna, *ja?*"

Madison nodded and explained the plan to switch back on Saturday. "I'm not sure how I will get to town."

"I will send Malachi on an errand. You will go with him."

Madison was about to point out that Malachi might present a problem, but Rachel looked as if she were about to fall asleep and Madison knew she needed her rest. She tiptoed from the room, closing the door behind her.

The cleaning trio was now preparing lunch, and Madison remembered that since it was Thursday, Malachi would be working on the farm today. She hadn't seen him yet, but she knew it would be impossible to avoid him.

Sure enough, he came to lunch with Daniel and Jeremiah. Madison tried to avoid his eyes, but she could tell he was watching her. When she accidentally glanced up, she could see the questioning look. She knew she had to speak to him.

As lunch was winding down, she excused herself and went outside. Without looking back, she hurried over to the pond, where she sat on the bench and waited. Minutes later he sat next to her.

"I have to tell you something," she said without looking at him. "It isn't going to be easy to say, or to hear."

"I am waiting."

She turned and looked at him. "Malachi, you are a great guy."

He nodded. "I know where this is going."

"No." She shook her head. "You do not. Believe me, you have no idea." She had his attention now. "I need to be able to trust you." She paused, watching his eyes.

"You can trust me. I swear you can trust me with anything, Anna."

"I am not Anna."

His brow creased. "Who are you?"

For the second time that day, she told her story. He listened with a shocked expression, shaking his head from time to time, saying he couldn't believe it. She simply continued, trying to make him understand. When she was done, he looked angry.

"I'm sorry," she said quietly.

"You tricked me."

"No." She shook her head. "At least I didn't mean to trick you. I'm sorry."

He stood with balled fists. "Whether you meant to or not, you tricked me, Anna." He shook his finger at her. "No, you are not Anna. You said that, right?"

She told him her real name and waited as he stood there glaring at her.

"I really am sorry, Malachi."

"I do not understand you." He shoved his hands in his pockets.

"But I can trust you still?" she asked. "You won't tell anyone? Rachel knows, but—"

"Rachel knows?"

"Yes. And she understands—"

"She understands?" He looked skeptical.

"She knows we meant no harm."

He shook his head. She could tell he was hurting, and it hurt her to see it. Still, what could she do? What was done was done. There was no undoing it. "Rachel said that you could drive me to town on Saturday."

"Why?" He stared at her with angry eyes. "Why should I do that?"

"So Anna and I can trade places again."

"Fine," he snapped at her. "I will do that. I will be glad to see you gone, Anna—I mean *Madison*. I will say good riddance!" He stormed away.

Madison's stomach felt like it had tied itself into a dozen tight little knots. This was not how it was supposed to go. She felt so sorry for what she'd done to Malachi. In a way, he was right—she had tricked him. She never should've spent time with him. But really, what could she do about that now? The damage was done. He would get over it. Everyone did . . . in time.

She stood and headed back toward the house. As she walked, she told herself that in all fairness, Malachi didn't even know her. They had spent a total of maybe two hours together. Perhaps not even that much. What they had both experienced was a bad case of infatuation. A plain old crush. Not true love. Not really.

Still, she felt guilty and regretful. It was wrong to toy with anyone's heart. If she could go back and do it all over again, she would definitely do it differently.

As Madison got near the house, she began to pray silently, asking God to help Malachi through this heartache and bring something good out of something messed up.

19

On Thursday morning, Anna rose early to call her father's phone in the barn. He was surprised to hear from her again so soon. Inserting an excited edge to her voice, she told him the good news about Rachel's baby entering the world, repeating the parts of the story that Madison had told her.

"I will go tell your mamm now," he said finally. "Thank you, Anna."

They said goodbye and Anna set the phone down, sighing to see that it wasn't even eight o'clock yet. This was going to be a very long day. It was also Nadya's day off and, in Anna's opinion, a good reason to stay home because she wouldn't have Nadya watching every move she made, scowling at her if she accidentally picked up after herself. Fortunately, she had only two more full days in New York City. While she knew she should do something to make the most of her time here, perhaps even see some of the sights, she had no desire to do anything. So that is what she did. Nothing. Or almost nothing. Finding a novel that looked interesting—and unlike anything she'd be allowed to read at home—she lost herself in it for a few hours.

A bit before noon, Madison's phone rang again. Assuming

it was Garret—since he never seemed to give up—she prepared herself to make another excuse for not seeing him. She was surprised to hear Lucinda's voice.

"Anna!" she exclaimed. "Wait until you hear this."

"What?"

"My aunt found Jacob Glick."

"My Jacob Glick?"

"I think so. Anyway, he has the right birth date and name."

"Jacob is here still? In New York?" Anna's heart was pounding hard. "I can see him?"

"Absolutely. My aunt gave me his phone number. You can call him."

Anna's hand trembled as she opened a drawer in Madison's desk, grabbed a pen and pad, and wrote down the numbers in shaky-looking penmanship. "Thank you!" she cried. "Thank you so much!"

"Let me know how it goes, Anna. I'd love to hear the end of this story."

"Yes," Anna promised. "I will tell you all about it." As soon as Lucinda was off the phone, Anna punched in the numbers, holding her breath as she waited, listening to the rings. One . . . two . . . three.

"Hello?" answered a familiar deep voice.

"Jacob?"

"Yes?"

"It's me—Anna!"

"Anna? Anna Fisher?"

"Yes. A friend found your phone number and—"

"Where are you? Home still?"

"No. I'm here in New York City. In Manhattan."

"No way."

"Yes!" she cried. "I am. I really am. Where are you?"

"Brooklyn."

"Where is that?"

"Not far from where you are. What are you doing there?"

"I came looking for you." There was a long pause, and Anna felt worried—did he not want to be found? "I would like to see you, Jacob . . . if it is all right."

"Of course it's all right. It's great. How about if I come over to visit you?"

"Yes. That's a good idea. I'm not clever at finding my way around this big city." She told him where she was staying and he sounded impressed, but when she started to explain why she was there, he cut her off.

"I can't make it over there until around three," he told her. "Is that okay?"

Anna felt a cold wave of disappointment. "Not until *three*?"

"Yeah. I have classes until then."

"Classes?"

"In fact, I'm late now, Anna. I have to go. See you around three. Okay?"

"Okay." As she set the phone down, she felt nothing close to okay. She had come all this way, made all this effort, and now that she had finally found Jacob, he wasn't willing to drop everything to run and see her? That did not make sense.

She decided to call Lucinda, explaining what had happened and how much it bothered her. "I have over three hours to wait now."

"Why don't you come down here and wait with me?" Lucinda suggested.

"Thank you." Anna was already on her way out the door. "I would like that."

Something about the smell of fabric, the textures, the colors, the sewing notions . . . it comforted Anna. "Please, let me help you again," she told Lucinda.

"Gladly." Lucinda handed her a long black dress with pins in the hem. "This is next."

Anna frowned at the hemline. "But it is uneven."

"That's how it's supposed to be."

"Uneven?"

Lucinda nodded.

"Oh." Anna tried not to think about the unevenness as she slowly stitched. It was not for her to understand the way the English thought. The more she saw on the television and on the streets, the less she understood—and the more she longed for home, where everything, for the most part, made sense.

"Did he sound happy to hear you're in town?" Lucinda asked.

Anna considered this. Happy . . . had Jacob sounded happy? "I am not sure," she admitted. "He sounded surprised." She remembered her conversation with Madison last night and relayed it to Lucinda.

"You're kidding! Madison helped deliver your aunt's baby?"

"I am not sure it was exactly like that. But she did help. She was very excited about it."

"That is totally weird." Lucinda laughed. "Madison Van Buren delivers an Amish baby."

"That may be overstating it." Anna frowned.

"Anyway, it's crazy." Lucinda got a funny look. "But in a way, it all adds up."

"It adds up?"

"Well, Madison used to talk about wanting to go back in

time. She was always reading funny old books. She secretly watched *Little House on the Prairie* too."

"The Laura Ingalls Wilder books?" Anna nodded. "I read those books too."

"You live those books."

Anna shook her head. "Oh no. Not like that. We are not in the wilderness."

"Anyway, I'm starting to get it. Madison is living out one of her childhood fantasies." Lucinda set the scissors down. "Who would've thought?"

"Madison said we cannot exchange until Saturday." Anna pulled the thread through. "At first I was upset. I wanted to go home today."

"But now Jacob is here." Lucinda grinned. "Aren't you glad you stuck around?"

"Yes."

"What does Jacob look like?"

Anna closed her eyes for a moment, remembering. "Jacob is tall and strong. He has brown curly hair and hazel eyes with flecks of gold. A nice straight nose, a good smile, good teeth. He is a handsome man, I think."

"Did he say what kind of school he's attending?"

"No. He has only been here for a few months." Anna frowned. "His schooling, like mine, ended after eighth grade."

Lucinda looked up from what she was sewing. "You're kidding. You haven't gone to school since eighth grade?"

Anna nodded. "It is how we do it at home."

"Wow, that would be totally awesome."

Anna blinked. "You would want no more school too?"

"Sure. Then I could start designing my own line of clothes."

"Oh."

"My mom says I can't start working in design until I've had at least two years of college. We argue about it all the time."

"You argue with your mother?"

"Absolutely. But she's a cool mom. I mean she lets me work with her and I've learned a lot. Not that I would say that in front of her."

"I have learned a lot from my mother too." Anna sighed. "I think I will say that in front of her, when I see her."

"On Saturday?"

Anna shook her head. "No. I go to my aunt's house on Saturday. I am expected to stay with her for a while, to help her with the other children and things."

"How will you get there?"

"I came on the bus. Madison got the ticket for me." Anna frowned. "How do I get the ticket back there? Do you know?"

"You go to the bus station," Lucinda explained. "Or you can get it online."

"Oh, Jacob can figure it out." Anna winced as she poked herself with the needle. "I hope he will go back with me."

"Do you think he will?"

"I think if he loves me, he will."

"And he'll be welcomed at home?"

Anna thought for a moment. "He will be welcomed if he speaks to the deacon and admits he was wrong and asks to be baptized."

"What was he wrong about?"

Anna pressed her lips together, trying to remember exactly. "It wasn't just one single thing. Mostly it was the way Jacob questioned things."

"You're not allowed to question?"

"He questioned important things like how we live, what we believe, the Ordnung."

"Ordnung?"

"It's the rules. We are a community with rules that we agree to keep. Everyone must work together and respect the rules."

"Or what happens?"

Anna tried to imagine what would happen if her family and neighbors and the entire settlement all quit obeying the Ordnung. "Chaos maybe." She wanted to say "chaos like how the English live," but that seemed ungracious. "We are different," she said instead. "It is because we are different that we continue."

"What do you mean by *continue*?"

"I mean it is our traditions—the way we dress, the way we live, the way we believe—that sets us apart. It is the setting apart that preserves us."

"I think I get it." Lucinda shook out the garment she was working on. "Kind of like the Tibetan monks in the Himalayas."

Anna tilted her head to the side. "What?"

"They're religious too. They keep apart from the outside world. I read somewhere that's why they're still around—although they do suffer a lot of persecution."

"Yes," Anna agreed. "It is like that. We have enemies too."

"The Amish have enemies?"

Anna explained, as best she could, the lessons she'd learned in history, retelling stories of religious discrimination dating back to the sixteenth century, of those who died for their beliefs, and of the price paid for their religious freedom. "It is what holds our people together," she finally said. "Our history, our beliefs, our Ordnung." She felt a strange sense of pride as she spoke of these things—as if she was starting to believe them herself for the first time.

"That's a pretty cool heritage," Lucinda said as she went over to use a sewing machine.

"The truth is I was questioning it myself," Anna admitted.

"Is that why you traded places with Madison?"

"Yes. That and my longing to find Jacob."

"Hey, speaking of Jacob, it's almost three."

Anna jumped up. "Oh! I should go down to the lobby. It's where I said I would meet him."

"Thanks for helping again," Lucinda called. "My mom does want to pay you. I can help you with the bus ticket stuff too."

"Or Jacob can." Anna waved.

"Have fun!"

As Anna hurried to the elevator, she considered her appearance. She hadn't even thought to change her clothes or do anything with her hair—and now it was too late. What would Jacob think to see her dressed like an Englisher girl? But she didn't have any other options. As she went down, she realized that he too would be dressed differently. Everything here was different.

With her phone in her hand in case he called, she began pacing back and forth in the lobby, looking outside the glass doors to see if he was coming. What would he look like? How would he act? What would she say? Would it be like what she watched on television last night—the couple who had been parted, running to each other, embracing, kissing?

She and Jacob had first kissed about a year ago. It was springtime, and he had declared his love for her and kissed her. Then they had sneaked out a number of times, holding each other and kissing, and Anna had felt ready for marriage. Now that seemed so long ago.

Seeing that it was fifteen minutes past three, Anna decided to go out on the sidewalk. Perhaps he was confused or lost. She might spot him and—

"Anna!"

She turned to see a young man walking toward her now. "Jacob," she called out as she ran to him—and just like old times, they embraced. She buried her head in his shoulder and took in a deep breath. He smelled different.

He held her at arm's length and looked at her, studying her closely, and then he laughed. "Oh, Anna, you look so different."

"That is like the pot calling the kettle black." She pointed to his very short hair. "You cut your hair."

"What are you doing here?" he asked.

"I told you, I am looking for you."

He nodded to the building. "But why are you staying here? This is a very expensive neighborhood."

She smiled. "I know. Would you like to see where I live?"

He blinked. "Sure."

Anna smiled at the doorman and he opened the door for them. "Right this way," she told Jacob as she went to the elevator and pushed the up button. Inside, she slipped in the card, then pushed number 26 and waited.

"Very slick." He nodded with appreciation.

"We're going to the penthouse," she explained.

"You live in a penthouse?" He threw back his head and laughed. "Did you marry a millionaire?"

She turned and glared at him. "No, I did not marry a millionaire."

The doors opened, and she pressed the code numbers for the security system and let them inside.

"Wow, Anna." Jacob stared at the penthouse with wide eyes. "This place is awesome. Really, you have to tell me what's going on with you. If you didn't marry a millionaire, how did you get all this?"

"Are you hungry?" she asked as she walked into the kitchen. "I haven't had my lunch yet."

"Yeah, sure. I'm actually starving."

She opened the giant refrigerator and removed some of the plates of food that Nadya had left for her lunch and dinner. She carried them out to the large dining room and set them on the huge table before she went back for the plates and silverware. The whole time, she could feel Jacob's eyes on her, and she knew he was completely bewildered. For that matter, so was she. Everything about this felt very strange. Almost like a dream.

"There," she said when all was ready. "We will eat now."

They both sat down, and Jacob looked thoroughly stunned. "Seriously, what is going on here?"

"Do you want to pray first?" she asked.

With a blank expression, he shook his head.

"In that case, I will." She bowed her head and prayed silently, but when she finished, Jacob seemed even more perplexed.

"Please, Anna," he pleaded, "what's happened to you?"

She smiled and passed him a plate of fresh fruit. Finally, as they ate, she explained about meeting Madison on her way to her aunt's, and the life swap.

"Anna, that is unbelievable." He stared at her in wonder.

"Yes, and I must admit it was unwise. I regret doing it now."

"Why?" He helped himself to another portion of macaroni salad.

"I feel badly that I have deceived my family."

He frowned. "What if they've been deceiving *you*, Anna?"

"What do you mean?"

"Just that we were taught some things that aren't actually true." He took one of the little sandwiches, examining it closely.

"Such as?"

He began to ramble on about things like doctrine and theology and world history until Anna felt completely lost and frustrated. It seemed that Jacob was questioning everything, including God and the Bible and the future of the universe. Did he really believe what he was saying? If so, how could he sleep at night? She would be terrified.

"What are you really saying?" she finally asked him. "I mean about our community."

"Just that I think the church leaders are not only mixed-up but also misleading."

Anna wasn't sure how to respond. As much as she cared for Jacob, she knew he was greatly changed. Not just in appearance either. What made this even more unsettling was that she felt she'd just reached her own spiritual crossroads. How could she turn away from what felt genuine and important? How could she back out of her promise to be baptized? She'd made it not only to her parents but to God.

20

Madison felt torn on Friday. Of course, she was glad it was her last day on the farm, and she would be so happy to take a long hot shower, wash and condition her hair, and sleep in a comfortable bed. Yet there was something about this simple lifestyle that appealed to her. Enough to give up her other life? Probably not.

There was also Malachi. As she and Rebekah, who had thankfully come for another day, finished up the laundry, Madison could not stop thinking about him. She couldn't erase the image of his disappointed face. The way the sparkle had seemed to be extinguished from his eyes when she'd made her confession yesterday. She knew she had hurt him deeply.

Rebekah stood up straight and squinted up at the sky. "The clouds look dark, don't you think?"

Madison nodded. "It feels like it's going to rain."

Rebekah tossed a sheet onto the top of the laundry basket. "We better haste to hang this. Maybe it will partly dry before the rain comes."

They both grabbed one handle of the large wicker basket and ran it to the clothesline near the garden, where together they hung up the sheets. Madison was surprised at how much easier this task was with someone else helping. It looked much better than when she'd done it earlier this week.

"I can finish hanging the diapers," Madison told Rebekah, "if you want to go help your mother with lunch."

"*Ja*, das a good idea." Rebekah headed toward the house.

"Here, Elizabeth," Madison called to the toddler, who had wandered into the garden. "Come and help."

Elizabeth turned, but not before she had grabbed and pulled up a baby carrot and popped it into her mouth with a wicked little grin.

"No, no." Madison went over to fetch her. "Your mamm said wait until the carrots get bigger." She used the edge of her apron to wipe the dirt off Elizabeth's lips. "Come now, I need your help." She set Elizabeth under the clothesline and handed her the can of clothes pegs. "You hand them to me."

Elizabeth didn't seem to grasp the concept of working together. Instead she dumped the pegs onto the ground and sat down to play with them. At least it kept her busy and nearby.

Eventually, Madison got the last diaper hung. "It's no wonder disposable diapers caught on so well," she said to Elizabeth as she helped her toss the pegs into the can. "Now let's go help in the kitchen."

Madison had noticed that the house not only looked much cleaner, but it smelled better too. She would never say as much to Rachel, but she suspected that some of the rumors about Rachel's housekeeping had been based on truth. Not that it made it right for her neighbors to treat her like that. Hopefully things would start to change now that Rebekah and her family had decided to take Rachel under their wing.

"Here, Anna." Rebekah's mother had a tray with lunch ready. "You take this to Rachel now."

"Denki." Madison picked up the tray, careful not to slosh the soup as she carried it up the stairs. She hadn't seen baby Maddie since this morning. So far Daniel had not commented on the baby's name, so maybe Rachel would get her way this time. She had confided to Madison that he had chosen the names of the other four children. "Oh, dey are good names, all right," she said last night. "Only dis time I get to pick."

Madison pushed open the door with her elbow, glancing in to see if Rachel was sleeping, but she was sitting in the chair by the bed, brushing her hair.

"Here you go." Madison set the tray in Rachel's lap, then took her brush. As Rachel started to eat, Madison worked on her hair. It was long, nearly to her waist. But the color seemed faded and Madison suspected that it would be turning gray soon. "How old are you?" she asked as she brushed out the tangles.

Rachel chuckled. "I feel old, old today. Maybe one hundred."

"No, really, how old are you? I'm just curious."

"I will be twenty-nine in May."

Madison was shocked. Rachel was only twenty-eight? She could easily pass for ten years older. In fact, Madison's mother was forty-six, and she looked a lot younger than Rachel. But money could do that.

"It is all set for you tomorrow," Rachel said quietly. "I told Daniel I need you to run an errand. He says you must go early, at sunup, so Malachi can be back here to work by midmorning."

"So by this time tomorrow, the switch will be complete."

"You two girls." Rachel chuckled. "You crazy, funny girls."

"Anna will pick up where I left off," Madison said.

"*Ja.* The real Anna dis time." Rachel's voice sounded a bit sad.

214

Madison sat down on the edge of the bed. "The Lapp girls came to help again today," she said. "Their mother too. I like them a lot, Rachel."

"They are good people." Rachel set the spoon beside the empty soup bowl. "Good in the kitchen too." She grinned at Madison. "You did not cook today, *ja*?"

Madison laughed. "No, I did not."

"This is good."

"I think the Lapps want to be better friends with you, Rachel."

"I would like that too."

They talked a while longer, Rachel asking questions about what Madison's real life was like, Madison giving somewhat vague answers. Really, the less said seemed better. But she did tell Rachel about her parents getting divorced a few years ago.

"That is sad." Rachel shook her head. "I am sorry."

"*Denki*. Yes, it was sad. For all of us."

"Sometimes it happens here," Rachel said. "There is trouble . . . a marriage is not good. When one wants to leave community and one wants to stay. That is sad too."

"That would never happen to you and Daniel?" Madison suddenly felt worried. They didn't seem to have a very good marriage, but hopefully Rachel wasn't thinking of leaving him.

"No, no. Daniel will never leave."

"And you?"

"Oh no, I could not leave. I could not do that to my children. Never."

"You are happy?"

Rachel smiled over at the sleeping baby. "*Ja, ja*. I am happy. Happy to have baby Maddie. Such a good baby too."

"Would it be all right if I sent you something for her?" Madison picked up the tray of empty dishes.

Rachel's expression was hard to read. "You know how is here, Madison. If you send something that is English, I must hide it."

"Like the way you hide the dandelion wine and the hair shampoo?" Madison teased.

"*Ja.*" Rachel laughed. "Like that."

"I will see what I can find." She smiled at Rachel. "You should probably get some rest."

"*Denki*, Madison. *Denki schoen.*"

With the Lapp girls around to help with the kids and cooking and cleaning, Madison decided to put her best effort into getting that dress for Elizabeth sewn. It was slow going, and for some reason—maybe the machine did not like her—the thread kept getting all bunched up and then she would have to rip it out again. Finally, just before dinnertime, she had it nearly finished. She folded it neatly and placed it on Rachel's sewing basket. All it needed now was the hem.

To everyone's surprise, Rachel came down for dinner. When Daniel bowed his head to pray, after a few moments of the usual silence, he actually prayed aloud, giving thanks for his wife and their new child. Madison peeked over in time to see Rachel smile. Maybe there was hope.

After dinner, Madison cleaned up in the kitchen, then helped the children get ready for bed, but it was Rachel who came in to hear their prayers. While she was doing this, Madison heard the baby crying, so she went to check on her. She changed her diaper, which thankfully was only wet. She still wasn't sure how to deal with the other. She wrapped the baby back into the tiny quilt and walked her over to look out the window, out toward the pond, which was already glistening in the moonlight.

"Baby Maddie," she cooed as she rocked her in her arms. "You will grow up to be a fine young woman someday. I wish I could be around to see you. I will miss you."

"We will miss you," Rachel said from behind.

Madison turned to see Rachel with tears in her eyes. "I will miss you too," she told Rachel. "More than you can imagine."

"You will take us with you," she said, reaching for the baby, "in your heart."

Madison nodded. "Yes."

"And we will keep you here with us . . . in our hearts."

Madison reached out, hugging both Rachel and the baby. "Thank you, Rachel," she whispered, "for taking me into your home like you did, even when you knew I was a stranger."

"Das what we are taught," Rachel said, "when we welcome a stranger, it is like welcoming the Lord himself."

"*Denki schoen.*" Madison kissed both Rachel and the baby on the cheek. It wasn't until she was in her room that she realized she was crying too.

21

"Jacob has promised to take me to see the sights of New York," Anna told Lucinda as they met for coffee on Friday morning. "After he finishes classes at noon."

"Tell me everything," Lucinda urged. "How did it go? Was Jacob happy to see you? Is he going back with you? Are you—"

"Slow down." Anna held up her hands. "One question at a time."

"Okay." Lucinda stirred her coffee. "Let's start with Jacob. What kind of classes is he taking?"

"He said it's GED program. I am not sure what that means."

"It's a way to get a high school diploma."

Anna nodded, pretending she understood what this meant.

"Was he glad to see you?"

"I think so."

"You *think* so?"

"It was difficult to know. It is not like before. We are different—changed."

"Yes, but do you still love each other?"

Anna swallowed hard. "I do not know."

"You mean you don't love him now?"

"I love him still. *Ja*, sure. I cannot stop loving him so easy."

"Do you think he loves you?"

Anna frowned. "I am unsure."

Lucinda gave her a sympathetic look. "Maybe you'll know more after you spend more time together."

"Maybe."

"Do you think he'll return with you?"

"No." Anna firmly shook her head.

"Really? You know that for sure?"

"For sure and for certain. Jacob said he will never go back. Not to live there, though he said he would like to visit his family someday."

"Oh." Lucinda set down her coffee. "How do you feel about that?"

"I am confused."

"Yes, I can imagine. You want to go back, don't you?"

"I think I want to go back. But seeing Jacob . . . it makes me question things."

"What things?"

"The way our families live—and believe." She pressed her lips together, unwilling to say more.

"Yesterday you seemed quite certain about those things."

"I felt quite certain—yesterday. Before I saw Jacob. Now I am unsure of much."

"If Jacob asked you to stay here with him, if he asked you to finish your schooling like he's doing, start a new life, would you?" Lucinda looked hopeful.

"I—I don't know. I could not stay here with him unless we were married. That would be wrong."

"But if he asked you to marry him, Anna, would you stay here? Would you marry him and start a new life?"

Anna felt close to tears, as if something inside of her were tearing. "I do not know for sure. Maybe."

"Wow." Lucinda shook her head. "That just blows my mind."

"Blows your—"

"Sorry. That's an old expression—something my dad says a lot. I mean it's just incredible to think that you're the same age as me and that you might give up everything to marry a guy you love. It's so romantic."

"Romantic . . ." Anna considered this. She supposed there were some things about her situation that were similar to some of the novels she had read. But for some reason it did not feel quite the same. Perhaps because this was real life, not a storybook. Maybe her father had been right all along about reading storybooks. She felt torn.

"You know, Anna, if you decided to stay in New York and marry Jacob, my mother would probably hire you for sewing. She was really impressed with your work."

"Really?" Anna blinked. "She would give me a job?"

"I think so."

Anna thought of Daed and Mamm, of Katie and her brothers, of the land, her home, the life she would be saying good-bye to. Then she thought of Jacob—how long she had loved him, what their life here might be like. She felt completely and utterly bewildered. Which choice was right for her?

"You could probably stay with me or Madison until you and Jacob got married," Lucinda said. "Maybe you could start working on your GED too."

Anna nodded, only partially listening as Lucinda rambled

on about all the reasons it would be good for Anna to remain in New York City and eventually marry Jacob. The more Lucinda talked, the more believable it all sounded, until Anna was almost convinced this was a good thing indeed. Perhaps it truly was meant to be.

"What are you wearing for your big day?" Lucinda pointed to Anna. "Not that, right?"

Anna looked down at her clothes. "I dressed in haste," she explained. "Madison's phone kept me busy this morning."

"Who called?"

"First of all, *you* called to invite me for coffee," she reminded Lucinda. "Then Madison's father called, asking about my cold." She made a coughing sound. "I told him I was still sick but that I would call him as soon as I was better. He told me all the things to do for a cold and offered to come take me to the doctor. It was not easy to make him believe that was a bad idea. After that, Garret called."

Lucinda frowned. "What did Garret want?"

"To see me—I mean to see Madison."

"Did you tell him about finding Jacob?"

"No. I was worried he would want to come meet him. He was curious to see him before."

"Yeah, that would be complicated."

"*Ja.*" Anna sipped her coffee.

"Back to your outfit," Lucinda said in an urgent voice. "You can't spend your big day with Jacob dressed like that."

Anna shrugged. "I do not know how to dress."

"Sometimes you do okay." Lucinda cocked her head to one side. "And sometimes, like today, you could get arrested by the fashion police."

Anna blinked. "Fashion police?"

221

"Just kidding. But seriously, if you go running around the city like that, you could get photographed by paparazzi and really embarrass Madison." She chuckled. "Although that might be worth seeing."

"I do not want to embarrass Madison."

Lucinda looked at her watch. "Then we better get moving. It's already 11:30 and you are in need of a fashion intervention. Let's go up and give you a makeover."

Anna considered asking Lucinda for an interpretation for all that, but since Lucinda was obviously in a hurry, she decided not to. They had barely gone into Madison's closet before Lucinda was pulling out one item after another, finally carrying them all out to the bed and heaping them there. She went through the pile of clothing, finally deciding on a skirt with a black, pink, and gray pattern, some black stockings, and black boots.

"It's a good thing it's cloudy today," she told Anna. "You can still get by with black hosiery. But you will have to consider shaving those legs eventually." She handed the items to Anna. "Start with these while I pick out something to wear on top. Then we'll do your hair and makeup."

By the time Lucinda finished, Anna looked just like a real New York girl. Wearing a pink jacket and some accessories as well as a different purse, Anna felt she was, as Lucinda said, "put together." In fact, Anna thought she looked more like Madison than she had since the day Madison had helped her. Was that only a week ago? It felt like a lifetime.

Perhaps it was.

"You are good at this," Anna told Lucinda as they both stood looking into the mirror. Even Anna's hair looked right.

"Thanks." Lucinda grinned. "I like helping at my mom's fashion shoots."

Just then Madison's Blackberry rang, and it was Jacob saying he was downstairs waiting. "Thank you for helping me," Anna told Lucinda as they rode down in the elevator. "It makes me not so nervous."

"That's right." Lucinda nodded. "Good fashion is a great confidence builder."

Anna did not admit that she was still nervous, just not quite as much as before. When she saw Jacob waiting in the lobby, looking even more handsome than yesterday, she wondered . . . perhaps she could do this. She introduced him to Lucinda and the three of them talked for a bit in the lobby.

"Well, you two better get going," Lucinda said. "There's a lot to see in the city."

Anna thanked her again. Lucinda asked her to call when she got home, then she winked at Anna as if they had a secret.

"You look very pretty," Jacob told Anna as they went outside. "Just like a real American girl."

"Thank you." Tingles went down her spine as he cupped his hand around her elbow, walking her down the sidewalk.

"I thought we would take the subway," he said.

"The underground train?" she asked.

"Yes. It's a good way to get around."

"Better than taxis?"

He laughed. "Cheaper anyway. Maybe quicker too."

"You have learned so much in such a short time," she told him as he led her down a stairway tunnel.

He nodded. "It was like I belonged here, Anna. I felt it almost as soon as I arrived."

"Oh." She tried to comprehend this. "What did you do?" she asked as they got into the back of a line of people. "Where did you stay? Did you have money?"

As they rode the underground train, he explained how it was a little rough at first, but he quickly made some good connections. "We aren't the only ones who have left home like this," he told her. "There are good people who help people like us." He told her about a man named Robert who had found a place for Jacob to live, a house with a lot of other young men, and helped them to find jobs and to get into the GED program. "I take the test next month," he said as they emerged back up a tunnel stairway and onto the sidewalk. "Robert is already helping me to find some scholarship money."

"Scholarship money?"

"For college, Anna. I plan to go to college."

"Oh yes." She nodded.

"I want to get my law degree."

Again she nodded, but she really wasn't sure what that meant. "Where are we going?" she asked.

"This is Battery Park," he said. "I thought you might like to take a ferry to see the Statue of Liberty."

"A ferry?"

"A boat."

Anna had never been on a boat before. The idea of being out on water like that made her uneasy. "I would like to see the Statue of Liberty," she admitted.

"Robert brought some of us here a few weeks ago," Jacob said as they walked. "I thought you might enjoy it too."

When they reached the place where tickets were sold, Jacob looked uneasy. "I didn't know it was so expensive," he whispered to her.

She looked down at Madison's shiny black purse. So far she had been very frugal with Madison's money and credit cards. But this was her last day in New York, and here she was with Jacob, so she decided to set her worries aside. "I will buy our tickets," she told him. She used Madison's credit card, trying to remember how Madison said it worked, and told herself she could repay Madison with the money that Lucinda's mother was going to pay her for sewing.

As they waited to get on the boat, Anna told Jacob about what Lucinda had said about working for her mother.

Jacob looked surprised. "You are thinking about staying in New York?"

She smiled. "Maybe."

It was exciting to get on the boat, but when it started to move, Anna got queasy. Her legs felt wobbly and she was afraid she was going to vomit.

"Are you all right?" Jacob peered at her.

She held her stomach and shook her head.

"Come out in the fresh air," he urged, tugging her toward a door.

Being outside helped a bit, but the wind was cold and Anna began to feel that this boat trip was a mistake.

"You stay here," Jacob told her. "I'll go get you something to drink." He returned with a soda. "Here," he said, "drink this."

She didn't care much for soda, but after a few sips she did feel a bit better. When Jacob pointed out the majestic green statue standing on a building right in the middle of the water, she nearly forgot her queasy stomach. "She is so beautiful," Anna said.

Jacob told her about how the statue had been a gift from France and how all the immigrants to the United States had come past her, arriving on Ellis Island. "But not our ancestors," he said. "They came to America *before* the Statue of Liberty."

After the boat trip, Jacob asked Anna what else she wanted to see. "Nothing by boat," she told him. "I want to stay on solid ground."

He laughed. "No more boats." He decided on the Empire State Building, which was another tall, impressive building, but when he asked her if she wanted to go to the top of it to look down, she firmly shook her head. "It makes me dizzy to look down from the penthouse. I would not like to go all the way up there and look down. I keep my feet on solid ground."

"Maybe another time," he said. As he was taking her back toward another stairway tunnel, she stopped him.

"Can we ride in a taxi instead?"

He shrugged. "If you want to pay for it."

"I will." Going so fast underneath the ground made Anna nervous. It took a while for a taxi to stop, but finally they were riding inside one and she began to relax a little. At least the taxi didn't go as fast as the underground train.

"Grand Central Terminal," Jacob told the driver.

"What is that?" she asked. He explained that it was the train station, but well worth seeing. They walked around the enormous building for about an hour and then went back outside and waited, even longer this time, for a taxi to stop for them.

Anna was tired now, but she didn't want to admit it.

"Saint Patrick's Cathedral," Jacob called to the front seat.

It wasn't too long before the taxi stopped in front of an ornate-looking old building. "Wait for us," Jacob said to the driver.

They got out and walked around, looking at the giant

structure. Yes, it was pretty, and yes, it was huge, but Anna felt like a child who had eaten too many pancakes with syrup. She was full. Too full.

Back in the taxi, she let out a tired sigh, closing her eyes and leaning back. "I think I have seen enough sights for today."

"We're not too far from your building," he told her. "Do you want to go home?"

Home? Did she want to go home?

"Anna?"

"*Ja?*" She sat up and opened her eyes.

"Are you all right?"

"*Ja, ja.* I am fine. Just tired is all." She realized she hadn't eaten lunch. "Hungry too. Are you hungry, Jacob?"

He was, so he told the driver the address of the penthouse building, and when they got there, Anna paid him. As she slipped the wallet back into the purse, she realized that Madison's cash had dwindled considerably today. "We can eat in the penthouse," she told Jacob.

"Unless you want to go out to eat," he said.

"Go out to eat?"

"In a restaurant."

"Oh yes." She nodded. "We can do that."

"I think there are some good restaurants around here," he told her. "We can walk if you want."

Although the tall black boots were starting to hurt her feet, she agreed to walk. After about twenty minutes of painful walking, they finally found a restaurant, but before they went in, Jacob's phone rang. Anna waited as he answered. It still seemed strange seeing him in this setting, dressed like an Englisher and using a cell phone.

After he said hello, she saw his eyes light up. His voice grew warm and friendly, and she heard him say the name Monica. Suddenly it was like she had rabbit ears.

"No, no," he said. "I didn't forget. Don't worry. I'll still be home in time." He paused to listen. "Yes. I'm looking forward to it too. See you soon." He closed his phone and turned to Anna. She must have had a suspicious expression on her face because suddenly Jacob looked very uncomfortable.

"Who is Monica?" Anna asked.

"She is a friend."

"A *girlfriend*?"

Jacob shrugged, then smiled in a way that seemed to suggest guilt. "She is a girl. She is a friend."

Anna no longer felt hungry. "I have a strong feeling," she said softly, "that this Monica person is important to you."

He shoved his hands in his pockets and glanced over his shoulder.

"Please be honest, Jacob."

"I am being honest." He looked directly into her eyes. "I never—not in a million years—expected you to come to New York, Anna. I knew I was never going back home. I honestly thought that what we had was over."

She took in a quick breath. "So we are over?"

He took his hands out of his pockets and placed them on her cheeks. "I don't know, Anna. You bewilder me. First it seems you have no interest in leaving your family and that you will never change. Then I see you today." He smiled at her. "You are like a real New Yorker. A totally different person. I like it."

She didn't know what to say.

"Maybe I should ask you," he said. "Is it over?"

"What are you saying to me?" she asked. "What is your intention?"

"My intention?" His mouth twisted to one side. "I intend to go to college. I intend to make a life for myself."

"I mean what is your intention for me?"

"For you?" He looked confused. "I don't know what you want, Anna. If you like New York, you should stay here. Maybe you could go to school or get a job."

"And what then?"

He held up his hands. "I don't know. It's not for me to decide, is it?"

"Isn't it?"

"What are you asking me, Anna? Are you asking—will I marry you? Because I don't know the answer to that. I have a lot to do before I think about things like marriage."

"What about Monica?"

"I would tell her the same thing. She's not pressuring me. Monica doesn't want to get married any more than I do. We understand the way this world works. You go to school, you get a career, you establish yourself, and then you think about marriage."

Anna felt a rock in the bottom of her stomach. "I am not hungry anymore," she told him.

"Okay." He nodded in a brisk, formal sort of way. "Do you want me to walk you back to your building?"

She slowly shook her head. "No, I want you to leave, Jacob. I want you to say goodbye."

"Goodbye . . . forever?" His eyes looked sad, but his mouth was firm.

She closed her eyes, trying to keep the tears from spilling.

"Does this mean you're going back?" he asked. "To live the old life again? You could settle for that, after seeing this?"

"Yes. I am going back." She opened her eyes and studied

him for a long moment. He was not her Jacob anymore. He was someone else. "Goodbye, Jacob," she whispered. "God go with you."

He leaned over and kissed her forehead. "I wish you well, Anna." He turned and hurried away . . . almost as if he were relieved.

Her tears fell freely as she walked back to Madison's building. She tried to tell herself that her feet ached far worse than her heart, but she did not believe it.

22

After everyone in the house was quiet, Madison slipped out of bed, pausing to make sure Elizabeth was not stirring. She tiptoed down the hallway and down the wooden stairs, carefully avoiding the squeaky treads. Thankful for the moonlight coming in through the recently cleaned windows, she crept through the living room and the kitchen and went out the door.

Holding her skirt in her hands, she dashed across the yard to the barn, where she pulled a candle from her apron pocket and lit it with a match. She set the candle on the wooden ledge by the phone, and using its flickering light to see, she dialed the numbers and waited for Anna to answer. When Anna said hello, she didn't sound quite right.

"Is that you, Anna?"

"Yes. It's me." Her voice was gruff and flat sounding.

"Did I wake you up?" Madison asked.

"No. I am awake."

"Are you okay?"

There was a long pause, and then Anna began to pout out a sad story of how she'd spent the day with Jacob, how she'd dressed up and nearly gotten sick on a boat, gone to places she didn't want to go, gotten horrible blisters on her feet—only to find out that Jacob didn't really love her. Even worse, he had found someone else.

"I'm so sorry, Anna."

"It is for the best." Anna's tone didn't match her words. "Really?"

"I know it is better this way. I know I cannot live in the English world. I do not belong here. I do not like it. I wish I never came here."

"But if you hadn't gone to New York, you wouldn't have found Jacob. You wouldn't have discovered the truth about him. And you might've spent your whole life pining away for him, wondering if you two belonged together."

"*Ja*, you are probably right. Still, it is hard. It hurts."

"At least you know that it was never meant to be, Anna. You can get on with your life now. You wouldn't have known that without visiting New York."

"Yes, that is true enough." Her voice broke again. "Even so—I want to leave here. I want to go home!" Now she was sobbing.

"You can't go home yet," Madison reminded her. "Not to your parents' house anyway, because Rachel still needs—"

"No, no. It's all right. Being with Rachel is almost like home. I just don't want to be *here* anymore, Madison. I wish I had never come to this big place. I want to leave right now."

"That's why I'm calling. You need to take an early bus tomorrow morning. Have you gotten your ticket yet?"

"No. In my misery, I forgot about it."

"Well, you need to be here first thing in the morning. Maybe by eight or nine at the latest. Can you figure it out and do that?"

"Yes." Anna's voice was firm with resolve. "I will be there."

Madison heard something rustling in the barn—probably a cow, but just in case, she knew she should cut this short. "Good. I'll see you in the morning. Just be there, okay?"

"I will."

"Things are going to get better, Anna."

"How do you know that?"

"I just know. I'll be praying for you."

"You will pray for me?" Anna sounded surprised.

"Yes. You don't have to be Amish to pray."

After they said goodbye, Madison replaced the receiver back on the phone, puffed out the candle, then listened to make sure no one was around. Satisfied that she'd only heard one of the animals, she put the candle back into her pocket and slipped out into the farmyard. The three-quarter moon was high in the sky now, illuminating the fields with a milky light that seemed to be inviting her for one last rendezvous with the nighttime countryside. As she walked through the field and the high grass, crickets were chirruping happily and the owl let out three hoots as if to say hello.

Madison stood looking out over the pond for a few minutes, soaking in the sounds of night creatures, the smells of the earth and the blooming fruit trees and the water, and the beauty of the moon reflected on the black glassy surface of the pond. She sat on the now familiar bench and sighed.

She was going to miss this place. She wondered how she could replicate this part of her day once she was back in the busy city. Central Park was right by her building, but she knew better than to go down there by herself at night. Perhaps there were other ways to find this sort of place—perhaps it was a spiritual place as much as it was a physical one.

233

She would have to explore these things another time, because right now she wanted to keep her promise to pray for Anna. It had been disturbing to hear Anna's deep sadness tonight. Madison felt somewhat guilty for her pain. If she hadn't encouraged the life swap, Anna would not have discovered that Jacob no longer loved her.

Yet, like Madison had suggested, it could be a blessing in disguise (as Rachel would say) that Anna had learned the truth. At least she could move on now. So that was how Madison prayed—that God would help Anna to shake off her grief and to realize that she had her whole life ahead of her.

Madison also prayed for Anna's relationship with her aunt. She asked God to help Anna see Rachel in a new light, and to deepen their friendship. Perhaps it would take a miracle, but wasn't that God's business? Then she prayed for the whole family, starting with Daniel and clear on down to her namesake, baby Maddie.

Next she prayed for Malachi. She asked God to bring good out of his heartache and to make himself as real to Malachi as he had to her. And to show Malachi that he should get baptized because he knew he loved God . . . not because he supposed he loved a woman.

Finally, she prayed for the people back in her own world. She prayed for family and friends, and she asked God to help her to take what she'd found here—this sense of peace and purpose and connection with him—back to the city with her. That, she knew, would take a miracle too. But she suspected God was up to it.

23

It was almost ten o'clock when Anna called Lucinda. She knew it was late, but this was something like an emergency. At least it was to Anna. "I'm sorry to call—"

"Hey, Anna." Lucinda sounded cheerful. "I'm so glad you called."

"It's not too late?" Anna asked.

Lucinda laughed. "No way. It's the last Friday night of spring break. In fact, I was just getting ready to go out to a club. Want to come along?"

"A club?" Anna tried to imagine what that would be.

"You know, music, friends, dancing. Why don't you come—"

"No thank you."

"Okay. How did it go with Jacob today? You promised to call me, remember. He is so good-looking, Anna. You didn't mention that. Tell me everything—did you have a fabulous time? Let me guess, you guys are getting married, right?"

"Wrong."

"Oh. But he did talk you into staying—"

"No. I am going home tomorrow."

"Anna!" Lucinda sounded genuinely disappointed.

"I have to go home—I need to—" Her voice cracked and she began crying again. "I'm sorry. But it is upsetting."

"Oh, Anna. I'm sorry too. You've had a rough day."

"A rough week."

"Yeah. Poor Anna. I won't even ask you for the details if it's too painful."

"Thank you."

"But you did call me," Lucinda reminded her. "So what's up?"

Anna explained her dilemma over how to get bus tickets and needing to leave early in the morning, but she wasn't sure how it was done. "I told Madison I could do it, but now I do not even know what to do. Can I take a taxi all the way to—"

"Wowzers, that would be expensive. Although Madison is good for it."

"I don't want to waste her money. But I want to go home."

"How about if I come up and we'll figure this out together?"

"Oh, thank you!"

"Besides, I have money for you."

"Money for me?"

"For the work you did for my mom. I told her the truth about who you are. I hope you don't mind. She promised not to tell. Anyway, she wanted to write you a check, but I thought that you might not have a checking account. She's paying you in cash."

"Please thank her for me."

"All right. I'm on my way up now."

Within minutes, Lucinda was sitting in Madison's bedroom with Anna. Using Madison's Blackberry, she soon figured out the bus schedule, purchased a ticket with a credit card, and called the doorman downstairs to request a taxicab at five in the morning. She handed the phone back to Anna. "There you go."

Anna threw her arms around Lucinda and hugged her. "Thank you!"

"Sure you don't want to go clubbing with me tonight?" She grinned. "Last night in the Big Apple."

Anna frowned. "Big Apple?"

Lucinda laughed. "Another name for New York City."

"Oh. The Big Apple." She frowned. "It has given me a big tummyache."

"Okay then." She pointed to the clock. "Maybe you should set your alarm and get some sleep."

"Set alarm?"

Lucinda chuckled as she reached for the clock. After fiddling with the buttons, she set it back down. "That will wake you at 4:30. Is that early enough?"

"*Ja*. That's good."

"I'd offer to go with you to the bus station, Anna, but I'm afraid I won't be able to wake up that early."

Anna waved her hand. "No. It's all right. You have done enough."

Lucinda handed her an envelope. "Here's your pay. My mom says if you ever change your mind and need a job, just call."

Anna forced a smile. "I do not think you will be hearing from me again. But thank you. Thank you for everything."

"See you around." Lucinda grinned as she stood. "Tell Madison hey for me."

Anna nodded. "I will do that."

After Lucinda left, Anna considered taking a bath. But

the last one she took had not been as wonderful as she had imagined it would be, and she figured this one might be even worse. No, she decided, better to go to bed. That way the morning would hasten.

It was dark when Anna awoke to the sound of voices talking. Lying frozen in bed, she felt certain that someone had broken into her room. As she listened, she realized the voices sounded like those of the television, and when she looked over at the clock by the bed, she discovered the voices were coming from there. According to the green numbers, it was 4:30. Time to get up and get ready to go to the bus station!

She had already decided to wear the exact same outfit that Madison had worn on the Saturday they'd met. First she opened the bottom drawer of the big dresser, removing her own undergarments from where she had hidden them last Saturday. She'd been afraid that Nadya would discover them and grow suspicious. She put them on, then put Madison's clothes on over them. She felt as if she should have a bag to pack and take with her, but she realized her bag was already at Aunt Rachel's.

No, the only thing Anna needed was Madison's purse, cash, and credit cards. She even decided to switch back to the orange purse that Madison had taken with her on that day. Everything would be the same. Everything except for Anna. She would never be the same.

At 4:55 a.m., Anna tiptoed through the penthouse, let herself out the door, and pushed the elevator button. Hopefully Nadya was not a light sleeper. Although even the stern-faced housekeeper would have a hard time stopping Anna at this

238

point. Anna was so eager to make her escape that she felt certain that no one—not even the police, although she hoped it wouldn't come to that—could keep her in New York City after the 5:50 bus pulled out.

"No luggage?" Henry the doorman looked surprised.

She forced a smile. "No. This is just a day trip."

He nodded, returning the smile. "Have a good day then, Miss Van Buren."

Outside, the taxi was waiting. Feeling like she was halfway home, Anna got in and sighed.

"Where to?" a man with a dark complexion asked with a thick accent that was unfamiliar.

She told him the name of the bus terminal Lucinda had written down for her, then leaned back, attempting to relax. Suddenly she grew anxious and clutched Madison's purse to her chest, wondering if the taxi driver might actually be a criminal of some sort. What if he was a robber? A kidnapper? One of those bad people she had been warned about since childhood? So far she had met none, but that didn't mean this man wasn't dangerous. She looked out at the still, dark streets and wondered what she should do. Should she jump out at the next stop? If so, what then?

Anna bit her lip and thought hard. What to do? Suddenly she remembered that day in Madison's closet, when she had been frustrated and frightened and lost, and she had prayed. It had made a difference. Why hadn't she prayed since then?

She knew the answer. It was because of Jacob. Somehow when Jacob had stepped back into her life, God had stepped out. Or perhaps she had pushed him out.

Anna bowed her head now and silently prayed. She asked

God to help her, lead her, and protect her. By the time she was finished, the car was pulling up to the bus station.

"Here you are, miss." The driver turned around and told her the amount of her fare.

She fumbled in Madison's purse, pulling out one of the twenties, which was too much. Remembering a line from a book, she decided to try it as she handed him the bill. "Keep the change."

"Thank you." He smiled broadly as he hurried to open the door of the car, then ran on ahead of her to open the door to the bus terminal. "Have a good trip, miss."

"Thank you." She smiled back. "I will." She took another deep breath and looked around, wondering what to do next. Seeing a counter where a few people were milling about, she decided to start there. She decided to go for the gray-haired woman, who reminded Anna of her grandmother.

"I am here for the bus," she said nervously. She explained where she wanted to go and that her friend had called last night. "But I have no ticket."

"Name?"

She was so nervous she almost gave her real name but stopped herself. Lucinda had purchased the ticket under Madison's name. "Madison Van Buren."

The woman pushed some buttons on her computer, then asked to see a credit card. Anna fumbled to get the wallet, extracting a card that she handed to the woman with trembling fingers. She did not want this to go wrong. Not now when she was so close.

Barely looking at Anna, the woman pushed more buttons, eventually handed Anna a slip of paper, and told her where to wait for the bus. "It should be here in a few minutes," she said in a friendly tone. "If you want to get something to eat or coffee, there's time. The bus won't leave until 5:50—but no dillydallying because it leaves promptly."

Anna thanked the woman, then went directly to the area where about a dozen other people were already waiting. Although her stomach was growling and she noticed a place to get donuts, she was not willing to take any chance of missing this bus. She would rather be starving on a bus headed home than stuck in New York with a full belly.

The minute the bus pulled in, Anna got in line and got on. She chose a seat near the front, moved next to the window, and leaned back. Finally, she could relax a bit. Just not too much. She did not want to miss her stop.

Anna's sigh of relief mingled with the loud hiss made by the bus as it pulled out. Soon this city and everything in it would be behind her—a murky memory. And not a moment too soon.

Anna closed her eyes, trying to block Jacob from her thoughts, but he was all she could think about. Her thoughts and feelings swirled round and round like a whirlpool in a fast-moving creek in springtime.

What if things had gone differently with him yesterday? What if he had fulfilled her daydreams by proclaiming his love for her? What if he had begged her to stay here with him . . . asked her to marry him? How would she have reacted?

A part of Anna wanted to think she would have had the boldness to say yes to him. That she would have chosen him above her family and her upbringing. That she would have given up her former life, her home, everything she'd been trained to believe—all because she loved him so much.

Another part of Anna knew that was a lie. She knew from

the top of her head to the tips of her toes that she could not—and would not—ever live in this city. Not even with the promise of having Jacob by her side. She knew that the English lifestyle went against everything inside of her. Even Jacob's love could not have changed that. If he had asked her, she would have said no.

But, she sternly reminded herself, Jacob had not asked. He did not love her. He had actually seemed relieved when she told him she was going home.

What if Jacob had reacted as she'd hoped? What if he had proclaimed his love to her, and what if she had insisted he prove his love by going home with her? If he had agreed, how would she have responded? That was a hard question because part of her felt certain she would have been delighted. She would have felt victorious. As if that was her reward for all she'd been through this week.

In the light of day, another part of her knew that she would have feared she'd been dragging him home against his will. Jacob had a strong will. Where would the victory be if he came with her reluctantly? What if they got home and he changed his mind? What if they married and he realized he'd made a mistake and left her? Or worse, what if he stayed but was miserable . . . made her miserable? No, she didn't want to live like that either.

The only thing Anna had truly wanted was for Jacob to come to his senses! She had wanted him to realize that he couldn't keep living on the outside and that he couldn't keep living without her. She had wanted him to get down on his knees and beg her to marry him. She had wanted them to go home together and to live happily ever after. Or something like that.

She realized now that she'd been daydreaming. Or perhaps she'd been trying to live out a scene from one of those English novels her father disapproved of. She suspected her only way to experience that sort of storybook happiness would be through the pages of one of those books. Maybe that would be enough.

Anna decided she would rather be an old maid than settle for what her options might have been with Jacob. In reality, she had no options with him at all. Sure, he had encouraged her to stay in New York, but not so that he could marry her. No, all he had offered was a halfhearted suggestion that she might create some kind of life for herself—with or without him. Why would she want to do that?

As the buildings outside the window grew shorter and spaces between them grew larger, Anna remembered what Madison had told her last night—that Anna should be thankful to have discovered the truth about Jacob. She supposed that was true. Maybe now she would finally be able to let him go. She would no longer waste time daydreaming about him as she did her daily chores. She would not nurture false hope for a life that would never be. She would grow up!

Wouldn't her parents be relieved to learn Jacob was finally out of the picture? Not that she could tell them how this had all happened or what had brought her to this place of freedom. At least she didn't think she could. Maybe someday. Hopefully her parents would not use this as permission to marry her off to Aaron Zook. She suspected her parents' pressure toward Aaron had simply been their reaction to her obsession with Jacob. They probably hoped the threat of being stuck with someone like Aaron would wake her up—make her start looking around for other options. Surely there were other options.

Anna looked out her window to see English homes, trees, and green grass. She realized the city was behind her—as was her anger. Anna had been angry for a long time. At first she thought she'd been angry at the leaders in her settlement, then at her parents, and most recently at herself. Now she realized the only anger left in her—and it wasn't much—was toward Jacob.

It had been wrong for Jacob to leave her like that, telling her that he loved her, that they would be together again. And then nothing. That had been selfish.

Suddenly, as if the sun had risen and illuminated the darkness, Anna realized that Madison was right. If Anna hadn't gone to the trouble of hunting that boy down, she could have ended up miserable for her entire life. As it was, perhaps her misery would end someday. In fact, it was ending right now! This really was a new beginning for her.

Finally, as the bus moved through farmlands that looked so much like home that Anna felt a lump in her throat, she was able to pray. She was able to thank God for what he had done with her life during the past week. No, it had not been easy. But it had been good. She could see that now. It had been very good.

As the bus got closer to her stop, Anna began to think about her aunt Rachel and some of the things Madison had been saying about her. For some mysterious reason, Madison had really taken to Rachel. This was truly puzzling. How was it possible that someone like Madison—a girl who by all appearances was spoiled, pampered, rich, decadent, shallow—could relate to someone like Anna's aunt? It made no sense. Yet it also made Anna curious.

She knew Aunt Rachel's life was not easy. Uncle Daniel was so much older and set in his ways. Aunt Rachel had grown up as the baby in her family and in a much less restricted community, and suddenly she was married and thrust into a new place where her neighbors turned against her. Plus she had her hands full with the children. Was it any wonder that she grew weary?

As the bus stopped in the small town, Anna's heart pounded with excitement and anticipation. As she got off, she realized again that she had changed. She was not the same girl who'd boarded this bus last week.

24

Madison felt a nudge on her shoulder, then opened her eyes to see Rachel, still in her long white nightgown, with a candle in hand. Madison sat up quickly. "What's—"

"Shush," Rachel whispered. "Time to rise."

Now Madison remembered—this was the day to exchange lives back with Anna. "*Denki*," she told Rachel as she slid out of bed and stood. Rachel handed her the candle, then kissed her on the cheek.

"God's blessings on you," Rachel quietly told her.

"And on you," Madison whispered.

Rachel left the bedroom and Madison hurried to gather her things—rather, Anna's things—taking them to the bathroom to get dressed by candlelight. She chuckled to remember how long it usually took her to get ready for the day—all the steps of showering, shampooing, drying and styling her hair, putting on makeup, choosing the perfect outfit. It all seemed such a waste of time now. Would she ever want to do all that again? Maybe she would just simplify the process.

She twisted her hair into a bun, pinned it, and put on Anna's cap. She carried the shoes and the candle downstairs and paused in the living room, looking around, taking it all in, then continued to the kitchen where she sat down and put on her shoes—Anna's shoes. She wouldn't miss those shoes. Oh, they were comfortable enough, but so ugly. Madison would be glad to get her own shoes back.

As she was about to go out the door, Madison noticed a brown paper bag on the wooden kitchen table, with the name Anna penciled on it. She peeked inside to see some pieces of bread and butter and some dried fruit. Breakfast on the road.

By the dawn's gray light, she could see a black buggy out front. Unlike Daniel's buggy, which had an enclosed space in the back, this one was open. Malachi was bent down, doing something with the horse's reins.

Bracing herself, Madison went out and walked toward him. This wasn't going to be an easy ride. But she was determined to do what she could to smooth this thing over.

"Good morning, Malachi," she called out.

He stood up slowly, looking at her with a dark expression. "Good morning."

"I want to talk to you," she told him after she was seated next to him. He shrugged, shook the reins, and the horse began to move.

"I know you're angry with me," she began. "You have every right to be angry. You said that I tricked you, and I denied it. The truth is I did trick you, but I didn't really mean to do it."

"If I wasn't watching where I was going and I ran this wagon over a small child," he said, "would it make the child feel better when I told him I didn't mean to do it?"

"Maybe not." She sighed. "I really did not mean to hurt you, Malachi."

"Then why did you smile at me? Why did you look at me

that way? Why did you cast your line and reel me in? You knew you weren't Anna. You knew you would go."

"You're right," she admitted. "The truth is I found you very attractive. You caught me by surprise that day we met, and I was swept up in the moment."

He glanced her way, then put his eyes back on the dirt road.

"You know how it is in the English world," she reminded him. "You've lived there too. Guys and girls act differently. I was still in an Englisher state of mind when I met you and was acting very much like an Englisher girl. I was flirting with you, Malachi. I can admit that."

"That's right." He nodded. "You were flirting with me."

"You were flirting with me too."

A very small smile touched the corner of his mouth. "But my flirting was genuine. I knew who I was, and I thought I knew who you were. I didn't know you were playing a game with me."

"If it makes you feel any better, I briefly wondered what it would be like to abandon my old life and actually become Amish and stay here."

He turned and peered curiously at her. "Is that the truth?"

She nodded. "It is true. It didn't take long before I figured things out. I knew that was not going to happen."

"Yet you led me on?"

"Think about it, Malachi. How much time did we really spend together?"

He shrugged. "I don't know."

"Less than two hours, not counting now."

"But I thought about you every day, and every night too. Almost every waking minute, you were on my mind, Anna." He cleared his throat. "I mean Madison."

"But can't you see you were thinking about who you *thought* I was?"

"What do you mean?"

"I mean you didn't really know me, Malachi. You only knew who you assumed I was, the person I was pretending to be. You were falling for an illusion."

"Maybe."

"Where I come from, that's called a crush."

"I know what a crush is."

"A crush is not something you build your life around, Malachi."

He stuck his chin out and shook the reins, causing the horse to move faster.

"Now that that's out of the way, I have something important to tell you."

He turned and glanced at her again.

"You will be driving the real Anna back here, right?"

He nodded with eyes forward.

"Even though Anna and I look alike and—"

"You and Anna look alike?" He seemed surprised by this.

"Don't you remember I told you that when I confessed I wasn't Anna?"

He frowned. "I was so mad . . . my brain might not have been working too well."

She chuckled. "I know how that is. Well, anyway, yes, Anna and I could pass for twins. That's why this whole switch seemed to make sense at the time. But even though Anna looks like me, she is very different."

"How so?"

"For one thing, she's just suffered getting her heart broken."

He nodded as if he could relate.

"She's feeling confused about a lot of things. And she doesn't get along that well with Rachel. I just think she could use a good friend. That's all I'm saying."

"And you think I'd make a good friend?"

"I know you would, Malachi."

Madison told him about how Anna was trying to find Jacob and how it hadn't turned out the way she'd hoped.

"Was Anna going to stay there if Jacob had asked her?" Malachi asked.

"I don't know for sure. That's something you'd have to ask her."

As he turned onto the main road, Madison began to tell him that she felt like she had discovered God here. She explained how it felt to be in nature, how she had started to pray, and how she planned to continue to do so when she returned to the city.

"I thought I was connecting to God too," he admitted.

"You thought you were? Meaning you're not now?"

"I don't know. I still feel confused. I'm still thinking about getting baptized. I don't think I can go back to the English lifestyle." He began telling her about how much he loved making furniture, how good it felt to take a piece of wood and work it until it turned into something useful. His uncle was a fine craftsman and felt Malachi had good potential.

"You're not into farming?"

He chuckled. "I only help Uncle Daniel because my uncles had an agreement when it was decided I should come here. I think Uncle Daniel would prefer someone else working his fields. My heart is not in it."

Madison shared her brown bag breakfast with Malachi as they continued talking. They were just coming into town when she realized she was sad that this relationship was ending. In some ways, Malachi was an even better person than she'd imagined—as good on the inside as he was on the outside. Yet their lives were worlds apart.

"Will you be glad to go home?" he asked as he turned onto a side street to park the buggy.

She looked around to see cars and people dressed the way she remembered, and the familiarity was comforting. "Yes, there are definitely a lot of things I missed about modern life."

"Not me." He firmly shook his head. "I don't miss it at all. I don't think I'm ever going back."

"I know there are things I'll miss about the Amish lifestyle," she admitted as he helped her down from the buggy. "I hope I can take some of the things I learned with me—like how to live more simply, to slow down."

"You think you can get the best of both worlds?" His expression was doubtful.

"I hope I can."

"Good luck with that." He smiled in a knowing way, then pointed down the street. "Uncle Daniel asked me to pick up a package for him. And Aunt Rachel had some errands for me to do."

"Why don't you just meet up with us at the coffee shop when you're done?"

"All right." He dipped his head, then went on his way.

As Madison walked toward the coffee shop, she felt an unexpected rush of regret and reluctance. If she could have done this whole thing differently, would she? If she could wave a magic wand that would make her family and friends all understand and accept it, would she become Amish for good?

Just then she saw herself—rather, she saw Anna dressed in

her clothes and walking down the sidewalk toward her—and Madison realized she did want to go back to her old life. She did miss it.

She wanted to run toward Anna, to hug her and exclaim how good it was to see her, but she knew that would draw attention. Instead she continued walking, and together they went into the coffee shop and discreetly headed back to the restroom. They both went in, and Madison locked the door behind them.

"Wow." Madison stared at Anna. "This is so weird. You look more like me than I do."

Anna giggled. "I know what you mean."

"Ready to switch back?"

Anna nodded. "Let's do this."

Madison turned her back and started to undress. After she handed the dress back to Anna, she realized her mistake. "Oh, Anna," she said. "I totally forgot to bring my own underwear."

"Oh, well, I guess you can just wear mine home." Anna handed Madison her shirt.

"I'm sorry."

Anna giggled. "Where did you leave them?"

"Under the mattress."

"It's good that Rachel does not clean too deeply." Anna handed over the jeans. "She will not find them."

Madison frowned as she put on her own jeans, surprised at how confining they felt as she zipped them up. They pinched at her waist as she bent to pull on the boots.

"Sorry." Anna looked contrite as they both stood before the mirror, making the appropriate adjustments to their hair and faces. "I didn't mean to sound like that," she said. "I want to be more positive about my aunt."

"That would be nice." Madison was digging through her purse, making sure her keys were there, and even pausing to put on some lip gloss and mascara. Maybe old habits really did die hard.

"Still, it's good Rachel won't find your Englisher girl underthings in my bed. I would have some explaining to do."

"Rachel already knows."

Anna stopped pinning her hair. "Rachel *knows*? You mean she knows about us—about the switch?"

"Yes. She figured it out after the baby was born. I meant to tell you, but we were talking so much and you were telling me about Jacob, and I guess I forgot."

"Oh no." Anna shook her head. "This is not good."

"No, Rachel is okay with it." Madison fluffed her hair, surprised at how much body it had after being pinned up so much. Still, she looked different. She knew it.

Anna looked stunned. "Rachel knows that I sent a stranger into her home, to be with her and her children, to sleep in her bed, and she is okay with that?"

Madison nodded as she slipped on her watch and bracelet, then closed her purse.

"What about Uncle Daniel? Surely he is not okay with it?"

"He doesn't know. Rachel said it's our secret."

"You are sure about that?" Anna looked skeptical.

"Positive." Madison reached over to help with Anna's hair. "You will not believe this, Anna."

"What?"

"Rachel named her baby after me."

Anna blinked. "She named her baby Madison?"

Madison giggled and nodded.

"Uncle Daniel said that was all right?"

Madison shrugged. "She said he'd named the others and it was her turn."

"Aunt Rachel must really like you."

"I like her too, Anna. She is a truly good person."

Anna just shook her head.

"The baby is so sweet. You will love her." Madison sighed. "All of Rachel's children are very sweet."

Anna looked unconvinced.

"Elizabeth is a darling. And guess what—I made her a dress."

"You made a dress?" Anna looked stunned. "You know how to sew?"

"Barely. It wasn't easy. It still needs to be hemmed."

"I can do that."

"*Denki.*" Madison stared at their reflections in the mirror—totally changed and yet totally the same. It was weird.

"Are you ready?" Anna asked. "Is everything in place?"

"Yes." Madison nodded. "We're all put back together."

Anna used a wet paper towel to wipe a spot of mascara from her cheek, then sighed. "It's such a relief not to be you anymore."

Madison laughed. "Same back at you." Although, even as she said this, Madison wondered if it was completely true. She wondered if she would someday look back and regret that she wasn't born into Anna's family.

25

"I have a lot to tell you still," Madison said as they emerged from the bathroom. "Let's get some coffee and talk until it's time to go."

"Yes. I am starving." Anna suddenly remembered the donuts in the bus station.

"It's on me," Madison said as they went to order.

As Madison paid with a credit card, Anna remembered the packet of money still zipped inside a pocket of Madison's purse. Perhaps she should just leave it there, to pay Madison back for the money she'd used.

They carried their coffees and pastries to the same table they'd sat at last Saturday. Anna could not believe it had only been a week. So much could happen in a week.

"What did you think of the simple life?" Anna asked as she broke her cinnamon roll apart. "A little different from Manhattan?"

Madison chuckled as she set down her coffee. "Just a little. At first I went into what I think is called culture shock. I mean how do you get used to living without hot water and—"

"That's right," Anna said. "I forgot that Aunt Rachel's house doesn't have hot tap water."

"Does your house?"

Anna nodded. "Oh yes. My father put in a propane-powered water heater."

"Really? That's not against the Ordnung?"

"Not where we live. Maybe not all of Aunt Rachel's settlement either. I think Uncle Daniel is old-fashioned about some things." Anna was remembering more now. "Like their old wood-burning cookstove—I assume they still use it?"

"Yes." Madison sighed. "What a pain."

"My mamm has a propane stove. Much easier."

"Not all Amish live the same?"

"Every settlement is different." Anna explained some of the other differences. "Not all English have homes as fancy as yours?"

"That's true."

"Lucinda said that your family is very, very rich, Madison." Anna took a sip of coffee.

Madison just nodded.

"She also told me about how you used to be her best friend."

Madison frowned. "Did she tell you what ended our friendship?"

"She said it was a boy. Then Vivian stepped in." Anna remembered something. "Vivian left you a lot of phone messages. Angry messages. I wonder if she is really your friend now."

Madison shrugged. "Maybe not."

"Lucinda is a nice person." Anna smiled.

"How do you know so much about Lucinda anyway?"

Anna told about helping Lucinda sew things for her mother's fashion show. "Her mother paid me. It's in the pocket of your purse."

Madison reached for her purse, removed the envelope, and set it in front of Anna.

"I left it for you," Anna explained.

"Why?"

"To repay you for—"

"No way." Madison shook her head. "It's yours, Anna. You earned it."

"What about the money I used, the credit cards and—"

"I told you to do that. After all you went through last week, it's a small price."

"Yes . . . freedom is not all I thought it would be."

Madison chuckled. "That's true enough."

"Back to Lucinda," Anna said. "When she still thought I was you, I promised—"

"Speaking of that, what gave you away?"

"Oh, she's smart. She figured it out."

"How?" Madison set down her coffee and waited.

Anna started to giggle. "My hairy legs."

Madison laughed. "Oh yeah, I never even thought about that."

"Anyway, when Lucinda thought I was you, she asked me to be in her mother's fashion show—and I said yes."

"After she figured out you weren't me, she knew that I hadn't agreed, right?"

"She had already told her mother. It was when she was fitting me for your dress that she found out the truth."

Madison frowned. "Didn't you explain that you couldn't promise me for the fashion show?"

"I told her she would have to work that out with you."

"Thanks a lot."

Anna pointed her finger at Madison. "You know how you

keep telling me to be nice to Aunt Rachel, saying how she is a good person?"

"Yes."

"It's the same with Lucinda. She is a very good person. You should be nice to her too."

Madison seemed to be considering this.

"She helped me a lot. She seems a lot nicer than that mean Vivian."

"Maybe so."

Anna told Madison about Nadya and how she had gotten a little suspicious. "Especially the time she caught me jumping on your bed."

"You jumped on my bed?" Madison grinned.

"Yes. It was so big and so bouncy." Anna shook her head. "I have a question for you. Why do English have so much comfortable things—beds, chairs, pillows, blankets, rugs . . . so luxurious—and then they wear uncomfortable shoes and clothes?"

Madison laughed. "I don't know. That's a good question."

Anna nodded vigorously. "I thought about it a lot."

"I thought about the opposite question," Madison said. "Why do the Amish dress comfortably, but all their beds and furnishings are uncomfortable?"

"It's not like that everywhere. Uncle Daniel is very, very conservative," Anna explained. "He does things the old ways."

"No wonder Rachel is so worn out." Madison sighed. "Will she keep having children until she's too old? She told me they don't believe in birth control."

"My mamm is worried about this too. She told Aunt Rachel there are some kinds of birth control acceptable to their Ordnung."

"So not everything is what it seemed," Madison said.

"Both in my world and in yours." Anna ate the last piece of cinnamon roll.

Madison looked at her watch. "I have a few more things to tell you before it's too late." She explained about the Lapp family, the sisters Rebekah and Lydia, and how they were all interested in helping and befriending Rachel. "I hope you'll encourage them. Rachel needs some good friends to watch her back."

"Watch her back?"

"You know. To be there for her." Madison told Anna about how she'd spoken to Berta.

"Not really?" Anna giggled.

Madison nodded. "I did. Everyone was happy when she and her friend left."

"Now Berta will be after me," Anna exclaimed. "Who will watch my back?"

Madison held up a finger. "That reminds me. I have something really important to tell you."

Anna leaned forward with interest.

"His name is Malachi, and he's a great guy." Speaking quickly since their time was limited, Madison explained how she'd stumbled onto this young man, Uncle Daniel's nephew, and how she had unwittingly flirted with him. Though they had spent very little time together, this young man had gotten it into his head that he was in love with her.

"How is that possible?" Anna demanded. "You are at my aunt's house for a few days and you make a man fall in love with you? It is not fair." She was thinking of Jacob, how it took years for him to fall in love . . . and then he had fallen out.

Madison chuckled. "Here's the deal, Anna. He fell in

love with who he *thought* I was." She pointed to Anna. "He thought I was you."

"Now what?" Anna frowned. "I will have to tell him the truth and—"

"He knows the truth."

"You told both my aunt and this guy?"

"Malachi. His name is Malachi, Anna."

"*Ja, ja.*" Anna shook her head. "How many others did you tell? Soon my mamm and daed will be hearing about it too."

"Malachi won't tell anyone. Neither will Rachel. Don't worry."

"That's easy for you to say. You won't get in trouble for this."

"You won't either, Anna." Madison reached across the table, took Anna's hand, and squeezed it. "You are so lucky."

"I am lucky?"

"Yes. I know you probably won't believe me, but I envy you, Anna."

Anna studied Madison.

"There are so many things I love about your simple life. You're so lucky to be born into it."

"You can become Amish if you want," Anna said. "You just have to accept our ways and be baptized. It happens sometimes."

"I plan to take some Amish with me," Madison told her. "I'm not sure how. But I plan to change some things in my life. I want to make it simpler."

Anna nodded. "You have so much stuff, Madison. It made my head dizzy. Your closet is as big as my room at home. There are things, things, things—everywhere. Why do you need so much?"

"I don't."

"Oh." Anna wondered at this.

Suddenly Madison pointed outside. "Look there, Anna."

Anna looked out the window to see a tall Amish man crossing the street toward them. His posture was straight, his strides were long and confident, and beneath his straw hat she saw blond hair.

"He is very handsome," she told Madison.

"He is Malachi."

Anna blinked, then looked again as the man came into the coffee shop. "The same Malachi? Uncle Daniel's nephew?"

"One and the same." Madison grinned.

"He does not look like Uncle Daniel."

"No. He definitely does not." Madison waved to him, and he approached with a truly bewildered expression.

"Hello?" he said cautiously.

"Malachi, I want you to meet the real Anna," Madison told him.

"Hello . . . Anna?" He looked back and forth from one girl to the other.

"Hello, Malachi." Anna smiled nervously. "You want to sit?"

"Yes." He nodded as he sat, still looking from one girl to the other.

"She really is Anna," Madison assured him. "We changed clothes in the restroom."

"You are Uncle Daniel's nephew?" Anna asked him.

"Yes. And you are Aunt Rachel's niece?"

"*Ja.* She and my mamm are sisters."

Malachi looked back at Madison. "You look different."

"I am different." She smiled. "It was what I was trying to

tell you." She pointed to Anna again. "I was trying to be her. But she is the real thing."

Anna felt her cheeks grow warm. "I was trying to be Madison, but I was not good at it. I am glad to be home."

Malachi looked relieved. "You are ready to go home now?"

"Yes. Please."

Malachi frowned at Madison. "How do you get home?"

She reached into the bright orange bag, pulling out a set of keys. "I have a car to drive."

He looked surprised. "Yes, of course."

"We should go," Anna told Madison. "I would hug you, but we already have people looking at us."

"I understand." Madison smiled but remained seated. "You two have a nice ride back home." She actually winked at Malachi, causing his cheeks to get rosy. "It will probably be much more pleasant than your ride into town."

Anna glanced nervously at Malachi, but he just smiled. Such a handsome smile too! She reached for Madison's hand, giving it a quick squeeze. "Thank you for everything, Madison."

"Thank you too."

"You have a blessed good life." Anna let go of her hand.

"You too."

Anna knew she saw tears in Madison's eyes as she and Malachi left the coffee shop. For that matter, Anna had tears in her own eyes. It felt as if Madison was one of her best friends, yet they had only spent a total of a few hours together. And now it was over.

Still, Anna was glad to be home. Or almost home.

"You are the real Anna?" Malachi asked as he helped her into the buggy.

"I am the real Anna," she assured him. "Although the truth

is I don't feel much like the Anna I was when I sneaked out of here last week." She watched as he walked around—he really was a handsome man—and waited as he got into the driver's seat. "I am very happy to be Anna again."

"I am very happy you are Anna again too." He released the brake and shook the reins, smiling as the horse began to move. "I look forward to getting to know the real Anna this time."

"So do I," she said. That was true enough. She did want to know the real Anna again. She wanted to reacquaint herself with the girl who had once loved doing her daily chores, the girl who got true pleasure from baking raisin bread and making a window shine—and sewing. She couldn't wait to hem up little Elizabeth's dress!

As Malachi drove the wagon home, slow and easy, a familiar song began to hum through Anna's head. It was an old song Grandmamm used to sing in the garden. A song about peace and home and family. A song Anna hoped to sing to the end of her days.

26

With the morning sun shining brightly, Madison decided to put the top down on her Mini Cooper. She was surprised at how exhilarating it felt, the wind whipping through her hair as she sped down the country road. Okay, she was only going the speed limit, but after living in the slow lane for a week, this felt really fast.

After an hour, she realized her car was on empty, so she pulled into the next town. As she was filling up, the sound of something ringing in her purse made her jump, and then she realized it was her Blackberry. To her dismay, it was Garret. Instead of ignoring the call, she decided to just deal with it.

"Hello, Garret," she said pleasantly.

"Hey, Maddie." He sounded happy. "Great to hear your voice again. We're still talking?"

"Sure. We're talking now, aren't we?"

"Where are you?"

"Just out for a drive."

"Your car's fixed?"

She considered this. "Uh, yeah, it's running great."

"So what happened with Jacob? Did he and that Anna chick get back together?"

"No." She had almost forgotten that Garret had been helping Anna. "It didn't turn out like she'd hoped."

"Too bad. Was she okay?"

Madison smiled. "Actually, I think she was better than okay. They weren't really meant for each other."

There was a brief pause.

"Do you want to do something?" he asked hopefully. "Now that your relentless search for Anna's missing man has been resolved, we could still go to Nantucket and—"

"No." She started her car, moved it away from the pump, and parked. "I think I want to take a break."

"Take a break?" He sounded mad. "Or break up?"

"I guess it could go either way."

Garret let out a foul word, which, after she'd lived in an Amish community for a week, felt harsh on her ears.

"I'm sorry to hurt you, Garret. But, like Anna and Jacob, I think it's for the best."

"You strung me along for all of spring break just to dump me like this?"

"You knew more than a week ago that we had some major problems, Garret. Seriously, the writing was all over the wall."

He let out another crass word.

"I have to go, Garret. Sorry to end it like this, but—" She didn't get to finish because he had hung up. While she felt a tiny bit sad, she was mostly just relieved.

She decided to listen to her other messages—a mix from her mom, her dad, and Vivian. All three of them sounded similar in that they (1) wanted to know what was wrong with her, (2) wanted to know why she wasn't returning their calls, and (3) were irked. She called her dad first, but only because he sounded genuinely worried about her health.

"Hey, Dad," she said lightly. "I'm feeling a lot better now. I just wanted you to know."

"You sound better."

"I'm sorry I didn't call sooner. I got busy and the end of the week just got away from me."

"It's okay. I got pretty busy too."

"Anyway, I was thinking, if you wanted I could drive up to Boston for the night, maybe hang with you tomorrow."

"Oh, Maddie, I wish I'd known sooner. I was so used to being blown off by you that I made other plans. I could cancel—"

"No," she said quickly. "It's okay. We can do it another weekend."

"Do you want to look into Harvard after all?"

"Actually, I wanted to talk to you about that, Dad. I know you want me to go to Harvard. Mom wants me to go to Yale. I've decided that I want to do something totally different."

"Really?"

"Yes. I don't want to offend you guys, but I feel strongly about this. I'm just not an Ivy Leaguer, not at heart."

"Hey, that's okay, Maddie. I want you to go somewhere you want to go. I didn't mean to pressure you. It is your life."

"So you'll support me in choosing a different college—I mean if I have to stand up to Mom?"

"You know I'll support you."

"I don't want it to turn into a power struggle either."

"Yeah, I hear you. You're only a junior, you have time to figure this out. Especially if you're not going the Ivy League route."

"That's what I'm thinking too."

They talked a bit longer, and by the time she hung up,

Madison felt like she and her dad had made good progress. Unfortunately, her phone call with her mom was not quite as satisfying. After Madison apologized for not going to Tuscany with them, her mom launched into a lecture about how Madison would've enjoyed it, how disappointed her grandmother had been, and that maybe she'd think twice next time.

"I'm sure I will," Madison said. "If it's any consolation, I think I might've grown up some this week."

"Well, it's about time."

"Yeah." Madison sighed. "Tell Grandmother I'm sorry I let her down and maybe we can plan something this summer."

"Okay, dear, I'll tell her. It's cocktail hour now, so I'll have to let you go. Thanks for calling. I'm glad you're feeling better."

Madison told herself she couldn't expect too much from her mom, but she still felt slightly disappointed as she hung up. Next she called Vivian. Her messages had gotten increasingly grumpy, and Madison was hoping to simply leave a message. Unfortunately, Vivian picked up.

"Madison," she snapped, "where are you?"

Of course, it didn't improve Vivian's mood when Madison told her.

"I have had the worst week of my life," she said. "And I have you to thank for it."

"Why is it my fault?"

"Because I only agreed to come down here with my parents after you promised you'd come too."

Madison didn't remember any such promise, but she knew it probably didn't matter much at this point. "Sorry, Vivian."

"Sorry? That's the best you can come up with? Sorry?"

"It's all I have at the moment. In case you wondered, I had an interesting week and I—"

"Right! Now you're going to rub it in that you stayed in the city and had a fabulous time. Thanks a lot, but I really don't care."

"All right then." Madison was struggling to keep her voice calm and even. "I guess I'll see you next week."

"Whatever!" Vivian hung up.

Madison couldn't believe she was actually missing Rachel right now. And Anna too. Who would've guessed? Then she remembered what Anna had said about Lucinda and her mom's fashion show, so she called Lucinda's number.

"Hey, Lucinda," she said, "this is Madison."

"The real Madison?"

"Yeah. Anna and I switched back."

"Really? How did it go?"

Madison filled her in a little and they talked back and forth congenially almost like they were still friends. But eventually the conversation wore down.

"Anyway . . ." Madison decided to take care of one last thing. "Anna told me about your mom's fashion show and how she signed me up, and I want—"

"To tell me to forget it, right?"

Madison considered this—that had been her initial response, but not now. "No, I wanted to tell you that if you still want me, I'd be honored."

"You'd be *honored*?" Lucinda sounded skeptical. "Seriously, is this really Madison Van Buren?"

She laughed. "Yes, it's me."

"Okay, if this is really Madison, tell me about your thirteenth birthday."

"You mean the time we went skinny-dipping at the Ritz after the pool was closed?"

Lucinda laughed. "Yeah. And that was my idea."

"We used to have fun."

"Used to." Lucinda sounded a little bitter.

"Did you have any fun during spring break?"

Lucinda groaned. "All I did was work."

Madison was getting an idea. "So . . . what are you doing this weekend?"

"Not much."

"Well, I'm thinking about going to the Hamptons. Are you interested?"

"Really?"

"Totally."

"Who else is going to be there?" Lucinda sounded suspicious.

"Just you and me," Madison assured her. "Like old times—well, except no parents."

"Really? No Vivian? No Garret? None of your other snooty friends?"

"Just me . . . and you if you come."

"I'm in."

Suddenly they were making plans. Lucinda would gather up some food, Madison would be in Manhattan before eleven, and they would easily make it to the Hamptons by two.

<hr/>

"You're traveling light," Lucinda observed when she saw the overnight bag that Madison had quickly packed after she'd told Nadya to take the weekend off.

"I've been living light this past week," Madison confessed as she tossed her bag into the backseat. "It's kind of nice."

Lucinda stared at Madison as she started her car. "You really have changed."

Madison chuckled. "Are you making fun of my hair? Because I haven't washed it in days and then it was blowing in the wind with the top down. I know it's pretty bad."

"I'm not talking about your hair," Lucinda clarified. "You just seem really different."

"I actually feel really different," she admitted.

"You were really living with Amish people? On a farm?"

"That's right." As Madison drove, she told Lucinda all about her strange week. Not only was Lucinda sincerely interested, she seemed to actually understand how Madison was now longing for simplicity in her life.

"I want that too," Lucinda told her.

They talked about that all the way to the Hamptons. They both agreed that rather than stopping at any of the regular spots, they would go straight to the beach house, open it up, fix a late lunch, and enjoy a simple afternoon of beach and sunshine. And that's exactly what they did. Madison knew that her other friends would probably have spoiled a time like this—either by wanting to party hardy, pair off, or, as Lucinda put it, act "snooty."

In the evening, Madison told Lucinda that she planned to go out to the beach and just look at the stars. "Do you think that sounds dumb?" she asked as she gathered up a quilt.

"Not at all," Lucinda said. "Do you care if I join you?"

"Only if you promise not to talk too much," Madison said. "I mean once we're out there." As they walked outside, Madison confessed to Lucinda that, for the first time in her life, she was beginning to experience God in a real way.

"Seriously?" Lucinda sounded truly shocked. "Wow, you really have changed."

"I think I'm still changing," she admitted. "There's

something about being in nature, being quiet, calm, still. When the noise and distractions are cleared away, I feel more aware, more spiritually awake. Like I can almost hear his voice . . . like I'm starting to understand what God is about."

"Cool," Lucinda whispered.

They were out on the beach now, and Madison threw the quilt open and spread it out on the sand, where they both stretched out. Thankfully, Lucinda kept her promise of silence. The only sounds were the repetitive swish-swash of the ocean's waves and an occasional seabird settling in for the night. Overhead, the stars came out, and before long a nearly full moon crested over the ocean. Lucinda let out a little gasp, and Madison couldn't fault her for it. Truly, it was beautiful.

Maybe it was the aftermath of living with the Amish, or just her personal preference, or the influence of the Creator's amazing creation—or perhaps it was all three. But Madison felt certain that God appreciated simplicity. Because that was where she had found him. And that was where she was determined to remain.

Acknowledgments

I'd like to thank Suzanne Woods Fisher and Mindy Starns Clark for consulting with me in regard to how the Amish live today. Mindy has written a handy little booklet, *A Pocket Guide to Amish Life* (Harvest House Publishers, 2010). To learn more about contemporary Amish, check out her website: http://www.morefrommindy.com.

Melody Carlson is the award-winning author of over two hundred books for adults, teens, and children. She is the author of many novels for teens, including *Just Another Girl* and *Anything but Normal*, as well as several series for teens, including Diary of a Teenage Girl, TrueColors, Notes from a Spinning Planet, the Carter House Girls, and Words from the Rock. She has won a Gold Medallion Award and a Romance Writers of America Rita Award, and she was nominated for a *Romantic Times* Career Achievement Award. She lives with her husband in Sisters, Oregon. Visit her website at www .melodycarlson.com.

New School = New Chance for That First Kiss

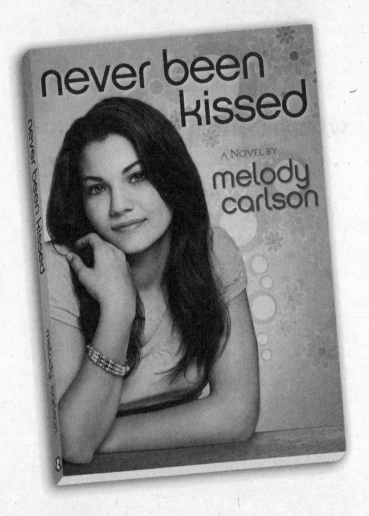

Just when it seems Elise is on top of the world, everything comes crashing down. Could one bad choice derail her future?

Aster Flynn Wants a Life of Her Own . . .

Just Another Girl

A NOVEL

melody carlson

But will her family get in her way?